CODE NAME KOMIKO

Naomi Paul

SCARLET VOYAGE

Copyright © 2014 by Working Partners Limited

Scarlet Voyage, an imprint of Enslow Publishers, Inc.

LCCN: 2013934268

Paul, Naomi.

Code Name Komiko / Naomi Paul.

Summary: In Hong Kong, high school senior Lian, code name Komiko,
begins to investigate the Harrison Corporation, a clothing business using
an illegal workforce, after a dead body washes up in Big Wave Bay. With the
help of her cyber-investigating group 06/04, Komiko plunges into a world of
corruption and danger to uncover Harrison Corps' crimes.

ISBN 978-1-62324-023-3

Future editions:
Paperback ISBN: 978-1-62324-024-0
EPUB ISBN: 978-1-62324-025-7
Single-User PDF ISBN: 978-1-62324-026-4
Multi-User PDF ISBN: 978-1-62324-027-1

Printed in the United States of America

112013 Bang Printing, Brainerd, Minn.

10 9 8 7 6 5 4 3 2 1

Scarlet Voyage
Box 398, 40 Industrial Road
Berkeley Heights, NJ 07922
USA

www.scarletvoyage.com

Cover Illustration: Photos.com/© Thinkstock.com (woman) and
Shutterstock.com (Hong Kong skyline)

With special thanks to Dave Justus

ONE

⁣⁣⁣llllllllllllllllllllllllllllllllllllllllllllllllllllllllllllllllllllllllllllllllllllllllllllllllllll

"The Dragon's Back is broken," Lian repeated, marveling at the poetry of the phrase.

"Seriously, you're being a weirdo," Mingmei said, rolling her eyes. "That's not even what he said, Lian."

True, that hadn't been exactly what the lifeguard had told them. He'd just said that the section of the Dragon's Back hiking trail adjacent to Big Wave Bay Beach was temporarily closed. It was no big deal; the girls hadn't come here to hike anyway but to bask in the late August sun on the last day before school started again. The mythological image had taken root in Lian's mind as they'd trekked across the white sands to stake out their tanning spot, though, and, as always, she found it hard to shake a good mythological image.

"You knew I was a weirdo when you signed on for this friendship," Lian said with a smile, smearing a big dollop of zinc oxide onto her nose. "Besides, who's around to hear me embarrass you?"

Mingmei lowered her sunglasses and shot her friend a withering look. "*Everyone,*" she said, gesturing to the crowded beach on either side of them. "Everyone's always around to hear everything. *Especially* when you're being a weirdo."

Lian laughed. Mingmei wasn't far wrong. Hong Kong had a population density so high that there were barely six inches between Lian's towel and that of the fat guy to her right. She kept her back to him and his snoring and watched Mingmei checking out the university boys emerging from the water, surfboards under their arms.

"One more year," Mingmei said wistfully, "and then we're done with high school boys forever."

Now it was Lian's turn to roll her eyes. "Well, it'll be nice to get rid of *that* burden at last."

"Sorry," Mingmei said. "I forgot who I was talking to for a second. I promise you, Lian, we'll find you a boyfriend by October so you can be sick of him by Christmas."

"That's a pretty ambitious timeline."

Mingmei shrugged. "I'm a pretty ambitious girl. Of course, we'll have to find a guy who's willing to overlook that gigantic hickey that Zheng gave you."

"Very funny," Lian said sarcastically, but her hand went self-consciously to her neck—to the pink welt where her violin nestled against her for two hours each day. Mingmei liked to joke about the "intense love affair" between Lian and her instrument. She'd nicknamed the violin after its maker, master Zheng Quan, and teased Lian about the "beautiful music" the two made when they were alone.

Lian didn't mind the jokes. Mingmei's relationships—if you could call afternoons spent watching a boy chase a ball around the park with his friends a "relationship"—tended to last a matter of weeks, so how could she understand the lifetime of dedication Lian had given to her violin, or the joy she felt when she drew a flawless performance from its strings? Lian had her doubts that any first kiss could rival the highs of Bartók's sonata.

Which is not to say that she wasn't a little curious.

"Not to mention," Mingmei said, catching Lian gently by the wrist, "all these calluses. Nobody wants to hold hands with a rock monster. You've *got* to ease up on the violin and spend a little time moisturizing."

"Hey," Lian said, pulling back her hand as Mingmei laughed. "These aren't *all* from violin practice, you know."

Mingmei did a double take. "Really?"

"Yeah. Some of them are from typing."

Now both girls were laughing. Lian felt easy and free today, set loose from her responsibilities for a few hours before family and school obligations came crashing down on her head once again. She wished she had more opportunities to hang out with Mingmei like this, just soaking in the sun, sights, and sounds of the Southern District.

She wanted to make the most of them now, while she could. Their final year of high school, with all its attendant exam prep and school activities, would make it hard for them to get together as much in the months to come. This year they shared only a single economics class, the rest of their time being spent pursuing their individual interests—biology for Mingmei, arts and music for Lian.

Not to mention another extracurricular pursuit that Mingmei knew nothing about.

"It's going to be strange, not sitting next to you for half the day," Lian said. "We'll have to spend the whole lunch period catching each other up on our mornings. There'll hardly be time to eat."

"Suits me fine," Mingmei said. "I've been looking for excuses to skip a meal or two, anyway. I just can't shake these last few pounds."

"Oh, shut up!" Lian scooped up a glittering handful of sand and tossed it playfully at her friend. Those "last few pounds" were nowhere that Lian could see; Mingmei could have been clipped right out of *Teen Vogue, Cosmo*, or any one of the beach magazines being read all around them.

"I am dead serious," Mingmei said, in a tone that was far from it. "Since that stuck-up Xiuying's *finally* graduated, I have to be the new standard-bearer for fashion in the hallowed halls of Island South High. I've got to be tanned, toned, and always dressed in the latest styles." Her cell phone's alarm chimed, and she stretched and rolled onto her stomach. Mingmei adhered to her tanning schedule with the kind of dedication Lian *wished* she would apply to her studies.

"How you don't crack under all that pressure, I'll never know," Lian said with a smile.

"I have you to keep me grounded," Mingmei said, winking over the top of her sunglasses. "Speaking of which, you're coming shopping with me in Causeway Bay next weekend. If we get there first thing, we can make it all the way through Fashion Walk before they lock up for the night. You can spend a whole day telling me what looks amazing on me, and what looks merely incredible. And of course, I'll find you some killer outfits, too. This is going to be the Year of Lian. The boys will all get whiplash when you walk down the hall."

Lian knew that Mingmei was sincere in her offer and that she had an uncanny knack for fashion—but being someone's dress-up doll was low on her to-do list right now.

"I think I'll take a rain check, Mingmei," she said. "It's, uh . . . next weekend's no good for me."

Mingmei sighed theatrically. "You always do this. What, is it about money?"

Lian widened her eyes and hissed at her friend to hush.

"I mean," Mingmei continued, pressing ahead but in a whisper, "your dad is loaded. And, despite all my efforts, you're a good and responsible daughter—so you must be earning some kind of allowance, right?"

Lian said nothing and rolled onto her stomach, burying her face in her towel. Her parents were generous, to be sure, but she had better things to spend her money on than the latest styles from America or Japan, or wasting a day in search of the perfect accessory to complement a dress.

"I've been saving," she said at last, mostly into the terry cloth. She turned her head toward Mingmei. "I need to upgrade my hard drive, you know. Get a new wireless trackball, network cables . . . um . . . Ethernet transponder uplink dongle." She was just making up tech terms now; Mingmei wouldn't know the difference as long as it sounded important—and expensive.

"You and your computer," Mingmei said, sighing again. "Does the violin get jealous?"

"Look, I just need this stuff, okay?" Lian said. "For school."

"For *gaming,* you mean."

Lian tried not to look too relieved. If that's what Mingmei wanted to think, she was content to let her.

The truth was messier than she wanted to get into.

"Honestly," Mingmei said, "you've got to unplug from those online games. They have this thing called 'reality' now. It's just like virtual reality but a little less virtual."

Lian made a show of grimacing. "Sounds awful."

"And, side note, you're *never* going to meet a hot guy in the World of Wargames or wherever it is you're spending your lonely nights playing. You've got to stop chasing down bad guys with your keyboard and join the rest of us here in the real world." Mingmei brightened as an idea struck her. "Why don't you drop the joystick tonight and come out with me? I'm meeting Jun for ice cream at Appolo. I'm sure he could bring a friend for you."

"Don't tell me how you're shedding pounds when you know you've got a crippling Magic Cone addiction," Lian teased. "Besides, I have to go to some boring business dinner with my parents tonight." Her lack of enthusiasm for the dinner was real, but it was also nice to have an excuse to avoid a blind date.

"Wow," Mingmei said. "If you can't be tempted by cute boys and Tiramisu Monaka, you may be beyond all hope."

"You've got your vices, and I've got mine," Lian said, hoping to end the discussion.

"Okay, okay," Mingmei said, springing up onto the balls of her feet. "You win this round. Let's go for a swim." Mingmei silenced her phone as the alarm chimed again, and they took off from their towels in a hurry.

Big Wave rarely lived up to its name, but today there was a pronounced choppiness to the water. It was warm where it lapped against the sand but colder than Lian expected as she and Mingmei swam farther out, avoiding the surfers and wakeboarders who rode the crests until they broke.

Soon, Mingmei was pulling away. She was such a good swimmer, Lian was sure she had a mermaid somewhere in her ancestry. Before long, Lian could barely see her friend knifing across the roiling surface, angling against the swells to decrease resistance. As she watched, Mingmei climbed effortlessly to the peak of a wave and seemed to pause, suspended, for a long second before disappearing over its backside.

Lian stopped giving chase for a moment and found herself in the wave's periphery, a brief sinking sensation capped with a short wet slap against her face. She blinked the salt water from her eyes and craned her neck; she was farther from the beach than she'd intended to go. A jaunt like this was nothing for Mingmei—who was nowhere to be seen now—but Lian wasn't so confident, and the continued rise and fall of the swells was doing nothing to help settle her nerves.

The waves had looked blue and inviting back on the shore; once they'd lured her into their domain, they'd turned gray and aggressive. Lian felt herself lifted again and bit her lip against the inevitable plunge. The South China Sea seemed needlessly angry with her in it, and she would have been more than happy to get out if she could just take a second to get her bearings.

She bobbed to the crest of a wave, trying desperately to find Mingmei in the distance, but it was no good. As she began to sink, Lian called out again—but she doubted her friend heard her. She could barely hear herself over the roar of the surf.

In contrast, a sudden sharp, loud voice hit her ears like something physical: "Move! Get out of the way!" A male, ferocious and bellowing; Lian couldn't tell where he was coming from until suddenly he was nearly on top of her, a fierce figure in an oil-black wet suit, riding a blood-red surfboard that scythed through the water inches from her face.

She twisted her body and jerked back her head in shock, just as the wave broke over her. Suddenly, the sea was everywhere, and she was nowhere. There was nothing to breathe but the cold leaden water.

Lian fought to the surface, her chest on fire, and spat out sea foam. It felt like the water had a hand around her neck; she coughed and sputtered, desperate to draw a single lungful of pure air. Her sense of direction had abandoned her as surely as Mingmei had, and through stinging eyes, she saw the next wave—larger and darker and coming straight for her. She was powerless in its shadow.

And then all at once there were two arms hooked under hers, and she was propelled out of harm's way, arcing up and over the wave's peak as Mingmei spoke close behind her.

"You got in a little too deep, huh?"

Lian had never been so grateful for their friendship. She took a few greedy breaths and then feebly admitted, "Yeah. Maybe."

Mingmei kept an arm around Lian and kicked her legs like pistons, steering them both toward a cove. It hadn't been that far away from her, Lian realized. She'd just been so panicked that she'd lost perspective.

"Lian, there's never any shame in turning back around when it gets too rough. Sometimes you've got to know when it's time to quit."

Mingmei didn't let go of her, even when they'd reached the shallows and could walk, rather than swim, up to the rocks at the water's edge and climb out. A path meandered up from the cove, festooned with bamboo and shrubs; the terrain was much rockier here on the outskirts of the bay, and nobody was tanning this far from the sand. They took their time, Lian feeling stronger and steadier with each step on dry land.

"Okay," she said at last, casting a wan look out at the water and the gray clouds slowly moving in from the south. "That sucked. I mean, that truly, madly, deeply sucked."

"No doubt," Mingmei said, pushing an overgrown bamboo stalk out of their way. "But you're fine now, and if that's the worst thing that happens to you today, then there's nothing to worry about."

Lian didn't really hear her, though; she was distracted by a dark shape at the edge of the water, in the craggier rocks a little way down from where they had emerged.

"You see that?" she asked, directing Mingmei's gaze. "What is that, a surfboard?"

She stepped off the path, moving the brush aside, and made her way back down to the sea. Whatever the thing was, it was bobbing in the rippling water, thudding against the rocks. It was too irregular in shape to be a board, she realized. Maybe a wet suit? Maybe some abandoned snorkeling gear? Or maybe—

Just behind her, Mingmei shrieked, and suddenly there was no "maybe" about it.

They were looking at a dead body.

TWO

The first detail Lian noticed was the saccharine Sanrio pink fingernail polish. Then her eyes focused and she saw that the corpse's left forearm was pinned between two rocks, mooring the body in the shallow water. The hand was small and feminine, slightly bloated, and an ugly goose-pimpled blue-gray hue. Against it, the nail polish stood out in sharp relief.

Lian stayed focused on that bright pink as she made her way down to the rocks at the water's edge, stumbling and skidding a little on the patchy terrain. She dimly heard Mingmei's voice behind her, calling out for Lian not to get too close.

But there was no way Lian could keep away.

The body was floating facedown, the arm trapped at an awkward angle. Midway between wrist and elbow, a silvery charm bracelet hung, the skin swollen on either side of it. Hardly daring to breathe, Lian drew up close, braced her foot in a crevice, and peered over the rocks for a better look.

The dead girl was about Lian's size and, she guessed, roughly her age. She wore a smart white blouse, a charcoal-gray pencil skirt, two socks, one shoe—which meant that she most likely was not planning on going to the beach when she set out on what she did not know would be the last day of her life.

Lian straightened, shielded her eyes, and shouted up to Mingmei. "Go! Get our phones, call the police, tell the lifeguards!"

Mingmei half shrugged and held out her arms, shaking her head. She was communicating that she couldn't hear what Lian had said.

Lian flashed nine fingers, three times, and then held her hand to her ear like a phone.

Mingmei stood stock still for a moment longer, and then finally seemed to understand. She took off like a shot for the beach. Lian was alone with a floating girl and a growing list of questions.

An hour later, the flashing blue lights from the police vans were turning everyone's skin the same color as the corpse's. The police had cordoned off the immediate area with an efficient, brusque manner, but a junior officer had been kind enough to offer Lian a blanket as she sat shivering on the rocky slope. Behind her, the sunbathers on Big Wave were being ushered off the beach, directed around the closed section of the Dragon's Back, and kept at a respectable distance from the crime scene.

"I promise, I'm fine, Mum," Lian said into her phone in the most reassuring tone she could muster. "Mingmei, too. We were both a little freaked out, but everything's okay."

"I can't even imagine," her mother said. "To be the one to stumble across. . . . I can't even imagine." Her voice was shaky, on the edge of tears.

"I'll be home soon, okay? The police have already taken my statement. I'm just waiting for them to finish with Mingmei."

There was a pause in which Lian felt certain her mother was dabbing at her eyes with a tissue. Her mom was a world-class worrier. "Just...be careful," she said at last, as if Lian were in any danger with all the cops around. "We'll see you soon. I love you, little panda."

Lian blushed. She generally wished that her parents would stop using the nickname, even when they only did so in private. This time, though, she was grateful for the warmth that the embarrassment brought to her cheeks. She said good-bye and hung up, wiping her phone's screen with the corner of the blanket. Her hair was still wet, and she pushed it back from her eyes as she cast her gaze back down to the sea.

A police boat had anchored a little way out from the shore. Two divers had gingerly freed the dead girl's arm from the crag and loaded her onto a floating gurney. Even from up here, Lian could still see that bold pink polish; it was a fun color, a young color, totally absurd as decoration for a now-lifeless hand.

On a nearly empty beach, under gathering clouds, Lian's mind had nothing to do but wonder about the girl. Who was she? What sort of person had she been; what sort of daughter, student, friend? What choices had she made in her short life that had led her here?

Had she taken her own life . . . or had it been taken from her?

An ashen hand fell on Lian's shoulder, and she tensed. But it was only Mingmei, finished with her statement and more than ready to leave the beach. The carefully regimented sunbathing had all been in vain, Lian thought as she stood; her friend was twice as pale as when they'd arrived at Big Wave.

Lian folded the blanket into a tidy square as the junior officer approached them. He was a baby-faced young man, maybe only a year or two out of training school, Lian guessed. "Oh, you're welcome to keep it," he said as Lian offered the blanket back to him.

She smiled slightly. "I'm declining on my mother's behalf. I don't think she'd be thrilled to have a souvenir from today in the house."

The officer nodded and accepted the blanket. "Of course, of course. Not a pleasant thing to be reminded of."

"Have you seen many cases like this?" Lian asked him, trying to keep her tone casual but keen to garner any insight she could into the case. The shock of discovering the corpse was wearing off—now her mind was going to work in the way that she had long ago trained it to.

The young officer sighed. "More than I care for. There are a couple thousand suicides a year in Hong Kong. The currents bring ones like this right back into our laps."

"So, you think this was a suicide?" Lian asked, wincing at the eagerness in her voice.

The officer gave her a curt smile, as if he'd already said too much. "We'll have to see what the coroner says," he told her. "You've both been very helpful, thank you. Can we offer you a lift home?"

Again, that courteous efficiency; it sounded like a kind offer, Lian thought, but it was really a way to hurry the girls off the beach now that their usefulness had expired.

"Thank you, but no," she said, reaching out to take Mingmei's clammy hand. "We don't want to be any trouble. We'll just take the bus back."

The junior officer nodded again and stepped aside so they could continue up the rocky slope to the trail. Lian didn't relish the hike back over to Shek O to wait for the bus, but a ride home in the back of the police van would have been more frustrating. She didn't trust herself not to pester the officers with questions, and she knew they wouldn't be forthcoming with any real answers. Besides, Mingmei looked like she could use a walk in the fresh air to get a little color back in her cheeks.

"You okay?" Lian asked.

Mingmei blinked a couple of times, and then said, "Yeah. Yeah, I'm all right. It's just . . . I've never been that close to a . . . a *dead body*. It freaked me out." She stopped in her tracks and looked at Lian. "Didn't it freak you out, too?"

"Of course it did," Lian said, giving her friend's hand a reassuring squeeze. "I didn't know what to think."

"You, uh, you handled it a lot better than I did. Staying down there, with that poor girl. I don't think I could have done that."

Lian cast one last look down at the rocks where she'd kept her lonesome vigil. The girl was on dry land now, the crime scene officers already swarming with their evidence bags in hand. A rising hum drew her eyes out past the body and to the bay, where a speedboat pulled in with a flourish. It didn't have police markings, but those were definitely Hong Kong Police Force uniforms on the men on board.

All but one of them, at any rate. Squinting, Lian could see a paunchy man in a blue tracksuit on the speedboat's deck, barking orders at the cops. With his aviator sunglasses, jowls, and potbelly, he didn't cut an immediately imposing figure, but the men all snapped to attention at his commands and set about their business.

Maybe a plainclothes detective, Lian guessed. A man with a plan, an expert at these kinds of scenes.

Lian realized that she and Mingmei had paused for too long on the hillside. A couple of the officers looked up at them, and Lian quickly dropped to one knee.

"What are you doing?" Mingmei asked her.

"Pretending to tie my shoes," Lian said, sliding her cell phone out from the towel in which it was bundled.

"But you're wearing flip-flops," Mingmei protested.

"Hence the *pretending*."

Lian propped her phone against her ankle and brushed its screen with her fingertip, scrolling to the camera icon.

"Come on, Lian. We're going to miss our bus."

"Just give me two seconds," Lian insisted, zooming in as close as she could to the man in the tracksuit. She clicked the shutter three times in rapid succession, then twice more as the man turned and she could capture his profile.

"You're being a weirdo again," Mingmei said, nudging her gently with her sandal.

"Maybe," Lian said, thumbing off the phone and slipping it back into the towel. She couldn't have articulated it, but something about the man had struck her as vaguely suspicious.

As they headed toward the roped-off section of the Dragon's Back, Mingmei hugged herself and shivered. Lian suddenly wished for her friend's sake that she'd kept the police blanket after all.

But the photos would have to serve as her sole keepsake of their strange, sad afternoon at the beach.

THREE

5:53 PM HKT — *Komiko has logged on*

> **Komiko:** Sorry I'm late, guys. I promise I have a good reason.

> **Crowbar:** Dont worry, youre not late, its not 6 yet!

> **Torch:** We agreed to 15 min, just us three, before the newbie signed in. So yes, Komiko *IS* late.

> **Torch:** But lay your reason on us.

> **Komiko:** Got delayed by a dead girl.

> **Torch:** ?

> **Torch:** That might just be a good reason, after all.

> **Crowbar:** 4 real what do U mean?

Lian sat back in her desk chair and took a deep breath. Every time she dove into one of these chats with the rest of 06/04, she had to brace herself against Crowbar's lack of punctuation and insistence on homophonic shorthand. But having to puzzle out whether "2" meant "to" or "too" or

22

actually just "two" was a petty annoyance, she knew, and a small price to pay for Crowbar's contributions to the cause.

Komiko: Body was found a little west of Big Wave. Young girl, about 16–18.

She'd very nearly typed "about my age," but that would have violated the first and most important rule of the group: no *identifying details*. "Lian" didn't exist in this chat room, and "Komiko" didn't exist outside it. She didn't know the age, race, profession, or even the gender of her two comrades, nor they hers. It was safer that way; they couldn't be coerced to spill information they'd never had to begin with.

Strength in anonymity.

Which is not to say that Lian hadn't formed her own mental images of her chat partners, based on the questions they asked, the causes they championed, and even the apostrophes they neglected to use.

Crowbar: U got 2 see the body? What stage? Macerated?

For example, Lian wouldn't have been surprised to learn that Crowbar—whoever he or she was—had something to do with the medical profession, or at the very least had several well-worn texts from the field. This wasn't the first time that Crowbar had tossed out a term that Lian had to look up in a separate browser window.

Komiko: Some swelling, yes. Her skin was kind of gray/blue. She was face down, I couldn't tell how much damage there was.

Crowbar: 99% of corpses face down in h2o . . . more bacteria in the torso means more gas so it floats & limbs hang

Torch: Appetizing image.

Crowbar: U snap any pix?

Lian ejected the memory stick—a 16-gig drive encased in a lucky rabbit's foot—from her laptop, clicked the USB cable into her phone's port, and quickly uploaded the photos of the man in the tracksuit. She was playing a hunch, and maybe it was nothing. But if anyone could identify the man or hunt down the facts on him, she felt sure it would be her compatriots in 06/04.

The name, of course, was a nod to the Tiananmen Square protests of 1989, and the unforgettable military actions on June 4. Students and intellectuals in cities throughout Mainland China had begun demonstrating in favor of liberalization. What started as a small-scale tribute to the late, deposed General Secretary Hu Yaobang soon became a sweeping, nationwide demand for political and economic reform. The conservative government declared martial law, and on that dark day in June, the People's Liberation Army mowed down thousands of civilians in the areas around the square.

Lian hadn't even been alive then, and learning the facts of the massacre had been an uphill battle. Her textbooks had contained no mention of this event, and the Chinese Communist Party blocked Web searches. For most of her life, the protests had been a mythical thing. They existed only in guarded whispers in the school hallways, or in overheard conversations when her parents thought she was asleep. Lian had become fascinated by these hidden injustices and by the smoke and mirrors that had been used to cover up the facts.

But a quote from Stewart Brand, lettered in tidy zhōngwén script and pinned to her corkboard, reminded Lian every day: *"Information wants to be free."* She had pieced together the whole story and had been stunned enough to seek out the like-minded souls of 06/04. Together, they would effect change in this nation—and in this world.

One tracksuited fat man at a time, if need be.

Komiko: No photos of the girl; didn't have my phone then. But this guy showed up and started bossing the cops around. He set off any alarms for you guys?

5:57 PM HKT — *Komiko has uploaded five JPGs*

Crowbar: I got nothing

Torch: Nice work with the full-on and side shots. That should make it easier for me to find something on him.

Komiko: Thanks. Eager to see what you turn up.

Whatever info there was on the man, Lian felt sure that Torch would root it out. Much of what she'd learned about Tiananmen, and about other abuses of government power, had come from following the 06/04 blog back when she lived on the mainland. Torch pushed reams of stolen data onto the short-lived mirror sites, and Lian had devoured as much as she could before each URL went dead. She didn't know anything about Torch as a person—though, from the proper grammar and the bullish attitude, she'd long suspected an educated male and had taken to thinking in terms of "him"—but as a hacker, he was without peer.

Lian dithered, though, on whether she thought Crowbar might be an older female health professional or a young schoolboy with anatomy textbooks tucked under his mattress; the depth of knowledge sometimes felt out of step with the juvenile typos and emoticons.

Crowbar: U guys think Blossom is goin 2 show?

Torch: Doubting she will, at this point. Maybe we work best as a trio anyway.

Komiko: Wait, why do you think it's a "she" we're talking about?

Torch: . . .

Torch: Seriously? With a handle like "Blossom," I think it's pretty obvious.

Komiko: What happened to never taking anything for granted? Besides, he/she/it, makes no difference. Blossom has earned a place in 06/04 and deserves a warm welcome.

Crowbar: Agreed x 1000

Lian smiled. At least two of them were on the same page. This wasn't the first time that Torch had suggested keeping their membership capped at three, but the group hadn't felt quite whole since Mynah Bird's arrest two months back. That had taken them all by surprise: Mynah had turned out to be a forty-year-old environmental activist, caught in the act of heavy-duty corporate theft. They had known from his sometimes-manic posts that he was a risk-taker who recklessly skirted the law, and he'd gone one step too far with a digital signature in his bank-hacking code. Now he was in jail—or worse—and, after weeks of discussion, the group was ready to fill his chair.

She was just thankful that Mynah had been the paranoid type who deleted all his 06/04 files every time he logged off. The authorities hadn't connected him to the group, which meant that their work could continue even in his absence.

Lian heard the click of her bedroom doorknob turning. She quickly keyed the letters "BRB"—"be right back"—and hit the function key to kick her laptop into screensaver mode. By the time her mother entered the room, there was nothing more damning on display than digitized woodcuts of pandas among bamboo.

"You always knock so quietly!" Lian said with a smile.

Her mother turned back to the door and gave a knock on the inside. "Sorry, little panda. I wasn't thinking. We're leaving for the restaurant in half an hour. You need to get changed."

"Fine, fine," Lian said, standing up and moving between her mother and the computer. "I just have to wrap up a couple of things online, okay?"

"You spend too much time online, Lian. There's a whole world that doesn't fit inside your computer. It's not normal for a pretty girl like you to hibernate playing video games all day."

"Well," Lian said, ushering her mother back into the hall. "You'll be horrified to know that you and Mingmei are on the same page about something. Why don't the two of you get together over bubble tea and figure out what's best for me? Let me know what you decide."

"Half an hour, Lian."

"Not a second later," Lian said, closing the door. She sat back down at her desk and returned to the chat just as a new message popped up.

6:00 PM HKT—*Blossom has requested access to this conversation*

> **Crowbar:** [Allow]
>
> **Torch:** [Allow]
>
> **Komiko:** [Allow]

And just like that, 06/04 had a new member.

> **Crowbar:** Welcome & glad U R on the team! So much 2 B done
>
> **Blossom:** Thank you. An honor and a little overwhelming. Not sure Im ready for the big leagues.
>
> **Komiko:** Nonsense. You wouldn't be here if we didn't think you were qualified. Torch vetted you like crazy.
>
> **Torch:** True. I have to admit, the Drax takedown . . . not too shabby.

Lian rolled her eyes. That sort of grudging respect, extracted like a pained tooth? Torch was definitely male.

Blossom had been responsible for compiling and crunching the mountains of data needed to prove that a company called Drax Plastics was breaking almost every environmental regulation on the books. The discovery of a temporarily unprotected subfolder on the Drax cloud drive had put all the pieces into place, with the names, account numbers, and staggering payoff amounts given to the lawmakers who looked the other way. It had been a major victory of the lone citizen against the big corporation, and 06/04 had certainly taken notice.

> **Blossom:** Thanks. Ive followed 06/04 for a while now, very impressed with the work you do. I think Im in good company. Crowbar, your stint in Junk Bay . . . Komiko, exposing the Wan Chai construction bribes—

> **Torch:** Okay, you've researched us, we've researched you, everybody loves everybody. If you've done your homework then you know our rules, but it's worth stating for the record:

> **Torch:** Don't *offer* personal info, don't *ask* for personal info. Strength in anonymity.

Lian grimaced. Blossom was just through the gates, and already Torch was posturing.

There was a rap at Lian's door, and her mother said, "Twenty-five minutes." Lian sighed. It was time for her to stop being an activist for the evening and slip into the role of dutiful daughter.

> **Komiko:** Guys, I have evening plans, so I need to log off. Don't haze the new kid too hard while I'm gone, all right?

> **Crowbar:** Goodnite Komiko

> **Blossom:** Cool, where you headed?

> **Torch:** WHAT DID I *JUST* SAY?

Torch: Personal details compromise the safety of the whole group. Komiko's activities outside this board are none of our business.

Blossom: . . .

Blossom: Sorry.

Crowbar: Dont sweat it, Torch is always prickly. U will learn to <3 it.

Lian wasn't sure that was quite true, but this wasn't the time to weigh in.

6:06 PM HKT — *Komiko has logged off*

She closed the laptop, set it on the desk, and moved to her closet. Her father had requested that she wear the cheongsam—the traditional Chinese dress—for tonight's event. Lian knew it was a beautiful and respectful article of clothing; that wasn't the problem. She just didn't like the way she felt in that clothing. She might as well drape herself in a neon sign that read PRIVILEGE. It felt like such a betrayal of the 06/04 ethos. What would the others have thought of her if they knew the truth—that she was heading off to smile and nod her way through a dinner in an exclusive Central District restaurant?

She unzipped the garment bag and felt a pang of unease. The dress was precisely the same deep shade of crimson as the surfboard that had nearly taken off her head earlier. It was hard to fathom that her carefree beach trip had been just a few hours ago. She'd showered and scrubbed, but somehow she didn't feel as if she'd been able to wash off the stain that Big Wave Bay had left on her.

She laid the cheongsam carefully on her bed and went back to the closet for a matching pair of heels. That she had so many to choose from suddenly made her feel sick.

Was it this? Was it guilt over her family's position here, and the niceties it afforded her, that had led her to join 06/04? Was she playing dress up as an activist just to ease her conscience over the high-rise living, the private schools, the closet full of shoes?

She shook her head to dispel these thoughts. No, she decided. She had read the blog back on the mainland. She had believed then, and believed more fervently now, in the group's causes. It was hypocrisy that she couldn't stand, that she strove to root out and expose.

And that meant capitalists and communists alike were in their sights.

Lian stood briefly at her window—looking down at the whole of Hong Kong Island that lay out at her feet—and then drew the shades so she could get changed.

FOUR

"You look uncomfortable," her mother said, barely louder than a whisper.

"Not surprising," Lian answered, "considering that I am uncomfortable." Penned in between her parents, she shifted in the backseat of the taxi, tugging at the hem of the cheongsam where it bit into her thigh.

"I understand," her mother said, pursing her lips. "But it's important that you not *look* it."

Lian sighed and turned to stare out the cab's window. Truth be told, it wasn't just the dress that was making her feel ill at ease. As they cruised through the Central District, the skyscrapers looming to either side seemed to glare down at her. She doubted she'd ever feel "at home" among these monuments to commerce.

But her mother was right; she knew the importance of this dinner to her father's business—they had been emphasized repeatedly and in no uncertain terms. She could play "dutiful daughter" for one night.

As if on cue, her father cleared his throat and inclined his head toward her.

"My little Xiao-Lian," he said, and Lian tried not to wince at the overly parental tone of his voice. "You look beautiful tonight. Like a little porcelain doll."

Lian tried to smile. She knew he meant it as a term of endearment, but she chafed at the thought that she was as fragile, or merely decorative, as a doll.

"I am counting on both of you," he continued, "to help ensure that this evening goes perfectly."

"Of course," Lian and her mother answered in unison.

As the taxi sped down Garden Road, her father detailed the guest list: a mixture of high-ranking Hong Kong officials, successful exporters, and wealthy foreign investors looking to diversify. Everyone who would be in that room tonight wanted a piece of Hong Kong, and he had to prove that he was the man who could get it for them at the right price and make the introductions that would lead to big windfalls for everybody.

But Lian tuned out the roll call and let her mind wander, gazing up at the HSBC Building, the Jardine House, the monolithic Bank of China Tower. Even at this hour, on a Sunday, more of the office windows were lit than not. The world of high finance and higher stakes—the world that her father had increasingly positioned himself in since their move from the mainland—took dedication, she knew. The work never stopped.

The cab turned a corner, their destination drifting into view—another in a sea of steel-and-glass towers, rimmed in color-shifting LED lights and flanked by bronze dragon statues thirteen feet high. Town cars and sporty European models amassed in front as parking valets dashed through the scene, coordinating the comings and goings of well-dressed patrons.

The opulence of it all felt oppressive. Just a few miles away, in the New Territories, there were people who had nothing—people who gazed across Victoria Harbor at the bright lights of Central District as if it were an alien city on some unreachable moon; people who could eat for a year on the food that would be scraped off plates into the trash after this dinner that Lian was about to smile through as best she could.

Again, she twisted in her seat, loud green neon splashing through the windows and shimmering against the gold accents on her dress. The lighting must have given her a sickly pallor, because her father's eyes softened for a moment.

"Do not be nervous, Lian," he said. "Just be yourself, and you will make me proud."

Lian nodded, but she knew that *herself* was the last thing she could be tonight.

They got out at the curb, her father paying the fare and leaving a generous tip. As the cab pulled away and became a distant red dot in a city full of them, Lian felt a flutter of unease in her stomach.

No escape now.

The elevator operator gave a curt nod as they stepped inside. He pressed a few buttons, and the elevator rocketed to the twenty-sixth floor. With an elegant chime, the doors opened directly into the foyer of Fàn Xī, all dark wood and decorative red lanterns. Lian's father strode to the host's stand, past waiting couples and small groups who sipped at overpriced cocktails and adjusted their cuff links as they held out hope for an open table.

The maître d' checked the night's reservations, realized he was talking to the man who had rented out the banquet room for the evening, gave welcoming nods to Lian's family, and led the three of them at an unhurried pace through the restaurant.

Lian caught the subtle signal the maître d' flashed the bartender, and as they passed the bar, the first in a row of multicolored liquor shots burst into flame and then cascaded into the next glass, the bartender's hands moving astonishingly quickly and finishing with a flourish, capping the final glass with half a lime to douse the fire.

The bar patrons gasped and gave polite applause, and even Lian flashed a genuine smile to the bartender as she passed. The spectacle, though, had been lost on her father, so focused on the impending dinner that he hadn't broken his stride or turned his head.

The maître d' led them past a decorative screen, hand-painted in delicate brushstrokes with a night garden scene, and into the Fàn Xī banquet room. Much as she didn't want to be there, Lian was momentarily taken by the beauty and care with which the room had been arranged.

More red lanterns made a graceful arc across the ceiling, highlighting the fine gold filigree set into the trim on the walls and the backs of the chairs. Crimson tea candles on the table cast flickering spotlights on the half dozen black porcelain vases that served as centerpieces, each containing an intricate miniature tree crafted in glass, every one unique. Even the table itself seemed carved from a single perfect piece of rich dark wood, unbroken by seams.

Her father, naturally, had his place card at the table's head: the zhōngwén characters, and below them, in copperplate pinyin, Hung Zhi-Kai. The seat to his right was marked for Lili—her mother. Lian looked to either side of these settings for her own name, but it wasn't there.

The farther she walked from her parents' chairs, the more resentful she grew until she eventually spotted her card—nearly all the way at the other end of the room.

Fantastic. Marooned down here, away from the only people she knew, stuck next to some stranger named— she squinted and leaned in to read the place card—Matt Harrison.

He was already there, his back to her as he gazed out the window wall. His suit looked expensive. Mingmei would have known the designer at a glance, no doubt. Messy blond hair curled over his collar, and he was shifting uncomfortably, tugging at his shirt collar to loosen his tie. Lian softened at the sight; maybe he was just as uncomfortable here as she was. It might give them something to chat about.

She pulled out her chair, and he turned in his. His eyes were a striking green, and his tan would have made Mingmei jealous. Taking a deep breath, she put on a smile and was about to introduce herself when he spoke first.

"Excellent," he said, his accent American. "I'll have a Diet Coke, please. Um ... " He made a show of searching for the right Cantonese word. "M̀hgōi."

She drew back, jerking her arm away from his hand.

"I am *not* your waitress," she said in English, picking up her place card and waving it at him.

The boy's cheeks flushed as red as the lanterns. "Oh. Oh, man. I'm so sorry. I just, I saw your dress, and I guess I thought ... wow. Sorry." His turn now to squint at her name. "Sorry, Hung."

She gave him a withering look and sat down next to him. True, the cheongsam was overly traditional looking; true, the waitresses she'd noticed in the restaurant were wearing dresses very much like it. Still, she couldn't help but feel offended.

"Hung is my *family* name," she corrected him, replacing her card. "Family first, then given name." It was such basic knowledge, but Westerners always got it wrong.

"Sorry . . . Zee-ow Lee-an," he said, taking a stab. Her name sounded like rotten cabbage in his mouth. She shook her head sadly.

"Lian," she said, pronouncing it like she was tutoring a slow child. "Just call me Lian."

"Lian," he repeated dutifully. "Nice to meet you. I'm ..." He paused. "I guess to you I'd be Harrison Matthew-Chase. Or just Matt."

He held out his hand. She gave it a light, cursory shake— after all, she was supposed to be on her "best behavior"— and then quickly busied herself with unfolding her napkin.

There had been eight or nine people in the room when they'd arrived, and now other guests were being led in by the maître d'. It was a mix of well-dressed locals, a handful of Europeans, a boisterous Australian quartet, and about half a dozen Americans. Lian watched her father greet each newcomer, make introductions among the guests, and nod to their places at the table. She had no doubt that he'd carefully seated everyone to optimize dinner conversation and facilitate deal making.

Everyone but her and this Matt kid.

He looked to be about her age, and he was admittedly pretty nice to look at—as well as the wavy blond hair and jade green eyes, he looked athletic, with broad shoulders. His teeth, she couldn't help but notice, were movie-star white. The only asymmetry was a dimple in just one cheek when he smiled. If she had seen him on a billboard or a mall marquee, she probably would have stopped to see what he was selling. Probably toothpaste.

But in person, he was losing points with her fast. He sniffed at the tea that the actual waitress—in her tight red dress with gold trim, Lian grudgingly acknowledged— brought out, then pushed it away in revulsion, splashing a few drops on the centerpiece. As the guests took their seats and the appetizers arrived, he poked at his food with a curious finger.

"What the hell is this stuff?" he whispered to Lian.

"Octopus carpaccio," she whispered back, swiftly moving the bite to her mouth with her chopsticks. "It's delicious."

Matt made a face. "No, thanks."

The salmon skin salad brought a similar response. Lian ate her delicate portion as she stole sidelong glances at the American boy as he fumbled with his chopsticks, trying to push aside the salmon and just nab a few daikon sprouts, spilling fish and onion on the table and into his lap.

Finally, he gave up, dropping the chopsticks rather noisily and flagging a waitress over.

"Look," he said in a hushed, earnest tone. "I'm sure this stuff is great, but is there any way you guys could whip me up some . . . you know . . . a bacon cheeseburger, some nachos? Anything I can eat with my hands would be killer."

Lian couldn't look at him. She hid her face behind her hand, not sure whether she was about to burst out laughing or berate him for his sad, dull palate. A cheeseburger? What an idiot.

The waitress frowned and left wordlessly. Matt picked up one chopstick and began doodling lazy curlicues around the edge of his salad plate.

"I don't think I'm getting nachos," he said after a moment. He flashed Lian a smile that was probably supposed to be charming.

"Yeah," she said. "Good guess. The next course is crispy pig throat, so I imagine you'll be sitting that one out, too."

"Are you kidding me?" he choked.

"It comes with rice. Can you eat rice?"

"That depends," he said. "Can I have a fork?"

This time she couldn't help but roll her eyes. "There is literally nothing easier than chopsticks. *Infants* use them."

She held hers up and demonstrated their operation. "This one stays still. This one does all the moving. Two pieces working in harmony, see?"

"Only one piece to a fork," Matt muttered.

"It is an *honor*," she said sarcastically, "to meet the first person who ever died of starvation while sitting at a banquet table. Congratulations, Matt Harrison."

"Hey, look, Chinese food just isn't for me, okay?"

Lian did her best not to sneer, but she wasn't sure she succeeded. "Yes, well. . . . Here, we just call it 'food.'"

"So this is really what you guys eat? Like, on a regular basis? It's like you found the weirdest possible things to put in your mouth, and the least convenient utensils to get them there."

She was incredulous. "Do you realize that, in one sentence, you just dumped on thousands of years of culture?"

He shrugged. "I didn't mean—"

"And that, rather than trying to assimilate, you have arrogantly suggested that we should be bending over backward to suit you? How typically Western."

"Hey, now, hang on a second, Lian. I'm not trying to start an international incident. But you're used to this type of food. I mean, you've lived on this island all your life, I bet."

She deftly maneuvered her last bit of salmon to her mouth and shook her head. "Not exactly. We lived on the mainland for most of my life. Our move here was relatively recent."

"Oh," he said with some concern. "So . . . I guess . . . you guys used to be poor?"

Lian almost spat out the tea she was sipping. "Did you seriously just say that?"

Matt backpedaled. "No, I just . . . I mean, I did a little reading on the Internet before we moved here, just so I'd know what to expect. I was under the impression that the mainland was . . . you know . . ."

Lian spun a chopstick in her fingers, fighting the urge to jab it into his thigh. "You're from America, right?"

"Yeah," he said, smoothing his napkin over his lap. "Colorado."

"So, how was it, riding a horse to school?"

"What?"

"And I assume that you owned several automatic weapons, to protect your stashes of drugs and pornography and burritos. Right?"

He shook his head in confusion. "What are you talking about?"

"Because that's what *I* read on the Internet," she said. "And it must be true. Everything I've ever heard about how Americans are lazy, violent, and morbidly obese must be true. Right?"

"Um," he said, still fidgeting with his napkin. "Well, I do like burritos."

The waitress came to collect their salad plates, and Lian took the opportunity to break from her conversation with Matt and speak to someone she didn't want to assault with a pair of chopsticks. The older gentleman to her left was engaged in an intense discussion of excise taxes; no joy there. Across the table, two of the Australian businessmen were leaning across one another to make their excited points to a local finance mogul. There wasn't much for Lian to contribute on that topic, either.

She cast a glance down the length of the table to her parents, who were chatting with a handsome man, whose gesticulations were as broad as his American accent. In a brief lull while the Australians whispered among themselves, Lian heard her father's voice, speaking flawless and deferential English.

"No need to apologize, I assure you."

The American man looked relieved. "Xie xie," he said, butchering his thanks. "I know just enough Chinese to order dim sum or find a restroom, but I'm sure I'm mangling every syllable."

"Not to worry, Mr. Harrison. We can speak in English . . . at least until you need a restroom."

The two men laughed at this, and then they dropped their voices to talk business.

"That's your father, down there?" Lian asked Matt.

He nodded. "Rand Harrison. The man, the myth, the legend." His tone suggested that at least two of those might be overstatements.

"He made his millions in burrito sales, I take it?"

This got a smile from Matt. "Clothing manufacture, actually. He owns a whole series of factories. I think he's up to nine now. Used to be headquartered out of Colorado Springs, but then he discovered Hong Kong outsourcing, and he never looked back." He tried a sip of his tea and grimaced. "Because, you know, you can pay people so much less here, obviously."

It was a good thing the entrées hadn't arrived yet, or she would have dumped his into his lap. "You are just a stellar ambassador for your country," she growled.

He just shrugged. Was he actually smiling? Was he enjoying this?

"Wait," Lian said, the facts clicking into place. "Harrison, as in . . ." She drew the stylized H logo in the air with three quick slashes of her chopstick. "Harrison Sportswear? Harrison Casual?"

"And just wait until you see Harrison Denim," he said, taking on the rich baritone of a runway announcer. "An upscale collection featuring classic designs with a contemporary twist. In stores this fall."

"So you're *that* Harrison." Lian was familiar with the Harrison Outfitters store at Fashion Walk—Mingmei had pulled her along to the grand opening, gushing over the styles and piling up armloads of clothing that even she could barely afford.

"No," he corrected her as the pig throat arrived. "My dad is '*that* Harrison.' I'm just the kid who got dragged halfway around the world with him."

"It's not all bad, though, is it?" Lian asked, raising an eyebrow as she nabbed a bit of crispy fat in her chopsticks. "You're getting to experience amazing cuisine like this."

"And talk to charming young women like you," he said. To his credit, he held the chopsticks as she had shown him and captured several grains of rice. He even got a few of them into his mouth.

"Hey, look at that!" she said. "You can be taught."

"I'm a C-plus student, at best," he said, smiling. "What about you? You a straight-A kind of girl?"

She shrugged. "I've made the honors list at Island South every year."

"And I'm guessing Island South is bigger than my living room."

"It's a private high school," she said. "So maybe not too much bigger."

He grinned. "Private school, huh?"

She felt her face flushing. He was smiling as if he'd caught her admitting something embarrassing . . . and the truth was, she felt like he had. It was just another reminder of the privilege Lian enjoyed while others did without. She sank in her seat and tried to gain some conversational high ground.

"Still," she said, looking for a casual deflection of the topic, "home schooling must get pretty lonely. You take away the social aspect of high school, and it's just learning. I'll bet you miss all your friends back in America."

"Um," he mumbled, attempting another bite of rice. "Not really. I mean, we stay in touch, you know? I Skype with them all the time." He looked up, as if making sure he had her attention. "Especially with my girlfriend. Like, every night. Morning, for her, I guess."

She nodded placidly and took another bite of pork. Was it supposed to bother her that Matt had a girlfriend?

Was he fishing for a reaction? Boys, she already knew, were impossible. Apparently, American boys were doubly so.

Delicate rosettes of medium beef arrived next, with the waitress pointedly informing Matt what the meat was. Lian couldn't help but smile at the simple gratitude on his face. Before she could say anything, he picked up one of the flower-shaped pieces in his chopsticks and tossed the whole thing into his mouth.

His eyes watered instantly, and she felt a pang of pity.

"That green stuff in the centers," she said, indicating on her own plate, "is called 'wasabi.' It can be a little spicy."

"No kidding," he gasped, managing to swallow his bite and then grabbing for his tea like it was the best drink he'd ever tasted. "I don't know how you guys haven't set yourselves on fire with this stuff."

Lian chose not to waste any time figuring out if what Matt had said was offensive. She ate a couple of the spicy rosettes, with no adverse reaction, and deflected the topic again. "So . . . assuming you make it out of this meal alive, what are you thinking of doing with that home-school education? Burrito magnate?"

He shrugged. "I don't know. My dad wants me to take over Harrison Corp after he retires, but I don't think I really have much of a head for business. Lately, I've been thinking it might be pretty cool to run my own surf shop."

She waited for the irony to dawn on him, but it clearly wasn't happening. "Wouldn't that require some kind of 'head for business,' too?"

"I guess it would," he admitted. "But you gotta figure it's a mellower clientele, with significantly lower expectations."

"Your faith in your own abilities is inspiring."

He caught the sarcasm but responded with a perfect, friendly smile. "And you? Loftier goals than selling board wax to white guys with ill-advised dreadlocks?"

She straightened in her seat. "I'm thinking of training to become a human rights lawyer."

"Ah," he said, raising his eyebrows. "So you're setting out to change the world?"

"Is there something wrong with that?"

"Oh," he said, carefully unwrapping a thin strip of beef from around its bright green nucleus. "There's nothing wrong with *saying* it. It's the *doing* it that's the hard part."

She was ready to argue. But, before she could, she was distracted by the conversation at the far end of the table.

It was really more of a monologue by this point, actually. Harrison Senior had slowly drawn the attention of everyone down both sides of the massive table. His voice carried through the room, as rich and dark as the wooden walls that reflected it.

"But none of these," he was saying, "hold a candle to the threats found online. Modern business can't survive without the Internet, of course . . . but the dangers are manifold. Every computer is a weapon if it's in the wrong hands."

Lian felt the little hairs on the back of her neck stand on end and hoped that no one in the room noticed that she was suddenly somewhat self-conscious.

"Every cyber-attack necessitates a rethinking of the firewall," Harrison continued. "Maintaining that kind of dynamism bleeds resources from companies trying to build shields faster than their attackers can forge swords. But I can at least appreciate the hackers' and coders' tactics. That kind of warfare takes actual skills, a talent for parsing ones and zeroes and using them like a craftsman would. It's not the programming geniuses who are the real threat to the corporations—what is stolen is insured. It can be recovered. No, the real threat to people like us is these . . . *bloggers*."

He spat out this last word like it was rotten fish.

Lian could feel her ears burning.

"Any monkey with a laptop and a Wi-Fi connection can jump online and post anonymously. The clever ones disguise their IP addresses or appear to be dozens of different commenters. They can post their slander without fear of reprisal, can spread their—often poorly spelled— thoughts to the world with no accountability. And they can cripple a company's reputation with no more than a few clicks of a mouse."

Harrison puffed up his chest for his big summation. "They are dangerous, they are irresponsible, and I am certain you all agree with me that, regardless of cost, they *must be stopped*." He pounded his fist into his hand with each of the last three words. The Australians and Americans applauded. Even the locals nodded vigorously.

"That's . . . not an entirely accurate portrait of the blogging community," Lian said. She felt riled by Harrison's speech, but she kept her words steady and strong enough to be heard as the clapping died down.

Heads turned; eyes drilled into her. Lian saw her father cringe with embarrassment, saw his neck muscles twitch as if he were straining to quiet her from across the room. To her right, she heard Matt suck in his breath, but whether he was impressed or frightened by her brazenness, she couldn't tell.

There was an interminable silence as Harrison seemed to appraise her. Finally, he gave her a perfect smile—like the one his son had inherited, but with all the sincerity leeched out—and said, "Do tell, little lady."

She had the room's attention; now she had to choose her words carefully if she hoped to change even one mind.

"The element you're talking about . . . they do exist, of course." Concede one of his points. Let him drop his defenses a bit. "But most bloggers have only the best interests of the public in mind. The best of them are the watchdogs who wake the rest of us up to tell us that something bad is happening." She emphasized *the rest of us*; better that the room not guess that she herself was one of the enemy.

"Watchdogs, hmm?" Harrison said. His tone suggested that he'd enjoy putting those dogs to sleep.

"Someone has to hold these shady business practices up to the light," she said, "to make these corporations take some responsibility for their illegal actions. It's . . . it should be the job of our government officials," she said, and immediately felt the locals turning on her. "But so often, they're afraid to act . . . or unwilling, since it would jeopardize their own connections, their own reputations. They've got their eyes on the bottom line instead of on the citizens they're supposed to represent."

An angry rumbling started at her father's end of the table and rolled toward her like the dark wave that had swept her away earlier. In the muttered chatter, she heard phrases like "know her place" and "improper" and "thought they were meant to be deferential." She felt hot all over and might have dashed for the door if her feet didn't feel like they were stuck in concrete.

It was Rand Harrison, surprisingly, who quieted the table with little more than a gesture.

"Now, now," he said, as if all the room were dull, unruly children. "I welcome this sort of discourse. The young generation has much of value to say, if we're willing to listen."

Lian thought she heard Matt stifle a snort.

"Th-thank you, Mr. Harrison," Lian said, genuinely grateful for his intervention even as she doubted its motives. "I mean . . . the closure of Drax Plastics, not long ago. That was all due to the actions of one blogger, turning a spotlight on some pretty dark corners of their environmental practices. And, to my way of thinking . . . that's a good thing."

"Oh, indeed," Harrison said, continuing to surprise. "To my way of thinking as well."

More muttering in the room, but it had a confused flavor, rather than an angry one.

"After all," Harrison said, "Drax was one of Harrison Corps' competitors. If the bite of a rabid watchdog takes them out of the picture, and I can keep my hands clean, then bravo to the blogger, I suppose."

He held up his hands to the room, turning them back and forth to prove their cleanliness. The dinner guests laughed at this, and Harrison launched into a self-important diatribe about what a "competitor" really was, and how Harrison Corp was outgrowing them.

Lian's moment had passed, and Harrison had let her off the hook, albeit in the most disingenuous way she could imagine. A glance at her father's face told her that she hadn't heard the last of it, though. She cast her eyes down to her hands and stayed silent until dessert arrived. Her appetite had waned considerably, but she tried a cursory taste and found it delicious.

Out of the corner of her eye, she saw Matt take one cautious bite, smile, and then go back for another, bigger one.

"So, uh . . . this isn't bad," he said quietly. If he had any thoughts about her tête-à-tête with his father, he was keeping them to himself. "I'm almost afraid to ask what it is."

"Steamed sweet egg custard," she answered, her affect flat.

"Okay. So far, so good. What's this thing in the middle?"

"Longan," she said. "'The dragon's eye.'"

"Um. But it's not a real dragon's eye, right?"

She finally looked up at him. The sincerity on his face was actually charming. Sad, but charming.

"No," she reassured him. "It's a fruit. But see how the seeds show through and look a little like the pupil of an eyeball?"

He nodded. "That's really cool. And this sort of sticky-sweet stuff around the edges?" He chewed a piece of it happily.

"Hasma," she said.

"And . . . what's hasma?"

"I don't want to tell you."

"Come on," he said, scooping up another bite. "It tastes great, so it's not gonna bother me."

"Fine," she relented. "It's rehydrated fat from around the fallopian tubes of a frog."

He paused with the spoon halfway to his mouth, and then burst out laughing. "I'm impressed, I really am," he said, taking the bite. "It takes a pretty twisted mind to make up something like that on the spot. Well done, Lian."

She smiled and slid her bowl to the right. "I'm glad you think so. Here, you can have mine."

He thanked her and dug into the frog fat with gusto.

Lian decided against telling him she wasn't lying. No matter how funny his expression would have been.

As the dinner began to break up and the guests stood up to mingle, Lian managed to slip past her parents—occupied as they were with the Australians—and out into the main area of the restaurant, past the bar and into the foyer, where she felt like she could breathe for the first time since she'd arrived. She took a seat on a plush, empty bench and tried to collect her thoughts, when suddenly she felt a hand on her shoulder.

"Hey," Matt said, looking down at her. "I'm glad we got seated together. I feel like I learned a lot tonight." He gave her that dazzling smile one more time, and then said, "Okay. So. I'll see you around, Lian."

He gave her shoulder a gentle squeeze and then walked across the room to where his father was standing, checking his watch. Lian quickly dropped her eyes; she wasn't in the mood to go for a second round with Harrison Senior. But the man's voice carried, and she heard him telling Matt to call a car.

"I'll see you at home later," Harrison told his son. "I've got some business to attend to."

"Surprising," Matt said. His tone told Lian that Rand Harrison must always be attending to some business.

"Don't stay up late on your computer," Harrison called after him. "You have class in the morning."

Lian looked up to see Matt hit the button for the elevator. She was about to turn and walk away when she saw the doors open a moment later. A man stepped out of the elevator, carrying what looked like a very expensive overcoat folded over one arm, and began to cross the foyer.

She had to try very hard not to look like she was staring at the newcomer; she focused on the exquisite red lanterns as he walked past her. But she was certain. He was in a tailored suit and expensive shoes now, rather than a puffy blue tracksuit, but there was no mistaking the jowls, the bald spot, the potbelly.

He was the man from the police boat, the one she'd snapped the photos of on her phone, who she had assumed was one of the cops.

He was now helping Rand Harrison into a very expensive overcoat.

FIVE

Her parents would be tied up saying their farewells for another hour. Lian found her mother at the bar, explaining the fragrances of the various *baijiu* liquors to a small group of Europeans who seemed genuinely interested in the topic.

"I'm going to catch a cab," Lian said, after begging the guests' pardon for the interruption. "I want to get home and check over my summer coursework one last time." That wasn't the real reason for her hasty departure, of course, but she promised herself she'd glance at the assignments once more before bed, just so she wouldn't have told her mother an out-and-out lie.

Hung Lili gave her a curt nod, said "Be safe," and returned to her conversation.

Lian tried to move stealthily back through the restaurant, but she caught her father's eye and momentarily stumbled in her heels. He said nothing but held her in his stern gaze for a long moment before breaking away to laugh at one of the Australians' off-color jokes. Lian took the opportunity to exit, but she didn't quite feel like she'd made it out unscathed.

Twenty-six floors below, the doorman was able to flag her a taxi so quickly that she doubled her standard tip. Three car lengths ahead of her, the potbellied man was just stepping behind the wheel of a pristine, new-model black Mercedes with Rand Harrison in its backseat.

"Where to?" her cab driver grunted.

"I don't know yet," she answered. "Go where that Mercedes goes, but not too close, okay?"

"Oooh," the driver said in a bored tone. "Intrigue."

Maybe his sarcasm was warranted. She did feel a little ridiculous ordering the tail, like she was in some bad American cop show. But she couldn't help but be curious about the fat man. Back at the beach, she'd figured him for a plainclothes detective, or a senior officer who'd been called out to the crime scene without the time to grab his uniform. So then why was he moonlighting as Harrison's chauffeur, fetching his coat and driving him to whatever "business" he was attending to?

Something stank about the whole situation.

"So," the cabbie said. "Are you his wife or his mistress?"

"Excuse me?"

"This part of town," he explained. "Wearing a dress that nice, chasing a car that fancy . . . come on. You're not the first pretty young thing to ask me to follow a two-timer."

"I'm *sixteen*," she said flatly.

"Intrigue, intrigue!" he replied, looking a million miles from even slightly interested.

It wasn't hard to believe that the cabbie was an old hand at tailing, though. He kept a respectful distance without ever letting a full city block come between the cars, and he seemed to know how the lights were timed so that he could hit them properly.

Harrison, for his part, didn't appear to be in any particular hurry. The Mercedes indicated a lane change, lazily drifted over, and headed up Gloucester Road for the Cross-Harbor Tunnel.

"Wave good-bye to the yacht club," the cabbie told her, just before the tunnel swallowed them up. "When we pop out the other side, I guarantee you're overdressed for wherever we end up."

Lian thought of correcting him—she was not some helpless rich airhead—but she didn't think he'd believe her. Let him think this was some petty, sordid affair—there was less chance of him remembering her that way, which was a good thing. Instead, she sat back in her seat, the tunnel lights moving over her in a steady rhythm, and tried to figure out some kind of plan.

The Mercedes emerged into the Hong Kong night and indicated for the Chatham exit. Lian peered through the cab's windshield, watching the sleek black car ease onto Gascoigne Road and then signal a right turn onto Nathan.

Every block they drove north seemed to grow louder, uglier, and more sinister. Lian had only ever been through the Kowloon district during daylight hours, and even then, she'd have shied away from most of these places. To either side of them were bars and clubs, beckoning with garish neon, bleeding music that boomed and thudded. Advertisements for fast food and hard liquor and plastic junk seemed bolted to every available surface above her head. The sidewalks were crowded, as they always seemed to be, with the sort of people who'd learned to keep their heads down, their faces hidden from passing cars.

"Your boyfriend's stopping," the cabbie said, nodding to the narrow alleyway into which the Mercedes had turned. The Mercedes' headlights shut off, and the black car was all but lost in the dark between buildings.

"Keep going," Lian instructed. "Pull over at the end of the block."

The cab slowed to let a bus by, then made for the curb. As she passed the Mercedes, Lian saw the potbellied man opening Harrison's door for him. The dome light threw odd shadows onto the man's jowly face.

"You sure this is where you want to be?" the cabbie asked, as she counted out the bills for the fare.

Lian certainly didn't want to be there, but she'd followed her hunch this far; she had to at least snag some photos of Harrison and the mystery man. She palmed her phone, brought up the camera app, and took a deep, calming breath. Out the back window of the cab, she saw the two men emerge from the alley and head up the sidewalk.

Now or never.

She stepped out of the cab and directly into a puddle of what she hoped was just dirty water. She swore lightly under her breath as the wetness seeped into her shoe. *Off to a great start.* She closed the car door and patted the fender to send the cab on its way.

Harrison and his companion had a substantial lead on her, but she narrowed the gap quickly; the portly man wasn't a speedy walker. The two men paused at a crosswalk, and Lian ducked into a doorway littered with used lottery tickets. She held out her phone and snapped a couple of shots, but they were useless: backs of heads, dark and blurry.

Another photo, taken as the men passed under the bright white neon of a beer sign, was a little better. She knew how ridiculous she must look, tottering down the Kowloon sidewalks in her cheongsam, holding her phone out at odd angles in front of her, heels going click-squish-click on the pavement.

"Fish ball?" a street vendor barked, startling her.

"I just ate," she said, breezing past him, hoping that she sounded cooler than she felt.

Up ahead, Harrison and his driver suddenly broke left and disappeared from view. Lian ran as fast as she dared to catch up. The men had slipped into a narrow alleyway between two towering, ramshackle apartment buildings. She craned her neck and squinted into the darkness.

Their destination was at the far end of the alley: what looked to be a tiny café, tucked away and calling as little attention to itself as possible. From this distance, she couldn't even read the signage.

Lian could feel her heartbeat's pressure in the back of her eyes. This was stupid and dangerous. There was no one in the alley but her and the men. This was the sort of dark corridor that a defenseless young woman might walk into but never come out of.

She thought of Mingmei, who'd had a very expensive clutch purse grabbed from her the last time she'd been in the Kowloon part of Hong Kong. Lian could almost hear her friend telling her to cut her losses and go home.

But she had come this far, and her curiosity was piqued. She brushed away her reservations and took a cautious step into the alley.

The potbellied man reached the café door and suddenly turned to check behind him. Lian dropped quickly behind some trash cans, her heart thudding. Her legs, constrained by the dress, were instantly wobbly, and she strained to keep her knees from hitting the grimy pavement.

From the alleyway's far end, she heard the fat man rap on the door—three fast knocks, a pause, then two more. She gingerly held the corner of her phone out around the trash bin, and watched on the camera screen as the men were let inside the building. From here, they were two small shadows. She had to get closer, had to get a clear enough photo to make this peril worthwhile.

The door closed behind the men, and Lian made herself count slowly to ten before she stood and moved down the alleyway, staying as close to the wall as she could. The sign over the door, she could now see, read THE FAMILY HAND CAFÉ. And below that, the characters for *mahjong*. A gaming house, then.

She thought of knocking on the door in the same pattern the fat man had used. But no; she'd be too out of her element.

Instead, she moved to the window to the right of the door. A cardboard placard filled most of the window's area, but around its edges she could peer into the café.

She spotted Harrison right away, just past the gaming tables. He was at a side door, on either side of which stood massive, burly guards. As the potbellied man stood silently by, Harrison spoke with the guards. Lian was no lip-reader, but as she watched she grew increasingly certain that Harrison was speaking fast and fluent Chinese.

Hadn't he stumbled over basic words at the dinner? Hadn't he prevailed on the whole room to switch to English? And yet here he was, and Lian was pretty sure he wasn't looking for a bathroom or ordering dim sum.

She thumbed the shutter on her camera app and managed to get a handful of decent shots as Harrison and his companion were allowed through the side door. Both men were in the frame, their faces clear even if their intentions were anything but. She powered off the phone, satisfied that her investigation hadn't been a waste after all.

She hadn't gone more than a couple of steps back toward the street when four shadows appeared in the mouth of the alleyway. Again, she felt her pulse jump.

"Leǐ ho," one of the men called as they approached. "Are you lost?"

"Can we help you?" another asked.

Lian wasn't sure whether she was just imagining the sinister undertones, but she didn't think it was wise to stick around and find out. She walked toward them, the only way out of the alley, with a purposeful stride and her head held high, her gaze level.

For just a moment, she thought they might close on her, and she prepared to scream for help. But at the last second, they moved aside to let her through.

As soon as she could see the street, she broke into a run. She made it to the sidewalk and fled from the alley mouth as fast as she could, waving at every cab until she spotted one with its "For Hire" flag up. As it pulled to the curb, she finally let herself breathe. She brought up the photos on her phone and flicked through them.

She wasn't quite certain what she was looking at, but she felt damn sure that Harrison and his buddy hadn't come to this part of town for anything as simple as a game of mahjong.

SIX

11:48 PM HKT — *Komiko has logged on*

Lian scanned back through the chat to see whether there was anything she'd missed since logging out earlier. Torch had laid out the group's guidelines for Blossom in terse, humorless sentences, with Crowbar trying to lighten the mood with cheery—if misspelled—levity. Blossom meekly agreed with Torch over and over, enough that Lian began to feel vaguely perturbed. She had to step back from her desk a moment and consider before she realized the reason: She, like Torch, was starting to think of Blossom as a girl, on the basis of the delicate user name. And in her head, she was hearing all the muttering from the dinner table. "I thought they were meant to be deferential."

The evening's trip into Kowloon had left her with a mix of emotions. She was thrilled to have captured a few decent photos and to take a tentative step toward linking Harrison with the poor dead girl. She was grateful to have made it back to the apartment in one piece and to have beaten her parents home, even though she'd been gone much longer than she'd hoped.

But more than anything, she was angry at herself for feeling so vulnerable, so unprotected . . . so much like a delicate, deferential blossom, nearly trampled into the dirty sidewalk of Nathan Road.

She'd taken off the high heels before she'd entered the apartment, treading lightly in case her parents were home. Now she shimmied out of the cheongsam, pausing to frown at the blotchy stain up its side before returning it to the garment bag; she'd have to deal with the dry cleaning later.

Once she'd changed into her pajamas, she felt less like a shrinking violet. "Comfortable and casual" beat out "dressed to impress" any day, in her book. With a smile, she even put on a spiked punk-rock bracelet that Mingmei had given her as a joke. She gave the mirror a sneer and pantomimed a quick jab; if those guys had tried anything in the alley, she could have taken out all four of them. No problem.

She carried the laptop over to her bed and sat down cross-legged, scrolling through the last of the earlier chat. Torch had logged off not long after she had—for no stated reason, as usual—and Crowbar had given a few upbeat reassurances to Blossom before they'd both signed off.

While she waited for the rest of 06/04 to log in, Lian poked through her e-mails—some spam, a useful coupon from an online electronics retailer, and a message from Mingmei saying she'd be by at 8:00 the next morning so they could head to school together on their scooters.

11:56 PM HKT — *Crowbar has logged on*

Komiko: What's the word, hummingbird?

Crowbar: Gettin sleepy, probably going 2 make this a short 1

Komiko: No arguments here.

11:57 PM HKT — *Blossom has logged on*

Crowbar: Hello again

Blossom: Hi guys! Or gals? Crap. Dont tell me, I dont want to know.

Lian laughed out loud at this.

Torch signed in with the customary precision, right at midnight, and brushed aside the small talk.

Torch: So you've got something new for us, Komiko?

Komiko: I do. I went for a casual stroll tonight and got a few photos.

12:01 AM HKT — *Komiko has uploaded three JPGs*

Komiko: I'm not going to quit my day job to get into portrait photography or anything, but does that look to you like our friend from the beach today?

Blossom: At first glance, it certainly does. Changing out of the tracksuit was a good move.

Crowbar: I agree . . . whos the other man?

Lian started to reply, but Torch beat her to the punch.

Torch: Rand Harrison.

Komiko: Correct. Clothing mogul, owns nine factories. Moved his operations here from the States. And apparently he likes a good game of mahjong.

She wasn't going to go into any detail about the dinner, but she was pleased to have gleaned a few facts from the man's son that she could share with the group.

Komiko: I don't want to jump to conclusions, obviously.

Torch: Obviously. That's not what 06/04 does.

Komiko: But seeing these two together, I have to entertain the thought that Harrison has something to do with the dead girl at Big Wave.

Komiko: Does he set off alarms for any of you?

Blossom: I dont know him, outside of seeing his logo on clothes and billboards and such. Seems like half of what anyones wearing right now is Harrison.

Crowbar: Hes shown up on the 06/04 radar B4

Lian grimaced. How hard was it to just type "before," honestly? But she paid close attention to what Crowbar said next.

Crowbar: Major investor in a Chinese silk factory, they were monopolizing a cluster of villages on the mainland

Crowbar: Right B4 the authorities cracked down harrison sold his stake & walked away clean. . . . Timeline always seemed suspect 2 me

Komiko: No kidding. I'll do some looking into that.

Crowbar: 2 bad Mynahs in jail, harrison was 1 of his pet projects

Lian sighed and massaged her temples. Hearing this was almost too frustrating, and she was suddenly feeling quite tired after one of the longest days of her life.

Komiko: That sucks. That means that A) Harrison's worth investigating, and B) we don't have a lick of Mynah's evidence to look at.

Blossom: . . . Can I ask, whos Mynah?

Lian braced for another upbraiding from Torch to the new kid, but when nothing happened for a good twenty seconds, she took it upon herself to respond.

Komiko: He was one of us. He got a little ambitious with one of his "pet projects" and they traced it back to him.

Komiko: The problem is, he kept all of his crucial data where no one could get to it: In his head.

Blossom: Thats impressive.

It really was. The group had agreed to never write down the ten-digit access codes that allowed them to log into the chats; Lian and the others carried that information nowhere but in their brains. But Mynah had been on another level entirely. He deleted all his chat logs immediately and didn't keep hard copies of anything. Still, when called upon, he could recite tiny details from months or even years back.

Mynah's paranoia had been 06/04's saving grace—in the wake of his arrest, there hadn't been a shred of evidence linking him to the group. But now he was behind bars, and there was no way for them to get in touch with him. Whatever he knew about Harrison, it was locked away along with him.

Komiko: But what that tells us is, there's dirt to be found on Harrison, so we'd better roll up our sleeves.

Torch: Piece of advice?

Torch: Don't look too hard into Rand Harrison. The man is dangerous.

12:22 AM HKT — *Torch has logged off*

Social graces were clearly not a priority for Torch.

His warning did nothing to dissuade Lian. If anything, she felt spurred to turn up every bit of info she could on Rand Harrison. Even if he wasn't connected to the dead girl, it was a sure bet that he had his hands in some dirty deals of some kind.

The others said their farewells, and they all signed off. Lian was just walking the computer back over to her desk when she heard her parents at the front door.

Quickly, she brought up the summer coursework file. She stared at the screen, counted to ten, then reached over and flicked off her overhead room light. *There*, she thought. *Now I didn't lie to mom. I'm still a good girl.*

Lian tucked herself into bed, still buzzing from the night's events but determined to catch a few hours' sleep so she wouldn't wind up drooling on her desk on the first day of classes.

Still a good girl.

SEVEN

Lian was distracted. Not in the pleasant, daydreaming way that a couple of the other students seemed distracted, as they gazed out the windows of Island South High School to the impeccably crafted gardens of Hong Kong Park. And not in the flirty way that Dingbang (who had, admittedly, gotten cuter over the summer) and some new girl in pigtails were distracted by one another in the back row of seats.

No, Lian was distracted by Rand Harrison. She'd eventually fallen asleep sometime around two in the morning, her mind churning with theories and ideas about Rand's impropriety, and had awoken almost itching to research him. But now she was stuck listening to an introduction-to-economics lesson, and the minute hand on the wall clock seemed in no hurry to turn her loose. She had a free period before lunch, and she intended to spend every bit of it in the school's computer lab, combing the Internet for information.

She looked down at her notebook and realized that, as she had been turning things over in her mind, she had absently doodled the stylized H logo of his clothing brand in the margins, again and again. She rested her elbow on her desk, her head in her hand, and slumped in her chair. The potbellied man was the common element, the link between Harrison and the dead girl in the water . . .

But who was the potbellied man? Would her 06/04 compatriots be able to turn up anything? For all she knew, they were also stuck in boring lectures, or day jobs, right now.

She flinched as Mingmei leaned across the aisle to nudge her.

"What's up with you?" Mingmei mouthed, furrowing her brow.

Lian closed the cover of her notebook and shrugged, but it was too late. The teacher, Mr. Chu, paused in mid-sentence and cleared his throat theatrically.

"Ladies," he said, and half the class turned to stare at Lian and Mingmei. Chu was Chinese, but he spoke English with traces of an American accent. Lian had assumed that he studied in the United States. "I am an old man, and my convictions are strongly held. And I find it absolutely *impossible* to believe that there is anything in this world or the next that could interest you more than the contrasting economic theories of Keynes and Hayek."

A few of the other students laughed. "Sorry, Mr. Chu," Lian said sheepishly. "It won't happen again."

He smiled back. "I hope not, Ms. Hung. Because you know the old quote, yes? If you don't learn this history, I'm destined to repeat it."

Another few laughs. The daydreamers and the flirters had even returned to the fold, no doubt grateful that Chu hadn't made an example of them instead.

"Now, where was I? Ah, yes. *The Road to Serfdom . . .* which was not, as one of you guessed in your summer work, a lost Bing Crosby/Bob Hope film."

Chu had a good sense of humor and peppered the dry statistics and social science models with little pop culture references and groan-worthy puns. Lian was buoyed by the thought that this might be a fairly entertaining course, after all. Any other day—once all this Harrison business was sorted out—she'd be an active participant, and bring home solid marks.

But today wasn't "any other day."

As if to drive that point home, Chu found his lecture interrupted again—this time, by a knock at the door. He opened it and greeted Island South's principal, Mr. Sòng, who stood at the threshold and exchanged a few polite words with the teacher. Then Sòng stepped into the classroom and smiled at the students.

"Class, I beg your pardon for this interruption. I had hoped to be here at the top of the hour, but the paperwork took a bit longer to process than I'd anticipated."

Lian had spent two years under Principal Sòng's roof; she thought of him as benevolent but terminally boring, the sort of man who used fifty words when five would have sufficed. As he rambled on about intake procedures and teacher-to-student ratios, never once in danger of coming to his point, she felt her attention drifting again.

"So," he said at last, taking a big breath for his finale, "I hope you will all join me in welcoming our new student to your class."

The principal announced the newcomer's name, but Lian didn't need him to. She looked up from her desk and straight at the marquee smile of Matt Harrison.

"Leĭ ho, everybody," he said, bowing his head briefly to the class. When he looked up and saw Lian, his grin somehow got wider.

Sòng had a few more paragraphs to say to Chu, so the students were free to kick up a quiet murmur—in Cantonese, mostly—about the new American import. Mingmei leaned over again and whispered, "Wow. They grow 'em big, blond, and handsome over in the States, huh?"

Lian just shook her head, dazed. Matt strode down the aisle, and Lian realized his destination moments before he slid into the empty desk to her right.

"I just got here, and I've already got a study buddy!" he said genially. "It's nice to see a familiar face."

Matt somehow managed to seem arrogant and sincere at the same time, just like he had when he'd said good-bye in the Fàn Xī foyer the night before. From the muttering around her in Chinese, Lian knew that several of her female classmates were already charmed by that smile and his glinting green eyes.

She shook it off and whispered, "I thought you said you were homeschooled."

He shrugged. "I was, up until my dad decided he wanted me to have a more 'normal' life, whatever that means. I guess he thinks I should have a few friends who aren't ten thousand miles away."

"Seventy-five hundred," she corrected him. "And you must have known last night that you were coming to Island South. Why didn't you say anything when I mentioned it?"

"Life's not full of surprises these days," he said, smiling. "I thought you might have liked one."

Chu finally managed to politely steer Sòng out of his classroom, and the lesson resumed. Lian wasn't finding it any easier to concentrate, though; she kept stealing glances over at Matt, who had opened his textbook to the proper page but was looking straight into his lap, where he appeared to be texting under the desk at a rapid rate.

Lian stared at him, debating whether to tut loudly, or give his shin a good kick. Five minutes through the door, and already he was blowing off the class. He may have had good looks, but he certainly had poor manners.

"Which leads us," Mr. Chu was saying, "to Keynes's *General Theory of Employment, Interest and Money*. Now . . . Mr. Harrison?"

"Hmm?" said Matt, not bothering to look up.

"Principal Sòng tells me that you did all the required summer reading for this course. So perhaps you can tell us a bit about the *General Theory*'s influence on modern economic thought?"

Lian felt a mix of dread and satisfaction. Chu did not accept slacking, and maybe being taken to task in his first five minutes would convince Matt to get his act together.

"Sure," Matt said, thumbing off his phone. "The *General Theory* is widely recognized as the foundation of present-day macroeconomics, and the primary inspiration for economic policymakers the world over from the late 1930s until the middle of the '70s."

"Excellent," Chu said, while Lian wondered what on earth had just happened.

"Although, if I can throw my own opinion into the mix," Matt continued, "it's a shame that Keynes's failing health kept him from being a more active participant in the debates surrounding his book. I think the classicists made it their business to water down his ideas because, frankly, he scared the crap out of them."

Chu nodded, clearly pleased. "Colorfully phrased and worth discussing. You're off to an impressive start here, Mr. Harrison."

"Please, call me Matt. 'Mr. Harrison' is my dad's name." He'd slipped the phone into his pocket and now made an arms-open gesture to the room. "That goes for everyone. Please."

Mingmei leaned forward so she could see around Lian and waved. "Hi, Matt."

Lian sank in her seat once again, willing the bell to chime so she could escape from this madness.

As class let out, several of the students clustered around Matt to welcome him. Mingmei was at the front of the group. Lian slipped out the door without a word to anyone. She'd catch up with Mingmei at lunch, and, if she was lucky, she would avoid running into Matt and his theories on Keynesian economics for the rest of the day.

The computer lab was about half full. It seemed to be mostly kids on their free period, mostly doing things unrelated to schoolwork. As the semester got well and truly under way, Lian knew, the lab would fill up quickly, and she'd have to sign up for a terminal ahead of time or risk missing out.

Today, though, she had her pick of computers, so she headed to one in the corner and quietly angled the monitor so that it wasn't visible to the rest of the room. Not that she expected them to look up from Facebook or Twitter or celebrity gossip sites, but better safe than sorry.

Lian didn't dare log on to the 06/04 group from here, of course. If any of them had turned up a connection between Harrison and the dead girl, she'd have to wait until she was at home, encrypted and firewalled, before she learned about it. But she couldn't shake the feeling that there was a connection waiting to be uncovered.

So she dug.

Her first search was for news reports on the tragedy at Big Wave. If the police had released the victim's name to the press, Lian would be having a significantly easier time compiling information on her. But no combination of search terms led to a story about the girl on the beach. Lian widened the parameters until the results were useless, and then resorted to frustrated browsing on the major news sites.

There was not one word about what she'd seen the day before.

She sat back in her chair for a moment, surprised and saddened. Life was sometimes cheap in Hong Kong, she knew, but it seemed odd that not a single news agency had picked up on this suspicious death. *Everyone deserves an obituary*, she thought. Everyone deserves justice.

Typing "Harrison Corp" into the search field, on the other hand, got her just shy of 70 million hits. It was feast or famine for the amateur detective with Web access. She clicked through on a handful of news stories, filtering to show the most recent items. Harrison had an industrial estate over the water, a massive factory and warehouse complex situated on Wan Po Road, on the city's east side.

She thought for a second, then opened a new tab and searched for maps of the currents around Hong Kong. There were about three miles between the Harrison port and Big Wave Bay Beach, and the gentle curves of the arrows in the waters of the Tathong Channel confirmed what she'd suspected. Anything, or anyone, departing from the Harrison complex stood a good chance of washing up right where Lian had been sunning herself.

This was one coincidence too many, when tallied alongside the ubiquitous potbellied man and Harrison's questionable "business" trip to the Family Hand Café.

Back in the original tab, she took down the address of both the factory complex and the Harrison Corp corporate offices in the Central District, entering them under the title "Economics lecture notes" into her phone's Notes application.

Many of those 70 million links, she discovered, led to photos of Harrison fashions modeled by pop stars, athletes, and the entire cast of some American show about attractive white people living in an enormous apartment and sleeping with each other. Two dozen different sites had what they claimed was an "exclusive" sneak peek at the Harrison Denim line: a photo set featuring a rugged black man in a cowboy hat, a buxom blonde whose jeans were so tight they looked spray painted on, and—for a bit of local flavor—the sultry lead actress in a high-rated Chinese cop drama on TVB.

Harrison's name kept cropping up as one of the sponsors for an American baseball team out of Colorado called the Rockies. A *New York Times* article had a photo of Harrison in a posh luxury suite at Yankee Stadium, wearing a black baseball cap with his team's CR logo and raising a celebratory tumbler. His other hand was on the shoulder of his son, Matt.

And Matt's arm was around the stunning blonde girl in the seat next to him.

He'd gone out of his way last night to mention a girlfriend. This wasn't new information. So why couldn't Lian stop looking at the photo? The girl could've been a model herself. She had her head resting against Matt's shoulder, laughing at something he had said.

When she heard Matt's voice calling her name, she had a moment of disconnect before she realized it wasn't coming from the picture. She turned to see him walking toward her, smiling wide.

"Mingmei told me I might find you in here," he said. "I thought I'd see if you wanted to walk to lunch together. I don't know my way around the halls here, and you were a big help in the menu department last night."

Lian said nothing, stabbing desperately at the keyboard, trying to minimize the browser window before he reached her. Maddeningly, she succeeded only in zooming in on the photo. The flawless faces of Matt Harrison and his girlfriend filled her whole monitor.

Matt put a hand on Lian's shoulder, just as he had when he'd said good-bye at the restaurant. But this time he drew back quickly.

"What . . . ?" he trailed off. Then she heard him chuckle.

"You know, if you spent a little more time studying Keynes and a little less time Googling me, you might have a shot at the dean's list again." He spun her chair so she had no choice but to see his grin. Somehow, she would have preferred him to be angry. She gritted her teeth and willed the ground to open beneath her feet and swallow her up. The ground did not comply.

"It's . . . I wasn't . . ." she stammered, her face burning in embarrassment. "You snuck up on me!"

He cocked his head. "That's your defense? I called your name from across the room, and you're claiming I 'snuck up' on you?"

She sank in the chair and rotated so she wasn't looking at him anymore.

"Man," he said. "Maybe I ought to forget about school and just become a ninja assassin. Clearly, I've got the 'sneaking up' skills for the job."

He reached over her to grab the mouse. "Here's how you close it," he said. "Pretty basic stuff. Even a dumb American can do it."

Lian searched her brain for a retort as he walked away, but nothing came to her.

Matt was gone.

EIGHT

Lian's hand was sweaty, clutching the phone. She'd never made this call before, and she wasn't sure she could pull it off.

"Wèi?" said the woman's voice on the other end.

"Ms. Fang?" Lian said, and then generated a brief cough. "This is Lian. I'm so sorry to give you so little notice, but I don't think I should come in for my violin lesson today." Cough. "I've come down with something, and I wouldn't want to pass it to you."

As lies went, this was a little one, but she still didn't feel great about it. She was probably imagining the sudden ache in the welt on her neck—Zheng's hickey—but it felt like an accusatory jab, a punishment for her fib.

"I understand," Ms. Fang said. "Thank you for your consideration. Add an extra half hour to each day's practice until we meet again."

"Of course." Cough. "I'll see you in a week."

Lian hung up, feeling guilty. Ms. Fang was not a warm person, but she was an incredible teacher; Lian hadn't always liked her but had always respected her. This lie was a violation of that respect. She resolved that she'd actually tack on those extra half hours of practice, so as not to compound the deception.

In the meantime, though, she'd effectively cleared her afternoon schedule, so she strapped on her panda-painted helmet and piloted her Twist N' Go scooter over the Eastern Harbor Crossing, headed out to Wan Po Road.

She passed the sleek and sprawling Shaw Studios complex on her left, briefly wondering who might be filming on its soundstages today. After that, though, the buildings became far less impressive: shorter, squatter, more about function than style. Huge gray warehouses sat impassively behind fences topped with razor wire; ugly beige field houses sprouted satellite dishes like mushrooms. Traffic cones and barriers directed her away from unfinished side streets and muddy service roads. Just before Wan Po Road seemed to give up pavement altogether, she took a hard right into the tree-lined entrance to the Harrison Corp complex.

Seeing that logo made her think back to the day's disaster in the computer lab. She knew her way around a PC keyboard; it was bad luck that she'd hit the wrong function key. Actually, bad didn't cover it. Utterly mortifying. She'd managed to duck Matt when she saw him at the far end of a hallway after lunch; he probably thought she was stalking him online, nursing some crush, and she certainly didn't want to make things worse by appearing to be tailing him in real life, too.

Okay, she thought. *Focus. Enough of this girly high school drama. This is a mission now. Stay alert, stay undetected, gather the intel, and get out clean.*

She pulled off next to a particularly thick-trunked tree and propped her scooter up behind it, concealing it from the road. As a heavy-duty Hino truck rumbled past her, exiting the complex, she stayed behind the tree and concentrated on calming breaths.

Lian was nimble enough to scale the high fence behind the trees, but she hadn't brought anything like shears or cutters to get through the double helix of razor wire on top. Even if she could jump from a nearby branch and clear the wires, it was a drop of probably twenty feet to the ground on the other side. She didn't imagine she'd make that without breaking a couple of bones in the attempt.

So the only way in that she could see was the front gate. She moved toward it furtively, keeping between fence and trees, and was able to watch the intake process at the guard station when another Harrison truck pulled up. Two guards—one, she could clearly see, was armed with a Taser, so she had to assume the other one was as well. No small talk, just a brusque demand for paperwork, a thorough review of it, and finally a code punched into a ten-key. At least six digits, and at this distance, Lian couldn't be sure of a single one of them.

The "walk up and smile" plan was out the window, then.

Lian began to despair. Had she driven all this way for nothing? Photos of far-off warehouses and guards playing

Tetris weren't likely to impress 06/04. Maybe she should have just gone to her violin lesson after all.

She'd started to thread her way back to her scooter when she spied movement at the far end of the drive. A truck was turning off of Wan Po, headed into the Harrison complex. As it drew closer, Lian could see that it was an old-model vehicle: ineffectual muffler, mud-spattered grille, and—most importantly—canvas sides.

In the moment, she made a decision. As the truck rolled past her, she broke from the trees, keeping as low to the ground as she could, and jogged up behind the left rear tire of the truck. From this angle, the guards couldn't have spotted her dash; so long as the truck driver hadn't checked his rearview in that split second, she was safe.

Lian reached up and grabbed one of the cords holding down the canvas, then leaped onto the thin shelf provided by the back bumper. The truck vibrated and shimmied, and she wound the cord around her right hand until the skin beneath it turned white.

With a hydraulic hiss, the truck began braking for the guard station. Lian flattened herself against the Harrison logo painted on the back of the truck. Over the juddering engine, it was hard to hear the guard request the bill of lading, and harder still to hear the driver's response.

Lian waited, willing her breathing to remain steady. Her palms were slick with sweat, and the cord slipped an inch or so in her grip.

This was taking so much longer than the previous truck's admission. There had to be something wrong.

She tried to prepare herself, to choose a course of action now rather than in the moment. What would happen if the guard decided to inspect the truck's interior? She could run, but could she make it to her scooter before being caught? She could stay, maybe take him by surprise with a kick to the jaw . . . but how much time would that buy her? And if she missed, how much time would she lose?

Swallowing hard, she relaxed her grip on the cord, readying herself for the sprint.

Then the guard gave the clearance, the gate lifted, and the truck started forward again. Lian counted to three, then pivoted to her right, coming face to face with the left outer wall of the truck. The toes of her right foot were all that touched the bumper; her left foot dangled in air. The cord dug deep into her hand. But if one of the guards happened to look at the rear of the truck as it passed, she'd be out of sight.

Somehow, she had made it into the Harrison complex. Chalk it up to dumb luck.

The truck took a left, out of sight of the guard station, and Lian pushed off with her left hand, feeling the canvas give a bit before springing back. She pivoted until, once again, both of her feet were on the bumper and her back was pressed against the truck's rear, giving her a view of the north campus of the complex as they drove in the opposite direction.

It was pretty drab: windowless corrugated iron warehouses, each adorned with a ten-foot-tall H logo; portable outbuildings where Lian supposed the paperwork was handled; a dozen or more trucks parked or idling. She could see a couple of men in short-sleeved white dress shirts, walking quickly from one of the portables, arguing over whatever was written on the clipboard that one of them was waving. They seemed too preoccupied to notice her, but she tensed just the same.

The truck turned right and began to slow; a shadow moved over her as they pulled into some kind of hangar. Lian quickly let the cord unwind from her hand and jumped from the bumper, stumbling for a moment on the concrete before she regained her footing. She slipped back outside, around the edge of the hangar door, and stayed as low as she could while rounding the building's corner.

There were no other buildings facing the rear of the hangar; no one was watching her. She took the opportunity to sit for a moment, steady herself, and consider the daring, thrilling, potentially very stupid adventure she'd just undertaken.

If she were caught here, she would probably face trespassing charges. Or maybe the guards would taze her.

Maybe she'd be found washed up dead across the bay in Big Wave.

But even if that didn't happen, she'd certainly be grounded until her dying day. For her parents—her mother, especially—trust was everything. This whole escapade, if it were found out, would be a massive and unforgivable abuse of that trust.

Lian tried not to think about "what if" and to focus instead on the task at hand. Getting back on her feet, she jogged the width of the hangar and peered around its corner. The nearest warehouse was about twenty-five yards away. No personnel around. At a flat-out run, she covered the gap in seconds.

The giant Harrison logos on every building were starting to intimidate her. She moved away from the front of the warehouse, down the vast length of its corrugated iron side, looking for a way in. Near the back corner, she spied at some distance a standing ashtray. It made sense that smokers would not want to walk halfway around the building; there must be a nearby door.

Lian walked toward the ashtray until she could see on its other side a black door with a metal handle and two locks. She was on high alert; at any moment, someone could walk out here to spark up a cigarette, and she'd be spotted. She could probably outrun a smoker, but . . .

Lian flinched as the caged fluorescent bulb over the door lit up and a bell inside the warehouse clanged wildly. Lian's heart leaped into her throat. No one was here; she hadn't even touched the door. How had they found her?

Turning, she banged hard into the ashtray, knocking it over and sending a cloud of ash into the air. Swatting it away from her stinging eyes, she ran forward, rounding the back corner of the building, coughing and half blind. She didn't know which way to run; she doubted that any direction was safe, or that she could fight anyone off in this state.

After about a minute, though, she'd rubbed the ash from her eyes, and nobody had grabbed her or shot wires into her. She edged away from the back of the building, where the loading bay doors stood open, and peeked back around the side wall. Distantly, she saw a truck pull up and park at the front of the warehouse, and people in black coveralls began to climb out of the back.

The light, the bell . . . they weren't an alarm. They were nothing more than the signal of a shift change.

This was the best chance she'd have of slipping in unnoticed. She went back to the side door and quickly righted the ashtray, grabbing a handful of cigarette butts off the ground and replacing them. Better to leave as little evidence as possible. Dusting off her hands, she gingerly tried the door handle. If this didn't work, she'd have to find a way to sneak in the front, and that would be a much harder proposition.

The door resisted for a moment, then gave with a satisfying click. Lian opened it just wide enough for her to slip through, and then gently let it shut behind her. It took a moment for her eyes to adjust to the darkness inside the warehouse; she was in some sort of service hallway, with a bathroom and a supply closet and an empty glass case where a fire extinguisher belonged. To her left was a ladder that led to an overhead gantry, so she climbed.

From this vantage point in the shadows, she could see much of the vast warehouse floor, with a clear view to the front entrance. The new shift workers had disembarked and were shuffling in. Lian couldn't be sure from this distance, but some of them looked very young: small framed, thin, maybe even junior-high age. And yet, all of them walked with the awkward, shuffling gait of the old and arthritic.

The previous shift—also in those black coveralls—was being herded to the doors and into the idling truck by a pair of bulbous, bearded men, who shoved and dragged the workers around, cursing at them to hurry up, and threatening a variety of punishments for disobedience. A skinny older man stumbled and was rewarded with a vicious boot to his ribs.

Lian winced at the impact. It seemed like the horror stories she had read about gang masters on illegal sites like this were true. She wanted to scream out, to protest the brutality, but giving herself away now would do nothing to ease the workers' suffering. Instead, she pulled out her phone and took a slow sweep of the scene below, recording it all on video. This would make 06/04's collective blood boil, she knew.

As she swung the phone to the near wall of the warehouse, the viewscreen showed two guards, uniformed and armed like the ones at the gate. One of them was nodding vigorously as he yammered into his walkie-talkie. After a moment, he holstered the radio and snapped his fingers; half a dozen guards trotted toward him.

"Fan out!" he barked. "There's an intruder in the building!"

NINE

A chill ran down Lian's spine. She'd been so careful, kept so quiet, and they'd still managed to detect her. The image of the dead girl washed up in her mind, and for a moment, she thought of surrendering herself, begging for a less dire end.

But then she rallied: no one had laid a hand on her yet, and that meant there was still a chance—however slim—that she could escape. *Focus*, she silently screamed at herself. *Find a way out. Now!*

Below her, she could see that one of the guards was headed toward the service hallway. Even if he didn't head up the stairs, she didn't think she could make it down them and out the side exit without being caught. That meant that the only option was to continue along the gantry one way or another, hugging the wall and hiding in shadows—deeper into the belly of Harrison's beast.

Directly opposite her, across the vast width of the warehouse, were a series of upstairs rooms that opened to the walkway. Lian decided that would be her best bet; if she could find an unoccupied room with a window to the outside, she'd risk the drop to the ground below.

The walkway across the front wall of the warehouse was a thin and perilous-looking affair. Not only was there a gap of maybe six feet where the railing had gone missing, the whole path was too well lit. If anyone on the factory floor looked up, there was a good chance they'd notice her edging along the gantry.

The better bet was along the back wall: shadowy, with large sections hidden behind pipes for, she guessed, an air conditioning system that clearly wasn't running. Here, the walkway overhung the loading dock below; she'd have to be quiet so the guards beneath her feet didn't notice, but she'd have much more space to maneuver.

Lian permitted herself a quick glance down the stairs as she moved back past them. She couldn't see anyone, but she could hear the squawk of a guard's walkie-talkie. It might only be a matter of seconds before he decided to check the second floor. She pulled up short behind a thick duct pipe, scanned to her right, and then made a mad dash for the safety of the next one.

The stop/start pace was infuriating, and doing it silently was nearly impossible. When she finally made it to the corner of the warehouse, Lian allowed herself a moment to rest on one knee, grateful that she'd gotten this far unscathed.

She heard a shifting footstep behind her and before she could turn, rough hands took hold of her. One covered her mouth, tightly enough that she couldn't move her jaw. The other locked onto her left shoulder, the forearm across her chest. She felt the attacker's breath on the back of her neck, and then she was being dragged into the inky corridor. Her feet scrabbled on the metal but found no purchase. She wanted to bite down on the hand but couldn't; wanted to shout but did not dare.

This must have been what that poor dead girl's final moments had been like.

Her assailant yanked her to the left and into a dimly lit storeroom. The hand on her shoulder released and moved to shut the door; she tried to twist out of the hold, but instead she was spun until her face was inches away from her captor's.

He wasn't a factory guard at all. He was a boy of no more than nineteen, his hair greasy and his skin smudged with dirt. His eyes were wild, almost shining in the gloom. An uneven patch of stubble decorated his chin and, from the stench of his breath, Lian doubted he had brushed his teeth this week.

"Jiao?" he hissed in the darkness. "Jiao?"

There was such desperation in his voice. She shook her head "no" as much as his panicked grip on her mouth would allow.

"Have you seen Jiao?" he asked. Lian felt prickles in her chest, up and down her arms—this young man's hysteria was almost infectious. She tried to speak, as loud as she dared, but it came out high pitched and muffled, lost in his hand.

"What did you say?" he asked, finally loosening up on her jaw and taking a step back.

Lian kicked out at him, the toe of her boot driving right into his groin. He hit the floor and went fetal, making little whimpering noises.

She stepped past him and grabbed a broom leaning against the wall near the door, holding it between them like a staff. "What I said was that I was about to boot you in the crotch. Maybe you should have listened better."

The boy coughed and held himself for a moment, then slowly put his palm down on the floor and brought himself up into a sitting position. Lian tensed and brought the end of the broomstick within inches of his throat.

"Don't," he mumbled, leaning away. "Please don't tell the guards I'm here."

She gave him a quizzical look. "Yeah . . . likewise." They weren't hunting her, after all, she realized—he was the intruder they were chasing. She'd just happened to stumble into this warehouse at the worst possible time for her stealth mission. *Fantastic.*

They had a common enemy, though, so that was someplace to start. Cautiously, she lowered the broom and offered him a hand getting up.

"What's your name?" she asked. "What are you doing in here?"

He held up a hand to quiet her, then steered the both of them behind a dilapidated filing cabinet.

"Hey—" she began, but he shook his head and motioned to the door. Now she could hear it, too: guards on the upstairs walkway, calling to one another, their footfalls growing louder.

Lian and the boy huddled behind the cabinet, waiting for the door to fly open. Again, she had to wonder whether she could connect with a fist or a boot or a broom before she was taken down.

But she never got the chance. The guards didn't venture into the blackness of the corridor, and after a minute or so she relaxed, unable to hear them anymore. The boy stayed vigilant and stock still for a long moment, and then he too seemed to unbend.

"I'm Zan," he said in a hoarse whisper. "I broke in here to find my sister, Jiao. You don't know her?"

"I'm a stranger here myself. I got in by the side door, and I've got no idea how to get back out."

"The dockside," he said. "At the rear of the building. If we can slip out through a loading bay, there's a path to the seawall. That's how I got in."

Lian bit at her lower lip. "There are bound to be guards on all the doors. How are we supposed to make it out?"

Zan smiled; it was just off kilter enough to make her nervous, though he was clearly trying for reassuring. "You're a size Small, I'm guessing."

He crossed to the other side of the storeroom and began rooting around inside a bin, tossing her a pair of black coveralls and selecting one for himself. She leaned the broom back against the wall and stepped inside the uniform; the material was rough, instantly itchy, and carried a powerful chemical stink that made Lian dry heave.

Zan went first out of the room, surveying the hallway as he skirted its wall back toward the gantry. After a quick look, he signaled to Lian that it was safe to follow. They crouched behind a duct pipe, and he pointed out the nearest staircase, an enclosed spiral that would deposit them in a recessed area downstairs. He took a deep breath and then moved, low and quiet, to the staircase and started down. She waited until she couldn't see the top of his head anymore, and then imitated his moves.

The factory floor was hot and loud, and thus blessedly easy to blend into. Lian kept her head down, watching Zan's feet as he moved purposefully past the chugging machines that tooled and dyed and sweated heat into the thick, still air. It was plain to see how her clothes had absorbed such a toxic smell; the warehouse was dotted with enormous vats emblazoned with the symbol for hazardous chemicals.

They marched to the loading bay doors. The gang masters were occupied elsewhere; the guards had convened near the front doors to rethink their strategy. Zan jumped off the platform and then offered a hand to help Lian down.

As soon as her feet touched the ground outside, she felt an urge to run flat out, but they kept their inconspicuous walking pace all the way down to the ladder at the seawall. Her heart leapt to see it; if she hadn't chanced upon Zan, she'd never have known that this was an option. She climbed down first and he followed, pointing to where the fence line began to curve back in toward the Harrison complex, eighty or a hundred yards distant.

Here, out of sight of the buildings, they broke into a trot over the rocky beach. When they reached a pile of driftwood and scrub brush, Zan moved it aside to reveal a hole where the wire fence had been snipped and bent back upon itself. Lian went through first, snagging the cuff of her coveralls on a bit of gnarled metal and swearing until she remembered that she didn't care about preserving them at all.

Zan squeezed through after her, and the two of them stood outside the treacherous sprawl of the Harrison complex at last.

"Okay," Lian said, ignoring the chemical taste that seemed to have coated the inside of her mouth. "If I have my bearings right, we should head this way, around the south campus. Stick to the trees and look for the dirt road that lets out by the main drive. Then we just need to walk far enough in to get to my scooter, and we're home free."

Being on the other side of that razor-topped fence made all the difference: Lian felt clear headed and triumphant, and the long trek back to the driveway seemed to take no time at all. They didn't make conversation, though. Talk could wait until they were miles from this place, when they could compare notes and Lian could learn about Zan's missing sister.

They let an exiting truck pass them as they hid, and then Lian jogged up to get the scooter while Zan played lookout at the mouth of the entryway. She righted the bike, strapped on her helmet, and zoomed down the drive to collect him. He didn't even wait until she'd come to a complete stop before swinging his leg over the seat and gripping her waist, and then they were off, back up Wan Po, toward civilization.

The road narrowed as they headed into the Tseung Kwan O Tunnel, and she leaned into the gentle curve. Headlights from the cars behind her played up the shiny walls. They emerged into the light of the sinking sun, and she angled toward the Autotoll lane of the plaza, whizzing through and steering where the cones directed her, hemmed in but still feeling freer than she had all day.

Just as Zan's hands tightened on her, she saw what he'd seen. A black sedan had roared through the toll lane to their right, sending the bright orange pylons scattering as it gunned its engine and rocketed toward her scooter.

TEN

||||||||||||||||||||||||||||||||||||||||||||||||||||||||||||||||||||||||||||||||||||||||||||||||||||||||||||||||||||||||||||

"Hang on!" Lian yelled back to Zan.

She gunned the scooter and shot the gap between two cars, just before one of them changed lanes. Tseung Kwan O Road was busy at this time of the evening. If she could just place enough vehicles between herself and her pursuers, she'd buy the time she needed to figure out what to do next.

Zan leaned into her and held tightly as she wove between lanes, the black car surging forward, getting mired, surging forward again. Zan tapped her shoulder and pointed down and to their left: the Kwun Tong Police Headquarters.

Lian shook her head vigorously. They'd been trespassing on private property; they were wearing stolen clothes. She hadn't had a spare moment to work out what she'd seen at the Harrison complex, and she had no idea what Zan's story was. For all she knew, appealing to the police for help right now was tantamount to walking in with her wrists bared, demanding to be cuffed and processed. Her mind was already processing worst-case scenarios, the look on her parents' faces, the cops taking her hard drive . . .

She checked her mirror again, cut off a flatbed truck, and powered toward the Lei Yue Mun exit. The black sedan disappeared from view, although the constant roar of its powerful engine reminded Lian that it was always close.

To their left were the industrial centers; with their grid layout and long, straight city blocks, they were no good for hiding. To the right were any number of winding little streets, dead ends and cul-de-sacs and one-way loops. Lian hooked a sharp diagonal path between two panel vans and raced into the semicircle around Kwun Tong Station.

"Move!" she shouted at a group of pedestrians dallying in the crosswalk at Hip Wo Street. She took the first left then the next right, onto streets she'd never heard of, lined with buildings she'd never want to enter. At last, when the black sedan's headlights were no longer in her mirror, she steered into an alleyway barely big enough to accommodate the scooter. She parked behind a trash bin filled with several days' worth of fish parts, and killed the Twist N' Go's lights and motor.

Zan and Lian crouched in the gathering darkness, not speaking but breathing hard. He kept watch at the near end of the alley, while she spied the far end. Cars drove by—some black, some sedans—but none stopped, and no one entered the alley on foot.

They stayed hidden until the sun sank completely below the horizon, and then Zan went to scan both alley mouths while Lian stripped off her pungent coveralls and threw them in the garbage.

"I think we lost them," he said when he returned to her.

"Good," she said. "We lost ourselves a little, too, but I think I can get us out of here."

"Do you suppose," he said, trashing his own black Harrison uniform, "that we could get something to eat, maybe?"

"Sure," she said, starting the bike up again. "It's time we talked, anyway."

Lian led them back to the main road, keeping watch for the sedan, and then into Kowloon City via the Kai Tak Tunnel, a long two-lane straightaway that would make it easy to tell whether they were being followed. From there, they crisscrossed the streets of Hung Hom until they made it to The Cat's Ear, a hole-in-the-wall noodle house off Bailey Street where she and Mingmei had been a couple of times.

Zan kept fidgeting and twisting around to keep watch behind them. She sighed in relief when they made it to the restaurant without his raising the alarm. "I have a confession," he said sheepishly after they'd ordered their meals. "I . . . I don't have any money with me."

"It's on me," Lian told him. "You look like you could use a good meal."

He also looked like he could use a scrub down with a fire hose and some industrial-strength cleanser, but she was too polite to say so out loud.

Zan shoveled his char kway teow into his mouth like it might be snatched away from him at any moment. As he ate, the color seemed to return to his cheeks, and he became more talkative. Lian had spent hours in his company and barely heard him speak two dozen words, but with a mouthful of prawn he was suddenly rather chatty.

"I live in Yah Tian," he told her, "About thirty miles north of here. My little sister, Jiao, came into the city a few weeks ago, looking for work." He took a gulp of tea and pawed at his mouth with a napkin. "Sometimes I think Jiao was born into the wrong family. She's smart as a whip, and all she has ever wanted was to go to university, but . . . my family's rainy-day fund got used up." He shook his head sadly, his lips thinning and his eyes narrowing. "Too many 'rainy days' where we live. So she decided that she was going to put herself through school."

Lian nodded. She understood that drive toward higher education and felt a pang of guilt that her family's finances would make it so easy for her, when there were people just as deserving who couldn't pursue their ambitions because of where they were born.

"Jiao called and said she'd gotten a job at the Harrison factory," Zan continued. "She told our mother that the money was decent and that we shouldn't worry . . . but of course that's what she'd say. Jiao's too proud to want pity. But she confided to me that she was staying at the cheapest place she could find, the Chungking Mansions, so she could put aside as much of her tiny paychecks as possible."

Lian frowned at this. The Chungking Mansions were a dismal, squalid firetrap where four thousand residents crammed themselves into tiny, and often not very clean, rooms. Crime and drug use was rife, and racial tensions among the residents often boiled over into violence. That it had inexpensive guest housing for backpackers and transients was by far the nicest thing that could be said of the place.

Zan captured a last bit of sausage in his chopsticks and tossed it into his mouth. "Like I said, she's smart, and she's always been able to take care of herself. But I'm her brother, you know? I worry. So we made a deal: she'd call me every two days, and let me know she was okay. That was enough to put my mind at ease. And then, three days ago . . ."

"She didn't call," Lian guessed.

Zan nodded gravely. "I called her number, but it just rang. So I hitched into town and went looking for her. The apartments where she was staying . . . scary place. If I'd known how bad it really was there, I'd have dragged her back home in a heartbeat."

He pulled a threadbare wallet out of his back pocket and opened it. Lian couldn't help noticing it was empty of money. Zan removed a well-worn photograph, bent at its corners, that he gazed at for a long, wistful moment.

"I showed her picture around the Mansions, but nobody knew anything. Half of them slammed the door in my face. I got called a lot of . . . ugly names." He paused, his eyes watering. "I don't understand how people could care so little. How they could see this face and not want to help find her."

He turned the picture around. Lian felt like she'd been punched in the gut.

"What?" Zan asked her.

"Oh," she managed to whisper. "Oh, no."

She was staring into the pretty, smiling face of the dead girl from the beach.

"Tell me," he said. His eyes were no longer teary; they'd turned intense and probing. "Something's wrong, isn't it? Lian, you have to tell me."

"Zan, I'm . . . I'm so sorry."

"For what? Why?"

"Your sister—Jiao—is . . . she washed up on Big Wave Bay Beach yesterday."

His voice trembled. "What do you mean, 'washed up?'"

"Zan . . . she's dead."

"Don't say that!" he shouted, slamming his palm onto the table. The few other diners fell silent. A busboy stuck his head out of the kitchen.

"Zan, please . . ."

"I've looked in every newspaper. There was nothing about a dead body on the beach in any of them. And, anyway, how would you even know about it?"

"I was there," she said. "I found her."

"You're sure?" he said, breathing hard. He held the photo up again, right in front of Lian's face. His hand was shaking, his knuckles turning white. "You swear it was her? You swear it was this girl, my Jiao?"

The face was seared in Lian's memory. There could be no doubt. She held Zan's eyes as she said, "I swear."

The anguish on Zan's face made Lian's eyes sting. "I'm going to the police," he told her. "Right now, right this minute."

"Zan, wait," she said, reaching for his arm as he stood. "I don't think that's a good idea."

"I don't care what you think!" he yelled, pushing her hand away. He knocked over his chair and ran out of The Cat's Ear, with all eyes on him.

Lian threw a handful of bills on the table—more than enough to cover the meal and the commotion—and chased after him. She found him walking in a chaotic circle on the sidewalk, distraught, clearly unsure which direction to go in this strange neighborhood.

"Zan," she said, catching him by his elbow.

"Don't touch me!" he shouted, rounding on her.

"Listen to me!" she pleaded, speaking quickly before he could refuse. "Just listen for a minute, okay? I don't think it's safe to talk to the cops. If I'm right, Rand Harrison has a man operating as a go-between with the police. Anything you say on the record, it's going to get back to Harrison, and that's going to get both of us in trouble."

"But we have to—"

"We have to be careful," she interrupted. "If you do something rash, they'll throw up a brick wall between us and the facts. Then Jiao's death will have been for nothing."

He stared at her, his chest heaving with each breath.

"I'm trying," she said. "I'm trying to find out what Harrison's role is in all this. To expose his wrongdoings, whatever they are." How had she phrased it at the dinner, to the man himself? "To turn a spotlight on all of his dark corners. But we have to build a case. We can't make a move until we have proof."

People were looking at them, curious about the argument in the street. Lian hoped Zan was done with the shouting, that maybe he could talk through this rationally.

"What is this, 'build a case?' 'Expose his wrongdoings?' Who the hell are you, Lian?" He looked at her hard, his eyes demanding an answer. "What were you doing, sneaking around that factory?"

She wasn't going to say a word about 06/04—not out on the street, where some onlooker might hear. Not to Zan at all, not yet. Instead, she chose a vague answer that she hoped would be enough: "I'm someone you can trust, Zan. We want the same thing."

"How can I know that?"

"I'll show you," she said, reaching into her pocket for her phone. The video footage she'd shot of the factory conditions, the foremen shoving and kicking the workers— that should be all the evidence Zan needed that she was there to take Harrison Corp down.

Except that her phone wasn't in her pocket.

She quickly checked all her other pockets; no joy.

"What?" Zan asked, when she growled in frustration.

"My phone. It must have fallen out when we were being chased!" She made one more pocket inspection, though she knew it was futile. "Dammit!"

A cold feeling spread over her skin. What if it had dropped out in the factory? When they were putting on the black uniforms. If someone with any know-how had gotten hold of her phone, she was finished. At least there was nothing linking her to 06/04.

The phone was gone, and with it, the only copy of the factory footage. The whole excursion had just been rendered a complete waste of time. She leaned against a nearby lamppost and fought the urge to cry.

The spotlight on Harrison had just grown a whole lot dimmer.

ELEVEN

As the Twist N' Go's purring motor echoed against the walls of the Cross Harbor Tunnel, Lian tried to talk herself down. There was a chance, however slim, that the phone had fallen out when she'd taken off the coveralls. All she had to do was go back to Kwun Tong tomorrow while it was light, try to retrace the turns she'd taken down unknown streets in the heat of panic, stumble across the alleyway where she'd shed the uniform, and pray that the garbage collectors hadn't beaten her to the punch.

Deep down, though, she knew she was kidding herself: the phone had probably been ground to powder under the unrelenting tires of Hong Kong traffic by now. But making a plan to look for it tomorrow was the only thing that was going to let her get any sleep tonight.

She'd offered to drop Zan off wherever he was staying, but after some hemming and hawing he'd admitted that he'd been sleeping on the streets since his arrival. This was more than Lian could bear; she'd practically demanded that he get back on the scooter, and together they were headed back to the Island, to Lian's family's apartment.

"We should make this fast," she told Zan, once she'd pulled into her assigned parking spot and killed the engine. Her father's car was gone; he and her mother were out for the evening, having dinner and drinks with the Australians to finalize some paperwork before the investors flew back Down Under the next day. Lian didn't know how late they'd be out, but if the previous night was any indication, the Australians weren't exactly teetotalers.

Still, better safe than sorry. She certainly didn't want to have to explain where she'd been or what she'd been doing when she'd met her new friend Zan.

They entered the building through the rear doors, closest to the bank of elevators. In part it was a practical decision on Lian's part, to draw as little attention to themselves as possible. But as much, or more, she did it out of guilt. Seeing Zan gape in awe of the spaciousness and clean white concrete of the parking garage was enough to tell her that he might well lose his mind in a trek through the lobby. The fountains, the landscaping, the rock gardens, the cathedral ceiling . . . all of it felt so unnecessary to her in the moment, embarrassingly opulent.

"This is . . ." he trailed off as they entered the apartment. "This is *astonishing*. It's so big, and so clean, and . . ."

She winced at every compliment.

"I feel like I'm in a museum or something," he said breathlessly. "Like I shouldn't touch anything." He peered into a curio cabinet filled with dozens of her mother's jade figurines. "How can anyone live in a place like this?"

"My . . . my father does okay for himself."

"No kidding."

Lian didn't want to talk about it anymore; she could feel herself blushing. "Stay here a minute," she told him, crossing the living room—so shamefully huge, all of a sudden—and letting herself into her brother's room.

Qiao—or "Karl," as he was now insisting everyone called him—was studying abroad in Switzerland for the year. He was meant to be splitting his time between business studies at Neuchâtel and the music conservatory in Geneva, but if his Facebook posts were any indication, he was more interested in splitting his time between a ski bunny named Elisa and a cocktail waitress named Naomi. The shirts, jacket, and pants Karl was about to unknowingly donate to Zan, Lian decided, would count as his penalty for two-timing the young ladies.

She returned to the living room with the clothes in a neatly folded stack and held them out—along with a handful of small bills totaling around three hundred dollars—to Zan.

"There's a youth hostel in Mount Davis," she told him. "Fifteen minutes from here. Any cab driver will know exactly where you're asking for. You can get a hot shower, sleep on a real bed, have some clean clothes to change into."

"I don't get it," he said, not yet reaching for the fresh clothes. "You live here, you have all this . . . you're so high up in the sky that when you gaze out that window, Hong Kong actually looks *beautiful*. And you could just stay up here and pretend that it really is. So why in the world would someone like you care what happens to a bunch of downtrodden factory workers? Why are you waging this one-woman crusade?"

"It's not just 'one woman,'" she said, a little quickly.

"What do you mean?" Zan asked. "There's more? Some kind of . . . group?"

"That's not important," Lian said, wondering if she had made a mistake going down this road.

Zan snorted derisively. "This world is an unjust place. What good do you guys think you can do?"

"Help those who need help," she said, crossing to the door. "Listen, Zan, I don't want to rush you out or anything, but . . . I have to rush you out. Get a good night's sleep, and we'll talk more tomorrow."

He picked up the clothes and pocketed the money, smiling gratefully. She walked him down to the elevator and hit the button.

"How do I find you?" he asked. "I take it you don't want me to show up here again?"

"There's an Appolo ice cream stand two blocks southeast of Island South High. I'll meet you there, 6 P.M. tomorrow. In the meantime, I'll get in touch with my group, tell them about you and Jiao. They may have already turned up something incriminating on Harrison."

"If you and your friends are going to be seeking justice on my sister's behalf, maybe I should meet them," he offered. "Thank them for what they're doing."

"I'm sorry," she said as the elevator doors opened. "That's just not possible." She thought of their motto: *Strength in anonymity*. And right now, they needed to be stronger than ever.

Zan paused and gave her a long look before stepping onto the elevator. "Thanks, Lian. For everything. I'll see you tomorrow."

The doors closed behind him, and Lian returned to the apartment from where Hong Kong looked beautiful. She made herself finish her day's school assignments—a blessedly light load—and change into her pajamas, and then keyed the ten-digit passcode into her laptop.

11:08 PM HKT — *Komiko has logged on*

> **Blossom:** . . . And Komiko makes four.

> **Komiko:** Good evening, everyone. I went on a field trip today and made a new friend.

> **Crowbar:** Were U checkin N2harrison?

> **Komiko:** Affirmative. I took a stroll around the Harrison Corp complex, and halfway through it turned into a guided tour.

> **Komiko:** I met a kid named Zan. His sister was an employee of HC who went missing three days ago. And you'll never guess where she turned up.

> **Blossom:** Out on a limb here, Im gonna say Big Wave Bay.

> **Komiko:** Got it in one, Blossom.

> **Crowbar:** Oh no thats horrible! Poor guy

Komiko: Couple that with the conditions I saw inside the factory, and I think the pieces are starting to fall together to build a case against Harrison.

Torch: I said it before and I'll say it again: we should stay away from that man. He gets a whiff of us, and we're dead.

Oh Torch, Lian thought. *Always such a ray of sunshine.*

Komiko: Well, for now, we're alive. And Zan's sister isn't. So I told him we'd do what we could to help.

Torch: Hold on. "We?" Are you saying that YOU TOLD HIM ABOUT 06/04?

Lovely. When Torch hits Caps Lock, rational conversation goes right out the window.

Crowbar: Whoa take it EZ Torch

Komiko: I didn't mention us by name, obviously. Just that I was part of something bigger than myself, a group trying to make things right.

Komiko: Or is that NOT the whole reason we exist, Torch?

She knew she was baiting him. But his little outbursts were getting tiresome, and she was fed up with him shaming the others anytime they stepped outside the lines of what he considered "proper" protocol.

Torch: You met this guy THIS AFTERNOON. You don't know the first thing about him, not really. And you couldn't WAIT to broadcast our existence to a complete stranger.

Torch: Really smart, K. Really good thinking.

Crowbar: Hold on, this Zan sounds like exactly the sort of person we R meant 2 defend

110

Blossom: Clearly hes got a beef w/ Harrison. That puts him on our side by default, right?

Komiko: That was my way of thinking.

Crowbar: If he can give us info abt his sister we could trace her records @ harrison corp

Crowbar: Prove a connection btwn the girl & the factory, thats a major scandal right there

Komiko: Right. Mynah Bird wouldn't have been digging into Harrison if there were no story there. He started the work, we owe it to him to see it through.

Blossom: What strikes me as weird is that there still hasnt been anything in the papers about the —

Blossom: Does she have a name, K? Can we start to humanize her instead of just "the dead girl?"

It was little things like this—the sensitivity, the kindness, the wanting to give a face and voice to the oppressed—that continued to make Lian think that Blossom was female.

Komiko: Her name is Jiao.

Crowbar: There hasnt been an official police report, hasnt been a postmortem done either

Komiko: Almost as if all trace of Jiao was being deliberately swept under the rug.

Blossom: . . .

Blossom: Komiko, do you think you could convince this Zan to pose as a worker? Get a job inside HC, see what he could find?

Torch: Terrible, stupid, HORRIBLE idea.

Lian hated to admit it, but she was in Torch's corner on this one.

Komiko: Let's put that one on the back burner. It's very high-risk. Once he got in, Zan might never get out again.

Torch: First sensible thing you've said since you logged in.

Komiko: ENOUGH. We get it, you're pissed off. The sky is blue and water is wet.

Lian smiled at her own joke. That certainly felt good.

Blossom: You mentioned the factory conditions. Did you get any evidence? Photos or video? That would go a long way.

Lian felt a little sick to her stomach at reading this question.

Komiko: Well . . . yes and no.

Komiko: I shot a ton of video on my phone . . . but my phone's not around anymore.

Torch: WHAT.

Komiko: Look, I had to escape, we were being chased, I dropped it somewhere along the way.

Crowbar: Uh oh

Torch: Sky = blue.

Torch: Water = wet.

Torch: Komiko = LIABILITY.

11:35 PM HKT — *Torch has logged off*

Lian hung her head and closed her eyes, but the word was seared into her vision in all caps, harsh and accusatory.

And, maybe, completely correct.

11:36 PM HKT — *Komiko has logged off*

She shut the laptop and flopped onto her bed, willing sleep to come but knowing that it wouldn't. If she could just switch off her brain for a few hours, instead of rehashing the whole day—from the humiliations at school to the dangers of the factory trip, from the new wrinkle that Zan introduced to the awful notion that she'd endangered 06/04—she might be able to wake up with a fresh perspective on it all.

Instead, over the next couple of hours, she tossed and turned and fretted her way toward a mild headache. When holding a pillow over her head didn't solve it, she got out of bed in a huff and shook an ibuprofen tablet into her hand. She'd long ago decided that such pills were best washed down with a iced coffee—the caffeine helping to rush the medicine through her bloodstream—and so made her way quietly down the hall to the kitchen.

She'd heard her parents come in sometime around one and had assumed they were asleep. But there was a light on in her father's study, so Lian went to investigate.

"Dad," she said quietly from his doorway. "What are you still doing up?"

He was at his desk, one hand on his forehead, his hair mussed. Towers of paperwork were spread before him, and Lian immediately understood that it was these, and not a night of social drinking, that had turned his eyes so bleary.

"I could ask you the same thing, little panda," he said, not unkindly. "But I think our answers would be the same. The work doesn't end just because the day does."

"You can say that again," she said. She walked into the study and took a seat on the other side of the desk. "How did your meeting go tonight?"

He sighed. "Much like how I imagine the meeting tomorrow night will go. There are so many conflicting interests in the deals I'm working with right now. It's hard to know where to begin. And our good friend Mr. Harrison is giving me the biggest headache of all, at the moment."

You and me both, Lian thought. Instead, she slid the coffee and the ibuprofen across the blotter to him. "Maybe you need these more than I do, then," she proffered.

"It's 2 A.M. already," he lamented. "I really shouldn't drink this now. It'll keep me up for hours." But even as he said it, he popped the top of the can and took a long swig. Lian smiled.

"The biggest sticking point is this proposed expansion of Harrison Corp's empire," he continued, swallowing the pill. "To say that it flaunts a number of monopoly rules would be putting it lightly. And it hasn't passed due diligence on several health and safety regulations." He sighed and flipped a few pages. "But you wouldn't believe the pressure I'm getting from above to push the deal through."

Lian believed it, all right. At the mention of "health and safety," she had to bite her tongue not to shout out "Ha!"

"If you're having doubts, Dad," she said, "you can't just cave. There's no reason you should sign off on a deal that you don't think is fair."

He fixed her with a very serious look. "It's business. 'Fair' doesn't enter into it."

She grimaced a little to hear him so world weary.

"Everyone's playing with loaded dice," he told her. "The ones who come out on top are the ones who realize that. This isn't about what's fair. This is about me delivering on the deal, or risking my job. Risking everything I've worked for."

His head fell back onto his hand, and Lian knew not to push any further. Instead, she stood up and walked around to his side of the desk.

"I'll leave you to it, then," she said, patting him on the shoulder. "I know you'll do what's right."

"Sleep well, little panda."

"And you, Dad."

Tuesday

TWELVE

Lian moved slowly through the corridors of Island South, the previous night's insomnia making the halls and everyone in them look like photocopies of themselves—faded and distant, indistinct and immaterial. Not surprisingly, the fact that she was headed for Mr. Chu's economics classroom wasn't spurring her to walk any faster.

She'd done the reading, of course; she wasn't about to be shown up again, by smarmy Matt Harrison or anyone else. But the question was whether she'd be able to recall any of what she'd taken in, or get her mouth to process her incoherent thoughts into actual words.

Currently, those thoughts were shifting from Matt to his father, who was, apparently, something of an expert in a certain shadowy segment of economic theory. Clearly, Harrison Corp played exclusively with loaded dice. How could anyone—from her harried father, to her splintering activist group, to a poor factory worker like Jiao—hope to stand up to a rule-flaunting behemoth like Harrison?

She slunk into the room, skirting its edges to get to her desk. Her eyes weren't focused on anything but her Converse hi-tops, so she slid her backpack onto the floor and nearly sat down before she realized that Matt was occupying her chair, leaning across the aisle to talk to Mingmei. The two had their heads close together, obviously enjoying themselves; Mingmei was doing that thing where she kept smoothing some imaginary stray lock of hair back behind her ear.

Lian didn't have time for this crap right now.

"I think you're in the wrong seat, pal," she said.

"Wow," he said, turning around and flashing his poster-boy grin. "You, uh, you look really tired, Lian."

"What a sweet thing to say," she muttered, as he rose from her chair. "No wonder you're such a hit with the ladies."

"Okay, let's start over," he offered. "Good morning, Lian. Did you have a restful and restorative night's sleep?"

"Of course not," she said, slumping into her seat. "I'm a proper student at a Hong Kong high school. I was up all night studying for the quiz."

"Oh, hell, the quiz!" Mingmei said, her eyes going wide. "I totally forgot!"

"Mingmei is a somewhat less proper student," Lian told him as he took his seat.

"Don't sweat it, Ming," Matt said. "I never knew we had a quiz in the first place, so you were already one up on me."

"You'll probably still do great," Mingmei told him cheerily.

Lian rolled her eyes. There were still a couple of minutes left before the bell called class to order, so she pulled her textbook out of her bag and pretended to focus intently on Friedrich Hayek's Nobel acceptance speech. The words blurred together on the page, and no amount of yawning seemed to straighten them.

"So, this Friday night," Mingmei said, tugging at her sleeve. "Matt's dad is throwing a party on his yacht. I'm considering it an opportunity to window-shop for all the features I'll want when I buy a yacht of my own someday. You want to come with us?"

Wow, Lian thought. *She's been in Matt's orbit for less than twenty-four hours, and it's "us" already?*

"I, uh . . . I think I'm busy," Lian said. "I've got to log a ton of violin hours. Plus, *Anna Karenina* isn't going to read itself."

"The audiobook does," Matt offered helpfully. "You can knock the whole thing out in about thirty hours, unabridged. You could even do it at the same time you're playing violin."

"Have fun on your yacht," Lian said, resisting the urge to ask him how he imagined she'd hear the audiobook over the sound of the violin. "I've got a date with Leo Tolstoy."

"You could probably score a date with a dude who hasn't been dead for a hundred years, if you eased up on the studying a little," Matt said. "Think about it, okay?"

She waved him off as the bell chimed, and Mr. Chu passed the quizzes down the rows. Lian stared at the paper until the words coalesced into sentences, and eventually she realized that she actually had a decent grasp on the material. The first few questions were straight from the text, a couple of true/false and a handful of multiple choice, one or two of which included some sort of humorous option E's appended by Chu.

She hesitated over a question on free banking, trying to ferret out the tenets of the system from its name. She shifted in her seat, running down the list in her mind, and felt certain that there were eyes on her. Turning her head just enough to see Matt, she found him looking in her direction. He smiled and raised his eyebrows.

Lian curled her arm over her paper and hunched down until she was sure his view of it was completely blocked. How much had he seen already? How many of her answers had he swiped? How dare he just sit there, letting her do all the hard work while he reaped the benefits?

Like father, like son, she thought.

Her mind then wandered to Jiao and Zan. She wondered whether he would show up that evening, like he was supposed to. Would he be patient enough to let 06/04 help him, or would he strike out on his own and disappear into the long shadows cast by Harrison Corp?

Chu called for the quizzes, and Lian was jolted out of her musings only to realize that she hadn't written anything at all for the last three questions. Her heart raced for a moment—she'd always been a straight-A student, and this was two flubs in as many days.

Calm down, she told herself. *It's only a small quiz, a tiny percentage of the course grade. There'll be extra credit down the line. You'll get those points back.*

And besides, she thought with grim satisfaction, *if you didn't answer those questions, Matt didn't have any answers to steal.* "Tough quiz," she whispered to him as the papers made their way to the front of the classroom.

"I guess," he shrugged. "What'd you get for the first blank? The one that just said 'Name'?"

It took her a second to realize he was making a joke. She didn't feel like laughing.

The lecture dragged, and in the last ten minutes of the period—while Chu checked over the quizzes and the class read about Kenneth Arrow's impossibility theorem—Lian was in danger of falling asleep with her face in her book. The chiming bell roused her, and she packed up her bag and joined the queue waiting to pick up their papers at the door.

"Eighty," Mingmei said, folding her quiz. "Not too bad, after all."

Lian stared at the 72% inked in red at the top of her own page. Chu hadn't said anything as he'd handed it back to her, but had she sensed a look of disappointment in his eyes? She supposed she wouldn't have blamed him.

"Hey, pretty good for the new kid," Matt said when he got his paper. He turned it around and Lian almost choked on air when she saw the red 100 in the upper right corner.

"Top grade!" it said, in Chu's neat script.

Mingmei gave Matt a playful, one-armed hug. "See? Told you you'd do great!" she said. "Hey, what did you get, Lian?"

"Embarrassed," Lian answered, and took off as fast as her tired feet would go.

THIRTEEN

"So, I need a hat."

The last bell had rung, and Lian was at her locker, selecting the books she'd need for the evening's homework. She double-checked that she wasn't missing anything, and then closed the locker. "You don't need a hat, Mingmei," she said. "You must have fifty hats in your closet, and yet you only ever wear the same three."

Mingmei ignored her. "Come on," she said, "let's get out of here and go hit up that new boutique over off Des Voeux Road. I need to find just the right seafaring look for Friday."

"No, that's okay," Lian said as they headed down the hallway toward the exit. "I've got some stuff I have to take care of this afternoon."

"But you love to watch me shop for hats. You've done it like fifty billion and three times."

"That does sound like an accurate count. But I can't today, okay? Have fun without me."

Mingmei frowned. "What's up with you all of a sudden, Lian?"

"What do you mean?"

"You're just being . . . kind of grumpy. And weird. You were all moody after economics, and then I didn't see you at all during lunch. And what was that phone call all about?"

Lian stopped short. "What call? When?"

"I don't know. Last night, around eleven o'clock? You call, you say nothing, you hang up. So I called you back, and you didn't answer." Mingmei shrugged. "What was it? A butt-dial?"

"No," Lian told her. "I didn't make any calls at eleven last night. Neither did my butt."

"How do you know? A girl can't be sure of what her butt's doing twenty-four hours a day."

"I lost my phone yesterday, sometime before dark. Maybe some upstanding citizen found it and was trying to figure out who it belonged to. I mean, it makes sense they'd call you, Mingmei. You're far and away my most frequently dialed number."

"That's the nicest thing you've said to me all day."

"But then," Lian wondered out loud, "why wouldn't they have said anything to you?"

"Maybe they changed their mind about turning it in."

"Yeah," Lian said, as they pushed open the double doors to the outside. "Maybe they weren't so upstanding, after all."

She waved good-bye to Mingmei and feigned interest in her Tolstoy novel for a couple of minutes, until she was sure her friend was well out of sight. Then she strapped on her panda helmet and cruised to the Appolo stand. Zan wasn't there yet. Lian ordered a red bean popsicle and took a seat on a nearby ledge, her eyes searching the crowd for Zan's face.

When he arrived, she hardly recognized him. Scrubbed, clean shaven, and sporting a recently brushed smile, Zan was much more presentable than he had been the day they had met.

"A decent night's sleep looks good on you," she told him.

"I figured, if you were taking me out for ice cream, the least I could do is make myself pretty." He did a little half turn to show off his new wardrobe: an inexpensive gray pocket T-shirt and black jeans, and a good effort to shine up yesterday's shoes.

"You'll note," he said, "no Harrison Outfitters logos anywhere."

"Yeah, I'd hope not." She read the hungry look in his eyes and spotted him the cash for a Black Jack Cone, which he accepted gratefully.

"So," he said a moment later, his mouth full, "did you talk to your friends? Can they help me?"

"Honestly? They're not sure, Zan."

He swallowed. "What's not to be sure about?"

"It's just a matter of proving that Jiao worked for Harrison."

"What?" he said, his brow furrowing. "You don't trust me?"

She was stung by the iciness of the accusation. "You have to understand, it's not about trust. It's about making an ironclad case. If we move forward with hearsay, we're setting ourselves up to fail." Her eyes pleaded with him for calm. "It's not personal. It's not about you."

"I can't imagine anything more personal," he said, crumpling his wrapper. "This is my little sister we're talking about."

"Of course, but—"

"But you want proof. Okay, fine." He looked thoughtful for a moment, chewing his bottom lip. Then he seemed to come to a decision. "Okay. This is what we'll do. I'll go undercover—get a job at the Harrison complex. I already know my way around it, and this way I'll have access to the records buildings. I'll find her file, her payroll info. There's your proof. A nice little paper trail for your do-gooders club."

Lian shook her head. "One of the 'club' already suggested a plan like that. But I don't know if it's such a good idea. I mean, your surname will slot right next to your sister's in a database. . . . They're bound to notice something like that."

"Right, right," he said, considering. "Well, then, I'll use a fake name. Honestly, I doubt they're going to look too closely. The way they churn through their workforce, all I'll have to do is show up desperate for a job and willing to take whatever they offer me." He seemed bolstered by having solved the problem. "This is a perfect plan. I'll apply first thing tomorrow."

He stood and took his trash to a nearby bin. Lian remained seated, watching him. There was almost a swagger to his walk now; he seemed somehow emboldened by the idea of the subterfuge.

Still, she was unsure. "Don't get me wrong," she said when he returned. "It's very brave of you, but it also feels reckless to go back there, considering how we left. Maybe tomorrow's too soon. Maybe we need to gather more information first."

"Screw that. I've lost too much time already."

"Listen, Zan, I really just need to talk to my group before any of us does anything."

He waved her off. "Talk all you want. Talk until you're blue in the face." He paused, and took on a mean look. "Just like my sister was when you found her."

Lian felt her blood go cold. "Zan . . . "

"Talking is useless. I'm planning to actually do something, unlike your little group."

"Just . . . just wait, okay? I'll be in contact—"

"You think things can be fixed by talking?" he said, glaring at her. "All right, then. Let me talk to this group of yours. Let me make them understand why it has to be this plan, and it has to be now."

She hung her head, shrinking from his angry eyes. "I told you. I can't do that."

"Right," he said with disgust. "I forgot. You can't do anything. You can just talk. Well, if you want to talk to me now, the word you're searching for is 'good-bye.'"

Lian didn't even look up to see which way he'd gone. She sat for a moment more, until the popsicle dripped onto her hand, and then rose to throw it away.

The weight of the books in her bag—especially once *Anna Karenina* rejoined them—was a reminder of how much she had to do that evening; add the requisite violin practice, and she was already looking at another late night. But her head was a jumble in the wake of Zan's abrupt departure, and she knew she was no good for schoolwork at the moment.

Instead, she took the scenic route home, steering the Twist N' Go down to Harlech Road and then cruising up Hatton, enjoying the path carved through the natural beauty of Lung Fu Shan Park. The warm air rushing over her face, and the long stretches during which she didn't have to dodge other vehicles, eventually brought on a sort of serenity.

Rather than piloting for Conduit Road and home, she smiled as she wondered whether it was too late to take Mingmei up on that hat excursion. No phone, of course, so she might as well just swing by.

Here, back on the edges of Central, there was once again traffic to contend with. Lian pulled her scooter to the curb to make way for an ambulance, its lights flashing and siren screaming as it raced past her. When it was gone, she fired up again and rounded the corner onto Mingmei's block.

There were more flashing lights.

Two police cars were parked right outside of Mingmei's family home, flanking an empty spot that the ambulance had clearly just left.

Lian's heart was in her throat. She popped her scooter over the curb and let it fall onto the grass in front of Mingmei's building. She hadn't taken more than a couple of steps before a police officer moved into her path, holding up a warning hand.

"This is my best friend's house!" Lian told the officer. "Is she okay? Who was in the ambulance?"

The officer stood, mute as a wall and just as impassible.

Through the open door of the home, Lian could see Mingmei, wrapped in a blanket, looking shell shocked as someone else in the house brought her a cup of tea, before putting a comforting arm around her shoulders. Lian squinted, sure that her mind was playing tricks on her in the blue wash of the police lights. But it was not.

That was Matt Harrison, all right.

Just as she was working up a good head of angry steam, Matt looked up, noticed her, and waved her in to join them; when she took a step forward and the policeman moved to block, Matt shouted out, "It's okay, officer, she's our friend."

The cop shrugged and stepped aside, and Lian rushed into the house. "What happened?" she asked.

"Burglars," Matt answered.

"They busted in and roughed up Meihui," Mingmei said. Lian gasped; she'd known and loved Mingmei's elderly housekeeper ever since she moved to the island. The thought of anyone assaulting the woman was abhorrent.

"They think she'll be all right," Matt told Lian. "But they wanted to take her to the hospital to check for internal bleeding, stuff like that. She seemed to be taking it all in stride. Tough lady."

"She is," Lian agreed.

"My poor Meihui," Mingmei said, her voice quivering. Matt readjusted the blanket on her shoulders.

"You said it was burglars," Lian prompted. "Did they take anything?"

"Just two computers," Mingmei said, dabbing at her eyes with a corner of the blanket. "Not the jewelry, not the

Blu-ray, nothing else. I guess Meihui startled them before they could really start getting their haul together."

Lian felt her brow crease. Mingmei's house was a treasure trove of art, antique baubles, and high-tech entertainment devices. There were thousands of dollars' worth of loot between the front door and the study, where the computers had been. So why had the thieves gone straight for the computers?

She was beginning to think the prank call Mingmei had received might have been more than just a good citizen trying to return a phone to its owner. She said nothing aloud, because she knew she was just speculating at this point; she had nothing to go on other than a gut feeling.

But it would nag at her until she knew for sure.

"I'm just glad you're okay," she said. Matt politely stepped back a bit so Lian could throw both her arms around Mingmei. "And Meihui will be okay, too. I just know it. She's going to outlive us all."

Mingmei smiled, and took a sip from the cup Matt had brought her.

"Oh, American boy," she said, making a face. "We're going to have to teach you how to brew tea properly."

He shrugged, and they all smiled, bathed in the blue light through the open doorway.

It was healthy, Lian thought, to find something—anything—to laugh about in the midst of all of this.

FOURTEEN

7:11 PM HKT — *Komiko has logged on*

Komiko: Hello, everybody.

Crowbar: you ok?

Komiko: A scary incident at a friend's house. Don't worry about it; nothing to do with you or 06/04. It's just on my mind.

At least, Lian didn't *think* it had anything to do with 06/04. Even if there was some connection between her missing phone and Mingmei's stolen computers, she didn't see how it would lead back to the group. She'd been scrupulous about not putting that kind of info on her phone in any form that would make sense to anyone but her.

Torch: Sorry to hear it. Hope everything's okay.

Lian almost typed a snarky comeback, but decided just to enjoy the sentiment. A note of humanity from Torch was sure to be fleeting.

7:13 PM HKT — *Blossom has logged on*

Blossom: Present and accounted for.

Crowbar: Good 2 see every1, whats the news?

Komiko: I talked to Zan this afternoon. He trusts us about as much as Torch trusts him.

Torch: He sounds like a smart guy.

Komiko: Well, he's exactly as smart as Blossom. He had the same idea, about going undercover at Harrison's complex. I tried to talk him into waiting, but he's too fired up.

Torch: I'll say again, it's not a good idea. As soon as we start involving a third party, things get messy.

Blossom: If Zan is willing to take that risk on himself, I dont see what harm itll do.

Torch: 06/04 works because we're a small, focused group. Every hand knows what the others are doing. Zan is a wild card; we can't predict what he'll do or police his mistakes.

Crowbar: Ive got 2 agree . . . Komiko U R maybe 2 close 2 him already. If harrison figures out what hes up 2 & questions him, whats 2 say he wont give U up 2 save himself?

Lian grit her teeth as she decoded Crowbar's distracting shorthand. Once 06/04 had vanquished all the evils in the world, their next mission should be to sit Crowbar down with a touch-typing program and a dictionary.

Komiko: I don't think he'd do that. He's got integrity.

Torch: Please. You've known him 24 hours, which means you don't really know him at all. If avenging his sister is his top priority, everything else — including you — is a distant second.

Blossom: BUT . . . if hes that focused on getting justice for his sister, hes going to try to take Harrison down however he can. Which sounds to me like hes on our side. The enemy of our enemy, and all that.

Blossom: If we back him, work together, and prove that Harrisons up to something... thats a HUGE coup for 06/04.

Crowbar: . . .

Crowbar: It would be nice 2 take Mynahs work 2 the finish line

Lian knew she had to be careful how hard she pushed. Blossom was in favor of Zan's plan, and Crowbar could be persuaded. Torch was Torch; he'd dig in his heels the whole way, but even he couldn't argue with results.

Komiko: One person is already dead because of Harrison. If we stand by and let that happen to someone else, we'll regret it forever.

Crowbar: Speaking of which Ive got the prelim post mortem for Jiao

7:24 PM HKT — *Crowbar has uploaded one PDF*

Nobody typed anything for a couple of minutes as they read over the coroner's report. There were two versions, one in basic Cantonese and the other in basic English. Lian scanned the genderless drawing of the victim; both the left and right flanks were circled. She checked this against the handwritten notes down the left of the form.

DESCRIPTION OF CORPSE: Body is that of Asian female approx 15 years, 65 inches, 106 pounds. Clothed in white blouse, gray skirt, white undergarments, socks, left shoe. No jewelry present.

EXTERNAL EXAMINATION: Unenbalmed body in early-stage putrefaction due to submersion in salt water. Rigor mortis in major muscle groups, livor mortis fixed anteriorly. Skin intact with no trauma save medical intervention.

Lian scratched her head at terms she didn't know: *sclerae, nares, irides, crepitus.* Context clues helped, but she got the feeling these weren't the important parts of the exam anyway.

HEPATOBILIARY: The liver weighs 2040 grams, edge blunted, cut surfaces discolored, blackish.

"Blackish" sounded wrong, even to a layperson like herself. The word cropped up again in describing the kidneys.

Crowbar: 1 important thing 2 note is under RESPIRATORY

Crowbar: No water in lungs = she didnt drown, she was dead b4 she went N2 water

Crowbar: Kidney & liver discoloration is concerning

OPINION: Unknown Asian female, approx age 15-17 years, prelim exam inconclusive. Toxicology screen out.

The exam was dated, and the box next to **FURTHER ACTION** had been ticked.

Crowbar: Tox report will tell if drugs were involved. I suspect yes

Crowbar: Not necessarily recreational, she could have been dosed

Komiko: I saw any number of vats of toxic chemicals at the factory. The whole place seemed like it was poisoning me slowly.

Crowbar: I wouldnt rule that out, we would need more 2 go on though

Lian sat back from the laptop. "More to go on." Such as, the papers her father had been sweating over the night before in his study? The ones detailing the health and safety concerns at Harrison Corp?

"Lian," her mother called. "Dinner in five minutes."

"I'll be right there."

Komiko: I might have an inside track on HC safety records. I'll have to get back to you guys later, though.

Komiko: I really think we're starting to see this puzzle come together.

Blossom: This is exciting. Let me say again how glad I am to be part of this.

Komiko: Glad to have you. Bye.

7:35 PM HKT — *Komiko has logged off*

Lian stepped into the living room, snagged the cordless phone off its cradle, and returned to her bedroom, shutting the door behind her. She Googled the number for the Mount Davis hostel and dialed. Zan had been incensed this afternoon, and he probably wouldn't appreciate the question she wanted to ask him now. But if he knew of any drug problems that his sister might have had—painful as they might be to admit—it could go a long way in helping make sense of the coroner's report.

"Lei ho," Lian said when a woman answered. "I'm looking for a young man staying there. His name is Zan."

"I'm sorry," the woman said after some shuffling of papers. "There's no one on our ledger by that name."

Lian sighed. Of course he'd used a fake name. It was probably a good idea on his part, but it gave her no way of tracking him down.

"Okay," she said. "Thank you for checking, anyway."

She returned the phone to its cradle and then entered the dining room, where her mother was just setting out the bowls. But for the stoneware, the scene looked much like the one in her father's office last night: he was surrounded by stacks of papers, rubbing at his temples in frustration.

"It never ends," he said with a sigh as Lian took her seat.

"Don't forget to come up for air."

"Air and ramen," her mother said, spooning out the broth, laden with noodles and the fragrant scent of spiced pork. "The two most essential things in life."

Lian blew across a spoonful to cool it. "Smells delicious."

"I'm glad that you decided to join us," her mother said. Lian detected an edge to her tone.

"Sure, why wouldn't I?"

"I didn't know whether you might prefer to skip out on dinner altogether tonight and just add half an hour to your other dinners this week."

Lian set her spoon back down in her bowl. "You spoke to Ms. Fang."

"She called here this afternoon to ask whether you were feeling better," her mother told her. "I had no idea you were under the weather. Of course, I didn't see you at all yesterday after school, so it certainly seemed possible. And the way you were dragging around this morning made me think you had told your teacher the truth. But tonight you're spry as ever, chatting away on your computer, making phone calls to your friends. And I haven't heard one note from that violin. So tell me, were you really sick? Or did you lie to Ms. Fang?"

Lian shot a glance at her father, but a bank of numbers seemed to be commanding his full attention, even as his soup grew cold.

The hesitation was enough to confirm her mother's suspicions. "A lie shows a lack of respect, Lian. For Ms. Fang, for your violin, for me, for your father. And one lie begets another. Soon, I won't know whether a single word out of your mouth is true."

Lian couldn't stop herself from rolling her eyes. "Seriously, mother? You always do this. You take one tiny thing and drag it out to the worst possible conclusion."

"I just expect more of you."

"And I expect that missing one violin lesson isn't going to spiral into me working a girlie bar over in Wan Chai, with a tattoo over my butt crack saying 'It's All My Mother's Fault!'"

Her mother fixed her with a stern look. "You need to think very carefully about what you say next, Lian."

Lian clenched her fist under the table and breathed hard for a moment. Then she felt something in her uncoil, and she relented. "You're right," she said. "I'm sorry. I'll make it up to Ms. Fang."

The apology seemed to soften her mother's dark eyes. "Is everything all right? Calling in sick—that just isn't like you."

"I'm just . . . frustrated. My last senior secondary year, I figured it'd be a cakewalk. But already schoolwork is piling up on me, and all the . . . extracurricular stuff on top of that, it's just a little overwhelming." She didn't need to detail what the "extracurricular stuff" entailed, but she was acutely aware of how much of her time it was eating into.

"And Mingmei," Lian continued. She elected not to mention the break-in, not until she knew more about what had motivated it. But her friend was still on her mind. "She's making doe eyes at the new boy at school. Who just happens to be the boy you seated me next to at the dinner the other night."

At this, at last, her father looked up. He hadn't touched his soup. "Rand Harrison's son?"

"Right," Lian said. "Matt. They became really friendly, really fast. Now they're even inviting me to some yacht party on Friday, which, let's be honest, is the last place in the world I want to be."

Her father straightened in his chair. "Oh, no, Lian—if you were invited, you must go. It shows good manners. It shows respect."

Lian had nothing like respect for Rand Harrison. She wasn't overly fond of his son, either.

But the pleading look on her father's tired face told her that there was only one response.

"Of course, Dad."

"Perhaps you and Mingmei could go shopping for a new dress tomorrow," her mother suggested with a smile. "Once you've finished all your violin practice, of course."

Lian gave a thin smile. "Good idea, Mother."

The soup had gone as cold and flat as her tone. She ate the rest in silence and then excused herself.

FIFTEEN

Lian scanned the back of the aluminum can, reading the ingredients as the lab computer booted up. Maybe there was something a little hypocritical, she realized, about researching dangerous chemicals when she was skipping her lunch period in favor of a cream soda and a quick energy bar full of things she couldn't pronounce.

One crusade at a time, she thought, swallowing a mouthful of soda.

She'd been on top of her homework the last couple of nights, using it and the extra violin practice as excuses—however valid—for not going dress shopping with Mingmei. It had actually felt nice to get reinvested in the semester, to take a break from the late-evening factory raids and car chases and just be a solid student again. She had managed to hold her own in a spirited economics class debate this morning, drawing praise from Mr. Chu and a clap on the back from Matt.

Not that she needed his approval.

But through it all, she'd still been distracted by the lack of word from Zan. She'd heard nothing since he'd stormed away from the ice cream shop Tuesday, determined to infiltrate Harrison Corp with or without her help. If he'd made it in, had he found anything? Had he uncovered his sister's records? Or had something sinister already happened to him, too?

It was with these thoughts in mind that Lian began her Google search in a private browsing session. She couldn't stop picturing the large vats of hazardous chemicals on the factory floor, so she began by querying what might be inside them.

The results were disturbing from word one.

Lian opened a separate tab to look up what "NPEs" stood for. These nonylphenol ethoxylates, she read, were detected in the majority of branded clothing samples worldwide. They were a common detergent that broke down to form a toxin known to turn male fish into females through hormone mimicry, among other baffling environmental effects.

Heavy metals in the wastewater. Alkylphenols and PFCs in factory discharge. The various dyes and bleaches and detergents formed what more than one site labeled a "poison cocktail" that ran into rivers, lakes, and eventually larger bodies of water, irreversibly damaging everything they touched.

Lian didn't know half of the chemicals she was reading about, and every link led her down a rabbit hole of runoff effects and biosphere endangerment. She sent herself an e-mail in shorthand with the toxins she needed to read up on and bookmarks to sites like Greenpeace and the World Wildlife Federation.

One compound she did recognize was formaldehyde. She knew it was used to embalm dead bodies. So why then was it showing up in clothing meant for living bodies? She eventually discovered a PDF report that detailed formaldehyde's use in preventing mildew during shipping. Easier to find, frighteningly, were lists of the harmful effects that the known carcinogen had been found to cause. Anything from eye irritation and skin rashes to, in higher concentrations, respiratory problems, wildly erratic menstrual cycles . . . even death.

What Lian made note of, as she clicked between tabs and read about formaldehyde and NPEs, were the commonalities. Both were banned in several countries, either outright or past maximum allowable levels. Both were the subject of increasing scrutiny from environmental concerns. And, not surprisingly, both were becoming battleground topics as the manufacturers pushed back. Both had been shown to have negative effects on kidney and liver tissue.

Lian wondered whether "negative effects" and "blackish" were roughly the same thing.

The bell chimed, and she logged out, careful to clear her history and cookies. As she left the lab, she downed the remainder of her soda, thinking. She had only scratched the surface; there were dozens more links she wanted to follow, dozens of search terms she wanted to pair with "Rand

Harrison," dozens of leads she wanted to tell 06/04 about. But it would all have to wait for tonight.

The rest of the school day went from a rush to a crawl, her energy flagging quickly once her sugar high wore off. By the time the final bell rang and she'd gathered her books for the weekend, she wanted nothing more than to head home and sneak in a quick nap before taking the bow to her violin strings.

"I literally cannot wait for tonight," Mingmei said, playfully bumping into Lian on the steps outside the school.

"You literally have to," Lian replied with a smirk. "Unless you can warp space and time. Or they redefined 'literally' while I wasn't paying attention. And nice shirt, by the way."

Lian hadn't been able to ignore the Harrison logo on the new charcoal gray sweatshirt Mingmei was wearing, its sleeves pushed up to her elbows. Like everything, it looked great on her, but now all Lian could think was how many fish had been emasculated to manufacture it.

"Thanks. It feels like a great big hug," Mingmei gushed. "Matt gave it to me, the night after the break-in. It's kind of like having him draped over my shoulders all the time."

Or wrapped around your finger, Lian thought.

"So you are coming tonight," Mingmei said. It was, characteristically, not delivered as a question.

"I told you already, I can't. How is it you can't remember that when I've said it a dozen times?"

"I suffer from an auditory impairment, Lian. You know I only hear what I want to. It's a very serious condition!" Mingmei made her best earnest face, daring Lian to laugh.

"It's true," Matt said as he walked up behind them. "That's why we're holding a benefit for it tonight on my dad's yacht. It's so important that we raise money and awareness of Selective Listening Disorder."

"I can't," Lian insisted. "Can't, can't, can't. It's a simple contraction. *Can . . . not.*"

Mingmei turned to Matt and shrugged. "I don't hear her saying she can't."

"My God," Matt said in mock horror. "It's getting worse! Please, Lian, it's such a worthy cause."

Lian had had enough. "Just drop it, all right?" she said, cutting him off. "It's not my kind of scene. You guys go, have a great time. You can try telling me all about it afterward, but I suspect Mingmei's disease is contagious."

She watched the two of them walk away, their bodies awkwardly close together, as if each was waiting for the other to begin the hand holding. Lian hoped they wouldn't hold hands—she feared she'd roll her eyes right out of her skull. How Mingmei got anything done at all when boys were in the mix was a mystery. Lian couldn't imagine trying to date on top of all the other demands on her time.

When she tore her glance from her friends, Lian felt a flush of relief.

Standing at a remove from the scooter parking, but keeping a close eye on it, was a familiar face. Zan. It was good to know he was alive.

"What are you doing here?" she asked after beckoning him over.

"I came to find you," he said. "I remembered your scooter, figured there was a good chance you'd stop by here sometime." His eyes flicked momentarily to Matt and Mingmei, across the lot. "The, uh . . . that guy you were talking to. That's your boyfriend?"

Lian laughed out loud. "No, no. No, he's not. No."

At least one too many "No's" there, she thought, inwardly cringing. *Probably two.*

"Ah," he said. "Good to know."

She wasn't sure, but she thought she'd caught a little smile on his lips.

"Walk with me," she said, strolling in the direction of Hong Kong Park. "Tell me what you've been up to the last couple of days."

"It's been a whirlwind," he said. "I was hired on the spot, no reference check or anything. There's a big group of Harrison employees sharing a rat's nest of an apartment at the Chungking Mansions. Since I didn't give a permanent address and didn't have any transportation, they set me up there. It's just as bad on the other side of the doors."

"Why not stay at the hostel?"

He shook his head. "Living where Jiao lived—how Jiao lived—is my best chance of finding out exactly what happened to her. Besides, it's a roof over my head, and a mat and pillow I can call my own until the next guy shows up."

"Next guy?" she asked.

"The factory runs in twelve-hour shifts, so the apartment does the same. They drop off the previous crew and load us onto the same bus. We see them coming and going. I don't

143

know any of their names, just that one of them clips his nails where I lay my head every morning."

She shivered. "Gross."

"Yeah, the whole setup is gross. I'd say they treat us like cattle, but at least cattle get to use the restroom whenever they want. They've got floor bosses looking for any and every infraction. But if you keep your head down, do your job silently, and have a huge bladder and a tiny appetite, you can escape their wrath."

They were ambling in the direction of the park's artificial lake and waterfall. The day was pleasant and the scenery equally so, but Lian's thoughts were on the dismal gray factory across the bay.

"Have you been able to ask anyone about your sister?"

He yawned before he answered. "We get two quick smoke breaks and staggered lunches, so I've used as much of that time as I can to ask around. A couple of the younger women there used to eat with Jiao, and, when she hadn't shown up for a couple of days, they asked a supervisor and were told that she'd left. Two or three other guys remember seeing her, but it didn't sound like they'd even noticed she was gone until I brought it up. I get the feeling that nobody bothers getting too close to their coworkers."

Lian frowned. "How sad."

"What's sad is how scared people seem to say anything about it. A lot of them wouldn't talk to me at all. The ones who did shut down pretty quickly when I brought up Jiao." His voice had become a hoarse growl. He was clearly frustrated. "And honestly, I'm starting to get a little scared. I don't want to push too hard, or ask too many questions at once. I'm nervous that someone's going to tell one of the gang masters about me and blow my cover."

"I know it can't be easy to be patient," she said. "But for what it's worth, I think what you're doing takes a lot of courage."

He gave a weary smile. "Thanks, Lian. Speaking of patience, has your . . . 'group' turned up anything that might help me?"

She wished she had more, and better, news to report. Finally, 06/04 was investigating something in her own backyard, and the intelligence seemed to be coming in a trickle rather than the flood she hoped for.

"It looks like there were some high levels of toxins in her body when she died," she said.

"What, like drugs? You think someone drugged her?"

"It's too soon to tell. But . . . I hate to even ask this, but was there any chance that she used drugs recreationally?"

Zan hung his head, and Lian stopped walking, giving him a chance to pick his words. Dragonflies chased one another in the air around them.

"She . . . briefly, one of her friends was getting a lot of ADHD medication," he said at last. "Methylphenelate, I think? She'd get together on the weekends with some friends, and they'd take it. But that was a couple of years ago. She stopped pretty quickly, and as far as I know, that was the only time she ever did anything like that."

He was clearly uncomfortable admitting it, and she rushed to reassure him. "It's okay. That's not what we're dealing with here. We think the chemicals she was being exposed to at the factory did a number on her liver and kidneys."

"Yeah," he said. "That makes sense. Some of the other workers there seem pretty sick, too. There's a guy, Tingfeng, who works the dye vats. They made him work through a kidney stone yesterday with just a handful of aspirin. He told me they'd stopped letting him leave work because he got one every few months, and they were tired of the lost productivity."

"That's barbaric!"

"He said the aspirin was the best medical plan he'd ever been offered."

Lian was, for perhaps the first time in her life, actually speechless. Such a specific detail made the whole situation seem much more real to her. She realized she could not imagine what it was like to be one of these poor factory workers. And she was extremely grateful for this.

"Do you think you can keep a list of the chemicals that are off-loaded to dye the clothes?" she asked Zan. "Anything that looks suspect, anything stamped hazardous?"

"I'll do my best," he said. "I'll write down everything I see come into the place and leave it to your group to figure out which ones are 'suspect.'"

"Awesome. Just . . . be careful, all right?" She gave an encouraging smile. Not once did he seem concerned for his own safety around these toxins; he just wanted to get the information, to solve the puzzle, to avenge his sister. In the moment, she felt guilty that she and 06/04 weren't doing more to help him.

"I just wish there were a way to get close to Harrison himself," Zan said, staring out past the water to the conservatory. "Figure out how high up this goes, how much of it he's signing off on. How many of his other employees have washed up on a beach."

Lian sighed. There was a way to get closer to Harrison. The invitation had been extended; it would be irresponsible not to accept it. Good manners, respect, et cetera.

"I'm going to try to do exactly that," she told Zan, making up her mind.

Just as soon as I pick out a dress.

SIXTEEN

"Honestly," Lian said to the guard. "Two pat downs to get into this thing? Where do you imagine I'd hide something in a dress like this, anyhow?"

The woman, clad in the uniform of the hired private security company Bǎochí Ānquán, had reached Lian's ankles with her scanning wand, and now stood back up. "I'm the only pat down here, miss," she said. "The guy who felt you up at the gate doesn't work for us."

Lian blanched. "What?"

The guard's straight face broke into a smile, and she laughed. "I'm joking. Trying to get you to relax, miss. It is a party, after all." She handed back Lian's clutch and waved her onto the walkway to Harrison's luxury yacht, the *Seaward*.

Lian took a deep breath. *It's a party, after all,* she thought, starting up the ramp. Just like any other party: drinks, music, hors d'oeuvres, snooping for secrets about a corrupt multimillionaire clothing mogul. Maybe a round of charades.

The boat had looked impressive from the dock, but it was almost unbelievable to behold once you were on deck. Every chrome surfaced gleamed, and every inch of teakwood was perfectly polished. Lian could only guess at the dimensions, but two decks rose above the main one she was on, and the guests standing at both the bow and the stern were a bit out of focus from where she'd boarded amidships.

This deck and the one above it were filled with well-dressed partygoers from seemingly every corner of the globe, men and women in designer labels to complement their diverse skin tones and bone structures. *These are the beautiful people,* Lian thought . . . *and the ones who aren't beautiful must have to find consolation in their insane wealth.* She felt acutely aware of being neither, and the same fraudulent sensation she'd had at the Fàn Xī dinner crept over her once more. Then she chided herself for the moment of self-pity: here she was, spending Friday night on a yacht, while people like Zan were stuffed into a musty shoe-box apartment in the Chungking Mansions.

Perspective was important, she reminded herself.

She looked both ways down the deck, then shrugged and started for the stern, hoping she'd spot someone she knew. As she rounded the corner, she did. Rand Harrison, glass of champagne in his hand and spiritless smile on his face, was holding forth among a crowd of his guests.

Lian stopped in her tracks. The European couple who had been walking behind her didn't notice, and bumped into her, causing her to stumble. So of course it was at that moment that Harrison looked up, pausing between words as their eyes locked. He just as quickly looked away and continued speaking, and Lian apologized to the European couple, ducking around them to walk the other direction. Harrison's gaze was an appraisal and a threat, all at once. She wanted to move away from it quickly. As quickly as she could in high heels.

On the opposite end of the yacht, she found Mingmei front and center like some exquisitely carved figurehead, the ivory folds of her dress rippling in the light sea breeze. Lian tapped her on the shoulder and called her name timidly.

"You traitor," Mingmei said when she turned around. She was all smiles, though, her eyes wide as she looked Lian up and down. "I've never seen that dress before! You clearly went shopping without me there to approve. It's my one joy in life, and you stole it from me!"

Lian blushed. Her black cocktail number had been a hasty choice, the first thing she had seen in her size. She had snatched it off the rack. It had a severe diagonal cut at the hem. She hadn't been at all sure about it as the clerk had run her credit card, but she'd been in a hurry and didn't want to linger at the shops. It was bad enough that she had had to shell out for a brand-new smartphone that week; add the dress to her tab, and this investigation into Rand Harrison was becoming expensive.

"How did I do?" she asked Mingmei. "Is it *completely* hideous, or just *mostly* hideous?"

Mingmei let her lip quiver and her eyes go moist; it was an act Lian knew well. "Oh, Lian," she said. "All this time,

I thought you were ignoring my fashion advice. But now I see that I taught you well. I really am amazing, aren't I?"

Lian smiled and hugged her friend. "You're not wrong, Mingmei."

"Sure. But one day I might be, and it'll be a humbling new experience."

"I'm sorry I've been a little 'off' lately," Lian said. "It's been a . . . *strange* week, starting at the beach and spiraling out from there. But that's no excuse for me to lose my temper with you."

Mingmei hugged her tighter. "Forgiven and forgotten. I'm just so glad you decided to come out tonight, after all. What changed your mind?"

Lian didn't think it was politic to mention that she was hoping to bring their host's empire to its knees, so instead she said, "The little miniature quiches they're serving."

Mingmei laughed as she let Lian go, then was immediately distracted by something just behind them. Lian turned to see Matt approaching, a drink in each hand and a brown-haired boy about his age close behind. When Matt caught Lian's eye, he raised one of the citrus-trimmed glasses as if to toast her arrival.

"Excellent," Mingmei said, switching to English. "Here comes Matt with something fruity!"

"I told you, his name is Taylor," Matt said as the boys joined them. "And just because he wears glasses and listens to Death Cab for Cutie records, that doesn't make him 'fruity.'"

The other boy smiled and held out his hand to Lian. "Taylor," he said to her, "as advertised. You must be Lian?"

She shook his hand and nodded. "Nice to meet you, Taylor. And way to nail the pronunciation."

"Yeah, Matt coached me. Said he'd been enough of a dumbass for both of us when he'd met you, so I didn't need to suffer."

Lian smiled at him and accepted the lime-festooned cocktail that Matt offered her.

"We were at the bar when I spotted you coming on board," he said. "So I grabbed an extra Long Island Iced Tea for you."

"Ooh," Mingmei said, taking a sip. "'Long Island.' It sounds like such an exotic place."

The boys looked at one another and cracked up. "Anyway, ladies," Matt said, "I hope it's about your speed."

"Lian's speed is usually both feet on the brake pedal," Mingmei said. "But tonight we're going to make her cut loose a little."

Conversation with Matt and Taylor came easily, and as Lian took tiny sips of her very strong drink, she was surprised to discover that she was actually having a good time. A waiter with a tray of the little quiches even passed near them, and she grabbed a couple. *Okay*, she reminded herself. *Don't forget why you're really here or anything, but admit that this turned into a decent Friday night.*

"Remember I was telling you how great David Bowie is?" Matt was asking Mingmei. "I slipped the DJ a couple bucks to put some on. If you don't love him through this sound system, then I don't know what to do with you."

Lian coughed as a bit of the hors d'oeuvre went down wrong. "Please," she said to Matt. "Please tell me you didn't request 'China Girl.' Please tell me you at least have that much tact."

He fixed her with a curious look, as if he couldn't believe she'd think so little of him. "No, Lian. I asked him to spin one I thought you'd dig. It's a little-known demo track called 'I'm Afraid of Americans.'"

She felt her cheeks flush. "Yeah. Well played."

Synth bleeps and a fuzzy bass line began to unwind from the speakers, and Matt grinned. "Hey, it's on now!" He took Mingmei's hand and gave a theatrical, courtly bow. "Care to dance, m'lady?"

"Of course," Mingmei said, handing Lian her glass—which had just ice and a lime slice in it now—and heading with Matt for the dance floor inside the main deck lounge.

"So, um," Taylor said to Lian. "You're not actually afraid of Americans, are you? Because that could make this conversation awkward."

"I'm only afraid of the ones who give me a reason," she answered. She didn't think Taylor was one of those; he was soft spoken, even a little shy, and kept pushing his black-framed glasses up his nose every time he made a joke. Charmingly nerdy.

"To be honest," she continued, "I haven't met many Americans in my life. You and Matt and his father are kind of my metric, right now."

"Huh. Well, two out of three ain't bad," Taylor mused.

"Meaning?"

"Oh. Well, um, I guess I put myself in the 'win' column," he said. "I'm biased, though. But Matt, he's a good guy. No question."

Lian thought that "no question" was a little generous.

"He and I grew up on the same street," Taylor said. "We went to the same school, always hung out together. He'd come over and we'd read my comic books, or play video games, or make up weird concoctions in the blender and dare each other to drink them. Now that he's moved out here, you know, that's the Matt I think of when I miss him."

Lian thought of a cynical reply but bit her tongue. Taylor's version of Matt was quite a lot different to her own.

"So when you're deciding which Americans to be afraid of," Taylor said as the song was winding down, "maybe give Matt a break. It's been a rough time for him, pretty steadily. I mean, on top of all that, being uprooted from his hometown to move halfway around the world, and he and Ashlynn breaking up, and everything."

"Ashlynn?" Lian said. "The blonde girl, his girlfriend?"

"*Ex*-girlfriend. Couldn't do the long-distance thing, so they called it off a few weeks ago. He's seemed pretty depressed the last month or so, when I've talked to him, so it's nice to see him enjoying himself again."

He pointed over to where Matt was instructing Mingmei on how to use the telescope mounted to the starboard deck near the stern. The two of them were laughing, his hand on her back, her eyes on the stars.

Lian watched them for a moment and decided she wasn't afraid of American Matt. She might actually be coming around to thinking he was a decent guy. But why, she wondered, had he lied about still having a girlfriend in the States?

"It's weird. All of this—" Taylor swept his hand to indicate the yacht party—"this isn't who he is at all. Deep down, he's still the kid wearing oversized hand-me-downs from his big brother, T-shirts of bands that were before our time." He smiled and glanced over to where Matt and Mingmei were dancing. "He was rocking Ziggy Stardust shirts before he'd even heard of David Bowie."

"Wait," Lian said. "Why was he wearing hand-me-downs?"

Taylor fidgeted a little, pretending to be fascinated by the label on his beer bottle. Clearly, he was thinking he'd already said more than he should have. "Well, um, his dad—"

"Taylor," Rand Harrison said, clapping him hard on the shoulder—aggression masquerading as familiarity? Lian wondered. Certainly Taylor seemed to chafe at the touch.

"I'm so glad you could come visit Matthew for a bit. I know it means the world to him," Harrison said. "But now I wonder if you'd allow me a moment alone with the lovely Ms. Hung here."

Taylor shot her a quick look, as if to make sure she'd be okay. She gave him a thin smile that she hoped didn't betray her unease.

"Sure thing, Mr. Harrison," Taylor said. "This is a pretty hip little shindig you've got going on, by the way."

"Be sure to fill out a comment card to that effect," Harrison said, dismissing him.

Lian stood at the prow, her elbows on the railing, gazing out across the harbor. She was acutely aware of Harrison's presence next to her: a little too close, a little too intimidating. His champagne glass was gone; in its place was a mostly empty tumbler of Scotch. But his tone was stony sober. "I'm pleased that you could join us here tonight, Lian," he said. "I know the *Seaward* isn't much to look at. I think of her as a 'starter yacht.' A test run toward something more substantial."

Maybe he was trying to joke with her, but he didn't crack a smile.

"Speaking of which," he said, turning on one elbow so he could look down the ship's vast length to where Mingmei and his son stood chasing comets. "You should know that Matthew's spoken very highly of you, these last few days."

"Really?" Lian said, genuinely surprised. "It's hard to believe he's spoken of me at all."

"Oh yes. He fears you're going to give him quite a run for his money in your economics course. If you'll pardon my pun."

"Leading indicators are that he's invested in doing well in that class," she said. "If you'll pardon mine."

Harrison appraised her with his plastic smile. "Very clever. I applaud your wit, Lian . . . or, rather, I give you an invisible hand."

She returned the smile, but with no more sincerity than she was being offered.

"My son, as I'm sure you know, is a very intelligent kid. So, understandably, it's a trait he values in others. And from your role as the devil's advocate at our dinner last Sunday, it's clear to me that you're a very intelligent kid, too. That your mode of thinking is very . . . *deep*."

As he said the word, he flicked his wrist, and the ice cubes from his glass sailed over the chopping black water and sunk with a quiet splash.

Lian felt a chill run up her spine. There were very few people on the decks, and none near them at the prow. Almost all of the guests were inside the lounge, dancing to a techno remix of some brassy big band tune or shouting their conversations at the bar. Even Matt and Mingmei had wandered somewhere out of sight.

No one would see Harrison push her over the railing. No one would hear her screams over the hubbub of the party.

"I like to consider myself a somewhat intelligent man, too," he said. "Intuitive, even. And I've intuited that you, Lian, don't think all that much of me. What I've done to cultivate that feeling, I can't imagine, but neither can I pretend I don't sense it from you."

She said nothing. What was there to say?

"All I ask," he said, leaning uncomfortably close, "is that you give me a chance. I just feel that would be the . . . *intelligent* thing to do."

She smiled and opened her mouth, knowing she needed to respond but not sure what words might come out. Before any could, Harrison's phone vibrated in his coat pocket. He pulled it out, glanced at the incoming number, and turned to her.

"If you'll excuse me," he said. "Duty calls."

He stalked away several paces, and then answered the call as he disappeared into a stairwell. Lian watched him go, unsure of what to make of their encounter.

A moment later, a light went on in the second deck cabin, and Harrison appeared, pacing the room: passing before the windows, vanishing for a moment, walking back the other way. If Lian leaned back on the railing, she had a pretty good view of him. He was agitated, clearly. As he talked, he gesticulated with his free hand. There was anger in his face and posture, to be sure. But as the phone call went on and Lian watched closely, she was certain she saw something else. Something unexpected.

Rand Harrison looked scared.

SEVENTEEN

"This one," Matt shouted over falsetto singing, scatting, and a two-note bass line. "This one is one of the all-time greats. It's him teaming up with this other band, Queen. It was huge! This was like 1981, 1982."

"You're making up years that never existed!" Mingmei yelled back. "Surely, the world was a void before I was born!"

Lian watched the adults on the dance floor, doing awkward, tipsy adult dances to the mid-tempo song. Clearly, they had all existed before Mingmei was born—several of them knew when to shout along with the singer's plea, "Let me out!"

Lian wanted to shout it, too. The run-in with Rand Harrison had left her shaken and had seemed like the perfect cue to call it a night. She'd only entered the lounge to say good-bye to Mingmei and the boys but had gotten swept up in Matt's pop music lecture.

"Hey," he said as the epic track quieted for a few measures of harmonizing and snaps. "It's so damn noisy in here, I can't hear myself think. Which is a shame, because I am *awesome* at thinking. Why don't we freshen up our drinks and head up to the second deck for a little?"

Before she could protest, Lian found her own voice drowned out again by swelling guitars. The others made for the bar, but she caught Mingmei's elbow.

"Listen," Lian said. "I think I'm going to make a break for it. I'm exhausted, and I've got ninety minutes of violin practice before I can sleep, so . . ."

"Don't even think about leaving," Mingmei chastised her. "One, you're on a yacht, which is an opportunity you might not have again until my fragrance line becomes an international phenomenon. Two, you look amazing in that dress. Three, Taylor said he was having a great time talking to you—that you were smart and funny and cute. I made him repeat the last one, so I know it's true. He really likes you, Lian!"

"Oh. Fantastic."

Mingmei's eyes narrowed. "Because there's something wrong with a boy liking you? Or because you've got so many guys throwing themselves at you that there's no room for one more?"

"Ouch," Lian said, though she smiled. "Words can hurt, Mingmei."

In truth, Taylor was a good-looking, quietly pleasant boy, and if she didn't have a corporate empire to topple, its evil CEO creeping her out, and a senior year schedule filled to bursting, Lian might have let herself be flattered by his attention.

"Just stick around a while longer," Mingmei begged. "Otherwise he'll feel like a third wheel. And, hey, if you wind up making out with him a little, even better! He'll be on a plane back to Colorado in a couple of days, so you're spared the awkwardness of running into him later."

Lian shook her head, even as she let Mingmei take her hand and lead her after the boys. "You and I are very different people, Mingmei," she said.

"Too true. But, slowly, I am lowering you to my standards."

The second deck boasted an impressive aft-facing sunken lounge, replete with billiards and foosball tables, an arcade *Galaga* video game, a flatscreen television that Lian judged to be sixty inches or more diagonally, and sofas swathed in the softest leather she'd ever felt. Matt let them in with a keycard and locked the door behind them.

"I nicknamed this the Fabius Maximus Suite," he told them. "Fifty bucks to anyone who can figure out why."

Lian wrinkled her brow and looked around. The whole room seemed designed for a guy Matt's age: two ergonomic, speaker-augmented gaming chairs rested against a side wall. An open cabinet displayed an impressively designed stereo with an iPod dock and a CD carousel. Dozens of discs lined the shelves—mostly American bands she wasn't familiar with, but some classical works as well. Ten or more books lay on various surfaces, all with bookmarks inside: some fiction, some history, a Nassim Taleb that Mr. Chu had recommended (but that wasn't on the syllabus). A Colorado Rockies pennant hung on the wall in between an oversized calendar of Marvel comic heroes and a framed poster of some movie about Brad Pitt and a bar of pink soap. A coffee table book on military engagements throughout the ages.

That was it.

"Retreat," she said, since no one else had hazarded a guess at Matt's question. "The yacht is already a retreat, and this is your own further retreat inside of it."

Matt looked impressed. "Got it in one, Lian! That's . . . wow."

Lian ignored Mingmei's look—somewhere between confusion and annoyance—and said to Matt, "Presumably you'll be waging a war of attrition against Carthage soon?"

"Yeah," he laughed. "Something like that. Man, remind me not to throw obscure references your way when money's at stake. You're too smart for me."

"Keep your cash," she said. "You can just loan me a couple of these books sometime, instead."

He nodded. "It's a deal."

"Okay, okay," Mingmei said, picking up the television remote. "Enough of the smart people being smart. Does this thing get MTV?"

They all laughed, and Matt brought up the channel, where two crudely drawn cartoon boys were insulting a rap video in what Lian thought was English, although it was hard to tell.

"Ahh," Mingmei said, sinking into the couch and taking a long pull on her straw. "*That's* more like it."

Lian had to admit that the show was pretty funny, and the company in which she was watching it was pleasant. But this wasn't why she'd come on board the yacht. If she deboarded tonight with nothing but a mild buzz and Taylor's e-mail address, the night might not be a total failure . . . but it wouldn't be much of a victory for 06/04, either.

She set aside her drink untouched and asked Matt where the restroom was. He opened the suite door and pointed her down a hallway and to her left. "If you end up in the bay," he told her with a smile, "you've gone too far."

Once she'd rounded the corner, Lian took stock of her surroundings. The speakers from below were still thudding, rattling her floor with their dull noise. There were a few partygoers down on the main deck, chatting or playing with the telescope. No one seemed to be up on the second deck anymore, and she didn't see any interior lights on in any of the rooms down the hall.

She made her way cautiously toward the fore of the boat, passing the bathroom and instead peering around the last corner of the hall. There was the study, the room she'd seen Harrison pacing earlier when he'd taken the call. If there was anything of value to her investigation on board the *Seaward*, it was likely to be in here.

Lian didn't dare turn on the room light, but she took her cell phone from her purse and scrolled to a flashlight app, dimming it so that it was just bright enough for her to see a few feet in front of her.

The study was disappointingly bare. No computer to search, no file cabinet to rifle through, not even an old-style rotary card index of business contacts. It was just a desk with a blotter and a banker's lamp, some pens, a framed photo of Harrison and, Lian presumed, his wife. Matt's mother.

She lingered just a moment on the photograph. The woman was beautiful, with Matt's blond hair and stunning green eyes. But her smile seemed sad, somehow. Her eyes seemed distant.

Lian shook the thoughts from her head. This wasn't why she was here.

She turned the glow of the phone onto the blotter, hoping to find an impression left in it by Harrison's handwriting: a name, an address, a written confession to Jiao's murder. But it was smooth and new, offering her no clues.

Distantly, she thought she heard a noise, and she spun around quickly, banging her shin on the desk chair. It was all she could do not to cry out in pain; she bit her bottom lip and stood there, breathing hard for a moment, willing the hurt to subside.

What she saw next sped up the healing process a great deal.

Rand Harrison's coat was draped over the back of the chair. The coat he'd been wearing earlier in the evening. The one from which he'd pulled his cell phone when it rang.

Lian slipped her fingers past the lapel, daring to hope. When she felt the plastic rectangle behind the silky fabric, she could have done a victory dance, if her leg wasn't still mildly throbbing.

She took it out and found the screen locked and requesting a pin. A mad part of her thought about pocketing the phone and just getting off the boat then and there. But that was nuts. She wasn't that desperate yet. Instead she thumbed four zeros—the manufacturer's standard pin. The phone unlocked and the screen flared to maximum brightness. *Lucky me*, she thought.

She punched up Harrison's call log and read the most recent number. Yes; this would have been right around the time he'd left her on the deck. Whoever had gotten him so steamed, and so frightened, was on the other end of those digits. She quickly scrolled to her own phone's contacts and punched in the number, filed under "RH scary phone call."

Another noise, closer this time. She'd risked enough; she slipped the phone back into the coat and was moving for the door when the overhead light came on. She slammed shut her eyes against the sudden brightness.

"Hey!" a male voice said from the doorway. "What the hell are you doing in here?"

Lian blinked several times, waiting for her eyes to readjust. As they did, the speaker swam into focus, and her heart leapt into her throat.

It was the potbellied man.

"I'm so sorry," she said, slurring the words a little. "I was looking for a restroom, and, uh, I stumbled in here and ran into the chair and, um, this isn't the restroom, is it?"

"No. It isn't."

"I'm so, so sorry," she said again, adopting a 'girlish' demeanor that, she suspected, was a pretty dead-on impression of Mingmei. "Just between you and me, I think I'm a little drunker than I thought I was."

"Bathroom's in the middle hall," he said gruffly. "And the party is downstairs. Not up here."

"Got it. Okay," she said, wobbling past him and back into the hall. He said nothing but gave her an odd look, as if he was trying to remember where he'd seen her before. She tottered quickly to the middle hallway, and then straightened up and dashed for the restroom, more sober than she'd ever been in her life.

Once inside, she locked the door and stood by it, listening intently for the fat man's footsteps. When she was confident he hadn't followed her, she lowered the toilet lid, sat down on it, and stared at the number she'd cadged from Harrison's phone.

She had signal here. No reason not to give it a call. She typed in the vertical service code to block her number, and then dialed.

"You've reached the Family Hand Café," a formal female voice said. "To whom may I direct your call?"

Lian recognized the name right away. It was the mahjong parlor where Harrison and the fat man had gone after the dinner.

"Who is calling, please?" the voice said.

Lian hung up and returned her phone to her purse, perplexed.

So she had the *where* of the call but not the *who*. Who was operating out of the Family Hand? What had they said to get Harrison so angry?

One thing she was sure of—if a man like Harrison was scared of them, they must be *really* bad news.

EIGHTEEN

"I'm surprised you're up this early, after your big party last night." Lian's mother gave her a sympathetic look across the breakfast table. "Do you need some aspirin?"

"I'm not hungover, Mother, just sleepy. I only had half of one drink last night," Lian said truthfully, rubbing at her eyes and padding over to the pantry for some cereal. "You must think I'm some kind of wild party girl."

"No, little panda," her mother said, turning the page of her newspaper. "I think you're my good and responsible daughter. But I like to have that notion confirmed every now and again."

Lian poured the puffed rice cereal into a bowl, replaced the box, and was opening the refrigerator for the milk when her father bustled into the room. He snagged his keys from the wall hook, grabbed and nearly dropped his briefcase, and was gone before Lian had said a word.

"What's Dad up to?" she asked her mother. "It's pretty early on a Saturday for him to be in a suit and tie."

"He would say that 'the work doesn't end just because the workweek does.' He was called in to some sort of urgent meeting with his bosses. Something that couldn't wait, apparently."

Lian didn't like the sound of that. She poured her milk and ate her cereal, careful not to seem like she was rushing through it. When her mother put down the newspaper and left the kitchen, though, Lian scoffed the last couple of bites, poured the milk down the sink, and quietly sprinted for her father's office.

The file cabinets and drawers were not locked; Hung Zhi-Kai trusted his family, and up until this point he'd had no reason not to do so. But if there was something in here, right under her nose, that could help with her investigation, Lian felt it would be irresponsible—possibly dangerous—of her not to take advantage of the situation.

The files, thankfully, were meticulously arranged, with tabs and cross-references making them simple to search. Lian quickly located the Harrison Corp materials—which was easy because they sprawled to fill most of a drawer—and, within them, precisely what she'd been hoping to find.

The report was thick, but luckily the local research company, MedVestigators, had summarized their findings on the cover sheet. The date on the findings was only about six weeks old. Keeping an ear out for her mother, Lian began turning the pages.

Analysis of ten Harrison samples indicates that chemical dyes are well within acceptable limits for toxicity.

"Damn," she mumbled, as she went to the next page.

Dye-fixing agents contain high to very high levels of mercury chlorides. Toxicity above acceptable levels.

She wasn't sure what "mercury chlorides" were, or what they did, but she knew that mercury was a poison, and she doubted that adding chlorine to it would help much.

Additional testing recommended on larger sample size.

This was more encouraging. She looked through the file for a follow-up report, but none had been submitted yet. Still, the one in her hands was enough to start on; she'd research mercury chloride's effects on the liver and kidneys, and see how it matched up with Jiao's autopsy.

Lian pulled up her phone's document scanner app, switched on the desk lamp for good contrast, and took a photo of the report's cover page. She nudged the edges of the preview and hit the "Scan" button, waiting as the program transformed the image into a PDF. Then she slid the report back into the Harrison file, exactly where she'd found it. She closed the drawer, made sure everything was in its right place. Then she switched off the lamp. Her mother was washing dishes; her father was still out. Lian headed down the hallway, her guilt over the snooping subsumed by her thrill at having uncovered a new piece of evidence.

Once back in her bedroom, she plugged her phone into her laptop and brought up the file. The findings had been signed by one Dr. Lan; a quick Web search showed that

Lan Ming was the owner of MedVestigators, as well as the head of its laboratories. Lian clicked the contact link next to Lan's name, which brought up a blank e-mail in a separate window. Her keystrokes were quick, and her lies were little and white.

Dear Dr. Lan,

Greetings. I am a high school student preparing an independent study on clothing manufacturing processes, and your company came highly recommended by my proctor. I write in the hope that you can spare some time to discuss acceptable toxicity levels for dyes and fixing agents used by companies who produce the most popular clothes among my peers (e.g., Roxie, Harrison Outfitters, Alien, etc.), and the effects of such toxins on the human body. Any assistance you can provide would be greatly appreciated.

Thank you,
Hung Xiao-Lian

That should open up the right kind of dialogue, Lian thought, *without tipping my hand as far as my true motives.* She sent the e-mail, and then typed in the ten-digit code she'd memorized for 06/04.

8:14 AM HKT — *Komiko has logged on*

Komiko: Anyone awake at this ungodly hour?

Blossom: Im here.

8:14 AM HKT — *Crowbar has logged on*

Crowbar: Got the ping, whats the news?

8:15 AM HKT — *Torch has logged on*

Torch: Yawn. It's much too early on a weekend for activism.

Komiko: Oh my goodness, Torch has a sense of humor!

Torch: I'm pretty funny when you get to know me.

Torch: Which you won't, because anonymity and blah blah blah. I say again, yawn.

Lian found herself laughing at Torch's words for the first time ever. He was claiming not to be a morning person, but this was the most pleasant he'd been in ages.

Komiko: Got a little something I thought you might like to see.

8:16 AM HKT — *Komiko has uploaded one PDF*

Komiko: Right there in black and white. "Toxicity above acceptable levels."

Torch: Very impressive find, K.

Blossom: OMG. How in the world did you get hold of a document like this?

Torch: Not important and not politic. We've all got our sources, and they need to stay protected.

Blossom: Sure. Just amazed, thats all.

Crowbar: I dont know much re: mercury chloride but I know where 2 look

Komiko: Fantastic. I was going to do that, but I'm happy to leave it to an expert.

Crowbar: Lets not oversell my abilities :)

Lian heard the apartment door open and close. Her father must be back from his meeting. She couldn't quite make out what he was saying, but his voice was louder than normal, his tone clipped and agitated.

Torch: If the known effects line up with the girl's autopsy report, C, this might just be enough to implicate Harrison.

Blossom: Not "the girl," remember? Jiao.

Torch: Right, sorry.

First the jokes and now an apology? Lian feared that Torch might be losing his edge.

Her mother's voice had grown louder as well. This sort of "verbal sparring" wasn't something Lian was used to from her parents. It gnawed at her for a long moment, and she decided to investigate, to at least hear enough of their words to know what had sparked the argument.

Komiko: brb

Still in her pajamas and socks, she tiptoed to the end of the hall and cautiously peered around the corner. Her folks were in the kitchen, but she could glimpse her father through the door. He looked twice as harried as he had when he'd left.

"No, Lili, I'm telling you," he said, sounding nearly manic. "If I don't push the deal through, they told me in no uncertain terms that there would be *consequences.*"

"You've faced consequences before, dear."

"Not some damned probationary week at work. Not losing the best leads to someone else. No. Consequences for me, you, and Lian. They're talking about transferring us back to the mainland."

Lian gasped. Whatever was happening, it was serious. In career terms, a transfer back across the bay was a black eye her father would never recover from.

"They wouldn't do that," her mother said, but she didn't sound very sure.

"They absolutely would. They showed me the papers. We're four signatures away from losing all of this."

"But," her mother protested, sounding as though she was searching for words. "But . . . that wouldn't be fair to Lian!"

"No. It wouldn't. That was my first thought, too."

Lian's heart swelled.

"And that's why I have to make sure this deal happens, regardless of my feelings," her father said. His voice had lost some of its energy; now he sounded defeated and hollow. "The negotiations are at such a delicate point. I can't afford to push them the wrong way."

He took off his coat, folded it over the back of a kitchen chair, and then sat down heavily, his fingers at his temples. His wife stepped behind him and began gently massaging his shoulders. The worry on her face was hard for Lian to look at.

"Damn this deal," her father muttered. "I wish I'd never in my life heard of Rand Harrison or his company."

Lian ducked back around the corner and let fly a string of foul, whispered curses. How dare Harrison cause her father such misery? Add that to a list of sins that might have no end.

She stalked back to her bedroom, furious, and pounded out her return on the keyboard.

Komiko: Sorry about that. Needed a little recharge of my righteous anger, apparently.

Komiko: We have to take Harrison down now. This has got to be our top priority. Every day he's still in business is a bad day for everyone else.

Komiko: And I can only speak for myself, but I don't care what the consequences are to me personally. I just want him stopped.

Blossom: Strong sentiment, K.

Komiko: I mean every word.

If Harrison's downfall meant that her father's company pulled the power ploy of sending the family back to the mainland, she would of course be sad to say farewell to the school and the friends she had made there. She and Mingmei would stay close—she hoped—but not living in Central would be a huge change otherwise. As much as she often felt guilty about the life of privilege she led there, she had to admit that the readjustment would be brutal. She worried more for her parents, though; they had earned this lifestyle and might struggle to deal with taking a "backwards step."

Crowbar: Glad U R back Komiko, I was abt 2 tell the others, got a look at the 2ndary postmortem on Jiao

Crowbar: Or on Unknown Asian Female, I should say, she still hasnt been IDed

Crowbar: This new report lists COD as drowning

Blossom: COD?

Torch: Cause of death. Cod don't drown.

Lian smiled in spite of herself.

Blossom: Got it. But I thought the first report said no water in the lungs, so drowning wasnt an option?

Crowbar: Thats just it

Crowbar: The 1st report has been deleted. Its not anywhere in the system.

Lian felt a chill. This wasn't some clerk accidentally clicking the wrong box. This was deliberate. A cover-up. There was no doubt in her mind.

Blossom: Look, maybe its time we talked to the police. If chemicals are making Harrison workers sick, the police have the resources to investigate.

Blossom: At this point, keeping this info from the cops is the same as standing by and letting it happen.

Torch: . . .

Torch: Well, I disagree. The local police have failed to come through in the past, in too many cases to name. They're not a safe bet.

Torch: I suggest that we go to the Labor Department. They have the power to shut Harrison down if they have just cause.

Torch: And I doubt they're as easily infiltrated as the police department. There's less of a chance of Harrison getting a heads-up from an inside man.

Komiko: Wait, we're losing sight of the human face of this. Jiao deserves justice, and someone is clearly working hard to prevent her from getting it.

Komiko: It isn't enough that Harrison Corp suspends operations for a couple of weeks while they figure out who to bribe. We need to close them down permanently so no one becomes the next Jiao.

Crowbar: I C your point & I dont disagree, but the Labor Dept is a good call

Torch: If nothing else, it's a start. It's a way to shine a bigger light on Harrison than anything the four of us alone can manage right now.

Blossom: Agreed. Contacting the authorities is the next step in the bigger picture.

Blossom: Jiao is important, but a full-scale look into the chemicals has to be the priority.

Lian's three compatriots seemed united in their course of decisive action, but Lian could not share their enthusiasm for the method. Only she had seen Jiao up close, and only she had heard the anguish in Zan's voice upon learning that his sister was dead. The others would never understand why it meant so much to her that the dead girl be avenged.

But maybe that meant that their method was the right course of action. For now.

Komiko: Fine. Torch, you'll handle alerting the Labor Department?

Torch: I'll send them an anonymous tip-off to look into the chemicals. Happy to hear any suggestions you guys have about the wording.

Komiko: I'll let you three hash that out, if you don't mind.

Komiko: I think I'm all crusaded out for the day. Going back to bed.

8:49 AM HKT — *Komiko has logged off*

Just before she closed her laptop, Lian was surprised to see a Facebook friend request. She really only used the social networking site to keep in touch with friends back on the mainland. She clicked through and saw a picture of a boy heading down a water slide on his stomach.

Accept friend request from Taylor Brandon?

Lian smiled and clicked "accept," along with the message: "Nice to meet you the other night, Taylor. The least scary American I've come across yet."

NINETEEN

"Were you asleep?"

Lian cleared her throat, but the words still came out gravelly. "It's three in the morning. Do you want the truth, or the polite lie?"

"I'm sorry," Zan said on the other end of the phone. His voice sounded agitated. "Normally I wouldn't call at this hour, but something strange happened, and I thought you'd want to know."

She sat up in bed, yawned, and switched on the lamp on her nightstand. "Okay," she said. "You've got my ear. The other four senses might need a minute to catch up."

"Right. So, the bus came to get the night shift, just like clockwork. We're most of the way to work when suddenly the driver turns around and takes us right back to Chungking Mansions. No explanation at all. And no space for us, of course, because the day shift's mostly asleep already."

"Huh," Lian said. "That is weird."

"It gets weirder," he said. "Within an hour or so, more workers show up. This time it's all the women and the youngest kids. They've got nowhere to go but into the apartments. It's standing room only, everybody's whispering, trying to figure out what's going on. But of course none of us knows any more than anyone else."

Lian was fully awake now. "Okay. I think you were right to call me. This sounds major."

"No, no, no," he said in a rush. "You haven't heard the major part yet. Because there's a knock on the door, and half a dozen government types come walking in. Dark suits, ear radios, just like you see in the movies."

"Government guys?"

"Hong Kong Department of Labor," Zan said.

Lian punched the air, even though it wasn't "like" her. Less than twenty-four hours from the tip-off to their arrival. Every once in a while, the wheels of bureaucracy spun in the right direction.

"They divided the room into small groups and interviewed a bunch of us," Zan continued. "Seemed to be concerned about payroll documentation, on-the-job injuries, eligibility for work, all that sort of thing. I think this is it, Lian. I think this is the beginning of the end for Harrison Corp."

"Zan," she said, smiling. "It is always okay to wake me up at 3 A.M. with news like that."

"I've gotta go," he said. "I'm in the next group to talk to them. I'll tell you more when I know more. Try to get some sleep in the meantime."

"I'll try," she said. "But this might be too exciting to sleep through." She hung up, switched off the lamp, and laid her head back on the pillow, prepared for her thoughts and speculations to keep her up until dawn.

But within moments she was out, and she slept more soundly than she had any night since seeing the dead girl's face.

When she woke in the morning, Lian was full of energy and in good spirits. It was tempting to phone Zan to see what he'd learned from his interview, but she didn't want to interrupt anything or risk waking him after his long, strange night.

So she channeled her restlessness into a spirited session with Zheng, nestling the violin at her collarbone and drawing the familiar notes of Mendelssohn's Concerto in E Minor from its strings. Just as she was about to transition into the second movement, the Andante, the doorbell rang. Her concentration broke for a fraction of a second, and she held a quarter note too long. *Always shy of perfection,* she thought, laying the instrument and bow on her bed and going to the door. She opened it without checking through the spyhole.

"Good morning, Lian."

She felt her blood turn to ice. Rand Harrison stood before her, his voice as sharp as his suit, his face wearing a tight smile completely without joy. On either side of him stood a dark-suited associate, their hands behind their backs and their stares unblinking.

"What can I do for you, Mr. Harrison?" she asked, hoping her voice wasn't betraying her terror.

"You?" he said, still smiling. "You can't do anything. I've come to see your old man." His eyes narrowed. "In a purely informal capacity, of course. Just two friends, chatting on a Sunday morning."

"Of course," she said. *Two friends and two corporate goons*, she thought to herself. It didn't sound very friendly at all.

But she saw no choice other than to invite them in and lead them down the hall. "Father," she said, knocking at the open door to her father's study. "Your good friend Mr. Harrison is here."

She left them in the hallway and returned to her room, closing the door and quickly bringing up iTunes on her laptop. Typing "Mendelssohn" into the search bar got her more than a hundred tracks, including several versions of the concerto she'd been rehearsing. She scrolled until she found the one she wanted—Janine Jansen, solo violin, no accompaniment—tweaked the volume, and hit Play.

Then she crept out of the room, closing her door behind her with a quiet click. She snuck back down the hall and stationed herself outside her father's study. The decoy music was just loud enough to sound like she'd returned to her practice (and become a much better violinist). She had nearly half an hour's worth of eavesdropping before she'd need to sneak back and restart the mp3.

"What's clear to me now," she heard Harrison saying, "is that the Hong Kong government doesn't look favorably upon my enterprise. Which, frankly, I find quite insulting."

"No, Mr. Harrison, sir," her father replied. Lian felt herself tense at the deference in his voice. "I assure you, your company's contributions to our economy are a great boon. The government would not dream of interfering."

"But that's just it, Hung. They did dream, and late last night their dream came true. And I found it very hard to sleep after that dream."

Well, thought Lian, *that's the difference between you and me.*

"A raid by the Labor Department?" Harrison continued. "It's embarrassing, Hung. It's offensive. When you and I both know that I've gone well out of my way to act on the recommendations made by Dr. Lan and her ridiculously named MedInstigators."

Lian's father cleared his throat. "The, ah, their name is—"

"Immaterial," Harrison interrupted. "You're right, of course. But nevertheless we bowed to their findings, and in so doing I was under the impression that you and I had an *understanding.*"

He spat out the end of the word like it left an awful taste in his mouth. Lian's hand began to hurt, and it took her a moment to realize that she'd made a fist so tight that her fingernails were digging into her palm.

"We do, of course," her father said quickly. "I don't know where any of these problems are coming from. But I'll get to the bottom of it all. That's my job."

"For now," Harrison uttered. "Though, I couldn't help thinking this morning that it wouldn't be hard to find someone else better suited for it."

"Mr. Harrison, no, I hope you'll give me a chance to make this right."

That was it. Her father's fawning words curdled in Lian's ears. The idea of such an honorable man being forced to suck up to a slimeball like Harrison was too much to bear.

Lian spun on her heel to stand in the study's doorway. The violin cadenza that had been building in the background swelled with expertly bowed semiquavers.

Her father was seated facing the door, and Lian saw his eyes go wide at the sight of her. Before he had a chance to wave her away, she spoke.

"You know, Harrison," she said, and the man and both his goons turned to drill their icy looks into her. "If the Department of Labor cracked down on you, they must have had a pretty good reason. They don't generally raid businesses that are on the level."

"Lian!" her father barked, his face reddening. "This is a business meeting!"

"Really?" she said, directing all her words at Harrison now. "I was told that it was just a 'friendly chat.'"

Harrison smiled his horrible smile at her. "What a lovely ruse you and Mr. Mendelssohn have concocted."

His face fell, and he turned back to her father. "I was under the impression, Hung, that you people took a stern hand to your children—kept them in line, kept them obedient. Or is that yet another myth I've been fed about the wonders of the Orient?"

Lian saw her father twitch. "To your room," he said, pointing at her. "Immediately!"

She stood seething for a moment, watching her father's eyes dart from her to Harrison and back. She saw the vein in his forehead throb, heard his clipped breathing.

At last, she hung her head and walked away, shutting the door behind her, retreating to the tempo of a coda being perfectly played, wondering if Janine Jensen ever got into this kind of trouble.

She doubted it.

TWENTY

Even with the pillow over her head, Lian heard a soft knock on her bedroom door.

"Come in," she said, though it came out muffled.

She heard the door open and felt the mattress sink as someone sat down near her legs. Felt a warm hand on her arm.

"Thank you for knocking," Lian said.

"I thought about not doing so," her mother said. "A knock is a display of respect, and respect appears to be in short supply this morning."

Lian groaned and rolled over, tossing the pillow to one side. "I hope you're not asking me to respect Rand Harrison," she said. "There's not a yacht party in this world that'll make that happen."

"You don't think your father felt disrespected when you spied on his meeting?" her mother said, her voice low in volume, but high in reproach. "When you shamed his guest? You don't think I felt disrespected, watching you slink back to your room when I thought you'd been in there practicing your concerto all along?"

Lian had no response. She looked away, out the window, to the skyline of the Central District. It was the most sickening vista she could imagine at the moment.

"Have we been terrible parents?" her mother asked. "Have we not always treated you with respect?"

You never knock, Lian wanted to say. But she knew these questions were all rhetorical; they were the perfect parents, and she was their dutiful daughter. That's the way things had always been.

How, then, to tell such parents that the life of privilege her father's work afforded her felt like a curse and not a blessing? That guilt gnawed at Lian when she opened her closet, or fired up her scooter, or dined on octopus carpaccio, or gazed from their apartment in the clouds down to where the money never touched?

Of course, these were unanswerable questions as well. Her mother wouldn't understand such sentiments, could never wrap her head around something like 06/04. Every day, Lian felt the gap between them widening. One day, she feared, she would no longer be able to see her parents from the other side.

"Despite your outburst," her mother was saying, "your father has been able to placate Mr. Harrison for the time being. Once the deal goes through, perhaps his sleepless nights will end. And perhaps you will remember where you last left your manners."

"Wait," Lian said, sitting up. "What do you mean, 'once the deal goes through?' The raid didn't kill the deal?"

"Why should it have?" her mother said. "The Labor men found nothing out of the ordinary at the complex. No toxic chemicals, no unsafe working conditions. All the paperwork was up to date, all the initials in the right place." She smiled. "They couldn't even find a dropped stitch on the new fall collection. If anything, the raid has made the deal more likely."

Lian felt sick to her stomach.

"The lawyers will be finalizing the contracts over the next few days, the press conference should be held next week. And after that, I imagine your father will sleep for days, and then we'll go celebrate his commission with the fanciest dinner any of us have ever eaten."

She looked delighted at the prospect. This was all just paperwork to her, Lian realized. Stacks of photocopied A4 sheets being pushed back and forth across desks, signatures in triplicate, corporate seals. The contracts went out, the money came in, a nice dinner was had to celebrate.

The human cost was not factored in—not for a single moment.

"I think I'd like a little time alone, Mother," Lian said. "I'm not feeling well."

Her mother gave her a concerned look, patted her arm again, and stood to leave. "Let us hope it isn't contagious."

Lian looked away. *Upper-class guilt is not in any danger of catching around here.*

She grabbed up the pillow again as her mother left the room, flopping onto her stomach and closing her eyes against the chalk-white cotton. Despair settled on her like a threadbare blanket; she wrapped herself in it and felt colder still.

Torch had once posted a quote she'd really appreciated, a handful of words attributed, perhaps incorrectly, to one Edmund Burke. She felt they were a perfect summary of 06/04's reason for existence: "The only thing necessary for the triumph of evil is for good men to do nothing."

But what happened when good men, and women, like 06/04 did *something*, and it still wasn't enough? What happened when evil was simply too well connected?

Clearly, Harrison had friends in high places. Someone had to have tipped him off that the raid was coming; there was no other explanation for Zan's bus being turned around, or for the women and underage workers being pulled from the factory floors. When the Labor Department had arrived, everything had appeared on the up-and-up. Strong male workers, no code violations, paperwork showing the government men exactly what they wanted to see.

She'd known that Harrison had his potbellied lapdog working within the police, but now it was plain that he had a mole seeded in the Labor Department—someone senior enough to know about the raid and give ample warning. And if that were the case, how many other arms of the government had Harrison infected? How informed was he?

Informed enough that 06/04's best play had been doomed almost as soon as it was set in motion.

Komiko: A bit of a roller coaster since last I checked in.

Lian scrolled back through the conversations that had taken place without her. Crowbar was despondent, all frowny emoticons and not knowing "what 2 do next." Blossom had made a couple of feeble stabs at encouragement and team spirit before largely falling silent. And Torch was on a furious tear, a raw nerve with a hair-trigger Caps Lock key.

Blossom: Roller coasters are fun. This isnt.

Crowbar: We did everything right, played by the rules, told the authorities . . . & we still lost

Torch: The battle. We lost the battle. NOT THE WAR.

Crowbar: Hard to C right now how 4 people can win a war

Lian typed quickly, hoping to post before Torch banged out an angry rebuttal.

Komiko: It's not just the four of us.

Komiko: Don't forget, Zan's working for HC now, spying for us. Our work is inspiring bravery in others.

Torch: Really? He's being brave? Because from where I'm sitting, it looks like he's being USELESS.

Torch: For a "spy," he hasn't fed us one bit of worthwhile information yet. Where's the list of chemicals? Where's his sister's paperwork?

Torch: Where is ONE SINGLE ADVANTAGE that brave, brave Zan has given us against Harrison?

Komiko: Okay, we're all angry at what happened with the raid. But let's remember who the enemy is here.

Torch: Oh, I remember. Believe me. And I'm actually DOING SOMETHING about it.

Lian pushed back from her laptop for a minute. The best way to handle Torch when he was in this mood was not to handle him at all. Just let him post uninterrupted until he started to run out of steam. She only hoped that Crowbar and Blossom figured out to stay clear as well.

Torch: Earlier today I hacked the firewall for the contractors who did the refurbishment on HC's Central offices.

Torch: I snatched every scrap with Harrison's name on it. All the blueprints, details of the layout—where the physical files are stored, where the server room is.

Torch: But that was just a warm-up. The main event is to crack that server and dig up the payroll files. They're required by law to keep them.

Torch: If Jiao worked there at all, there will be SOMETHING in their system. Even if they purged every mention of her, there are data ghosts.

Torch: Unlike in the real world, Jiao can't be erased completely online. And I will stop at NOTHING until I find her.

Torch: Any official document that places her at that factory will be enough to implicate Harrison.

10:58 AM HKT — *Torch has logged off*

Blossom: And just like that, Torch is gone. I guess the conversation was over.

10:58 AM HKT — *Blossom has logged off*

Crowbar: Maybe thats 4 the best, I dont feel like thinking about this right now NEway

10:59 AM HKT — *Crowbar has logged off*

Lian sat for a moment, pondering how utterly alone she was—in her bedroom, in her chat room, and in her fight against the forces of corporate greed.

At least she'd got in one good night's sleep before her whole world fell apart.

11:00 AM HKT — *Komiko has logged off*

TWENTY-ONE

By the time she got to the computer lab during her free period—after a trip to the restroom and a quick stop by the library to check out an annotated study guide to *Anna Karenina*—Lian's preferred workstation in the corner was already occupied. She stood at the room's threshold, watching Matt working the trackball, his eyes glued so intently to the monitor that he didn't even look up when she stepped into the room.

She watched him for a moment. The lab was sparsely populated, but somehow the four empty chairs on either side of him seemed to highlight Matt's isolation here—his *otherness*. He could have been outside with the other boys, chasing a ball around the grounds as if it actually mattered. But he was in the computer lab and was probably writing e-mails to his friends back home. Friends that he missed.

Lian backed out of the doorway, deciding not to disturb him. She had only taken a couple of steps when her cell phone vibrated in her pocket, two staccato bursts to let her know she had a new text message. She reached for her phone, and, in the same instant, Matt picked up his from the tabletop and read its screen.

Little wonder; it was a message from Mingmei, addressed to the two of them.

> *The Stephen Chow revival at Central Cinema rolls on, and tonight is Kung Fu Hustle with English subtitles. Something for everyone! I'm declaring this a double date, Lian, which means you pick a boy or I'll pick one for you. And as you know, my taste in men is excellent ;)*

Lian stepped out into the hallway and replied:

> *I'll pick my own prince; I'm scared you'll find me a frog.*

She had agreed to go to the film with Mingmei when it had been announced a month ago, before Matt was even in the picture. It seemed a little unfair that his arrival made it necessary for her to find a date as well, but she realized that she actually knew someone who might fit the bill very nicely.

She logged onto Facebook on her phone, and quickly messaged Taylor.

> *Short notice, but Matt, Mingmei and I are going to the movies tonight? Up for it?*

A message came back about a minute later.

> *Sorry, Lian. At airport now and heading home. Would have been nice to get to know you better*

Lian suppressed her disappointment, hesitated for a moment, and then texted Zan.

Call or text me when you get this; I was thinking I'd treat you to a movie tonight before your shift — Lian

"So how do you know this guy, again?" Mingmei asked hours later, as they stood in the concession line.

"He's a friend of my brother's," Lian fibbed. She'd decided that it was easier to go with this cover story than to pick and choose the bits of her life she could safely share with Mingmei (and Matt now, she supposed).

"Oh, of course. I think I remember him from Qiao's going-away party. How's your brother doing, anyway?"

Zan certainly hadn't been there, but if Mingmei wanted to fill in his backstory, Lian wasn't about to stop her. "It's 'Karl' now, not Qiao," she said, rolling her eyes. "And if his postcards are to be believed, right now he's into Swedish techno-pop and girls who favor berets. Between two girlfriends and a dozen ski slopes, I think he may have forgotten the 'study' part of 'study abroad.'"

She bought a large savory popcorn, and Mingmei bought the sweet kind, so they could pass both buckets down the row as needed. They rejoined the boys outside the theater doors.

"Lian makes a semester in Switzerland sound pretty appealing," Mingmei told Matt, in English. "Have you had a chance to go visit Qiao over there, Zan? Is the whole country one great big sexy chalet?"

Zan hesitated for a second, and then said, "Oh, yeah, I was there for a weekend in July. It's, uh . . . the weather was perfect, but those mountains were *freezing*." Lian breathed a sigh of relief—Zan was smart enough to hide behind his second language when under pressure. "And like Qiao's girlfriend said, 'once the cocoa runs out, there's only one way to stay warm.'"

"Ha. Which girlfriend was that?" Mingmei asked, smiling as she tossed a kernel into her mouth.

Zan shot a quick look at Lian; he hadn't been prepped with enough detail.

"The, um. . . . It's hard to remember. He went through them like tissues." He nudged Matt with his elbow, grinning: "The best part of being young, male, and good looking, am I right?"

Matt just stared at him. "Are you?"

Mingmei took Matt's hand, and the two of them walked into the theater. Lian lingered uncomfortably with Zan for a moment, picking at her popcorn.

"What's his deal?" Zan asked. "I was just making a joke."

"Don't worry about it. Matt's kind of a hard guy to read."

They entered the theater as well. Mingmei waved to them animatedly, but she needn't have bothered; Lian knew she'd always find her friend on an aisle seat in the very back row, her preference since the first movie they'd seen together not long after Lian's family had arrived from the mainland.

Lian made her way down the row and took the seat next to Matt, offering him her bucket of popcorn.

"Wait . . . has it got frog ovaries in it?" he asked.

"Tell him it does," Zan said as he sat. "More popcorn for us."

"Just garlic salt," Lian told Matt, who thanked her as he took a handful. He chewed one piece at a time as he held a steady sidelong stare on Zan. After a moment, Lian was wary of leaning too far forward in her seat, in case one of the daggers being thrown by the two boys caught her in the head.

"So, Zan," Matt said, his voice low and almost robotic. "Are you a student on par with Lian's brother?"

Zan laughed. "No way, man. I'm out there in the working world now, getting my hands dirty." He held up both his hands, and then plunged them into the popcorn on Lian's lap. "High school was just about all the reading I want to do for a lifetime."

"Sure," Matt nodded. "No need for it once you've gotten that diploma, obviously." Undaunted, he reached into the popcorn and pulled out a puff from directly between Zan's wrists. Lian wriggled in her seat; she hadn't realized her lap was going to be some sort of weird battleground for this machismo-off.

"Here," she said, lifting up the bucket and moving it over to Zan's seat.

"So what do you do for a living to get your hands so dirty?" Mingmei asked, pointedly not passing her caramel popcorn down.

Lian pressed her heel onto Zan's toes: a reminder to answer with anything but the truth. She tried to be subtle, but she couldn't be certain that Matt hadn't noticed the kick.

"Demolition," Zan answered. "I go in and set the charges, throw the switch, bring the whole thing tumbling down around me. Dangerous work, you know? Real men only need apply."

There was a light in his eyes as he spun his tale. Clearly, Lian thought, this imaginary profession was one that held a real interest for him, and he knew the topic well. Matt and Mingmei listened politely as Zan fabricated a story about his most recent project, naming the types of explosive used, describing the undermining process, stressing the importance of collapsing a building onto its own footprint.

"So if I screw up even by the tiniest bit," he concluded, "if I don't study every angle of the job . . . a whole lot of people could get hurt or killed."

"Well," Matt said, his tone still flat, "good thing you place so much value on education, then."

As the house lights went down, Lian saw Zan scowling. It was the first time she didn't feel annoyed to be force-fed commercials before a movie. They were a pleasant distraction from the mounting tension between the two boys, even the ones advertising the upcoming Harrison Denim line. Zan excused himself to use the restroom before the feature started.

"I know it was short notice," Matt whispered as a trailer for upcoming revival screenings started. "But I can't believe that guy was the best you could do, Lian."

"What's that supposed to mean?"

"I don't know, he's just . . . he isn't what I would picture as your 'type.'"

She straightened in her seat. "What would you know about my 'type,' anyway?" she whispered.

"Forget it," he said, staring straight ahead at the screen, which was playing the trailer for this year's *All's Well, Ends Well* syrup-fest, which seemed was promoted on the presence of a martial arts movie actor trying to prove he could do romantic comedy.

"No," she insisted. "If you're going to sit here and pass judgment on me for bringing him, you're at least going to tell me why."

"I want to see this movie," Mingmei whispered, tugging on Matt's sleeve and pointing at the screen.

"All I mean," Matt said to Lian, "is that you're a smart girl. And you're not unattractive."

Lian felt her eyes widen. It wasn't that she cared whether Matt Harrison thought she was pretty or not, but the caginess of that double negative was somehow worse than if he hadn't mentioned it at all.

"I'd just like to think," he continued, "that you value yourself more than to wind up with someone like him. Someone who thinks reading sucks, and that blowing things up is fun. Who asks for a high five from a stranger when he makes a crass comment about womanizing."

Lian was seething. Every ounce of pity she'd felt for Matt when she'd seen him in the computer lab had evaporated. If this was how he interacted with people, he probably had no more friends back home than he'd made here.

"I just hate to see an intelligent girl saddle herself to someone who isn't going to challenge her," Matt finished. A new preview started up, for some kind of war epic.

"I'mgettingawfullysickofyouappraisingmyintelligence," Lian countered. "I don't like you using it to insult my date, I don't appreciate you faking admiration for it when you're clearly better versed in economic theory than I'll ever be, and, most of all, I don't care for you bringing home reports on it to your daddy. So do me a favor and just keep your thoughts about how smart I am to yourself."

"What are you talking about, reports to my dad?"

"He told me, on the yacht," she hissed. "He told me you hadn't stopped talking about me. Which I thought was a little weird at the time, and now I've decided is plain creepy. So cut it out."

Matt shook his head, waiting until he had finished chewing his popcorn before he spoke again. "You're out of your mind, Lian. I haven't said one word about you at home. Maybe he had you confused with someone else."

"He knows *exactly* who I am."

"Well, then, maybe you're full of crap. Just because you've got some obsession with Googling photos of me and hunting me down like a stalker, don't think for one minute that the feeling is mutual."

Lian stood up, furious. "I'm done with this conversation," she said, not bothering to whisper any more. "Enjoy the popcorn."

She dumped the bucket onto his lap and stalked out of the theater before he or Mingmei could say another word.

Zan was coming through the door as she was pushing it to exit. She caught him by the sleeve. "Forget it," she said. "We're leaving."

"Everything okay?"

"It was getting a little bit cold in there, sitting next to Matt. A little cold and a little arrogant."

Zan jogged to draw up alongside her. "Don't you want to get a refund for our tickets?"

She sighed and kept walking. "I know this will come across like I don't care about wasting money, but right now I just want to get as far from this place as possible."

"Okay, okay," he said as she pushed through the glass double doors to the sidewalk. "But come on, what did he say to get you so riled up?"

She leaned against the building and pressed her fingers to her temples. *Yeah,* she thought when she became conscious of her action. *I'm my father's daughter, all right.*

"I don't want to get into it," she replied after a minute. "Just . . . when I tell you that his last name is Harrison, maybe you'll understand."

"Now I'm riled up."

"I kept wanting to give him chances because Mingmei's into him, and every once in a while there's a flash of someone decent beneath all the cockiness." She tilted her head to one side, trying to work out the tension in her neck. "But in the end, I just can't trust him. I can't trust that he isn't spying for his dad, taking everything I say and do back to headquarters so that Harrison is always one step ahead of us."

"There's a lot of middle ground between a decent guy and a corporate spy," Zan said gently. "You said it yourself earlier, he's hard to read. Maybe he's just an ordinary teenager."

"Maybe," Lian said, massaging her aching head. "But if so, someone really ought to weed that garden."

Zan offered to walk to the drugstore at the end of the block to buy her some ibuprofen and a drink. Lian thanked him and pulled out her phone. She had turned it off for the movie; when she powered it back up to call for a cab, she noticed that she'd received a new e-mail. She opened the message and read it silently.

Dear Ms. Hung,

As regards your enquiry to Dr. Lan, it is my unfortunate duty as her attorney to inform you that she will be henceforth unable to reply. In the event of her passing it falls to me to respond to her unanswered correspondence. Sadly, I am unable to provide assistance with the topics you named. If you have any further enquiries with which I may be of some assistance, please contact me via this address or the telephone number below.

Regards,
Shan Silman
Caffey, Carlson & Partners LLP

Lian reeled. She quickly brought up her Web browser and searched for recent news on MedVestigators. The first story that popped up told her the worst in its lead:

Doctor Lan Ming of Hong Kong was found dead this morning by neighbors, of apparent suicide by self-injection. This tragedy follows the loss of Lan's

202

business, research laboratory MedVestigators, to
fire just one week ago. Authorities have confirmed
that a suicide note was found on Lan's person but
have released no details of its contents.

Lian closed the browser and slid down the outside wall of the cinema until she was sitting on the sidewalk. The raid had failed, Zan's undercover work hadn't turned up anything incriminating, and now her next best hope had quite literally gone up in flames.

She took the pills and drank the iced tea, but this headache wasn't going to get better anytime soon.

TWENTY-TWO

12:08 AM HKT — *Komiko has logged on*

Komiko: Clearly, I'm not going to get any sleep tonight. Anybody up for some midnight conspiracy theorizing?

Torch: I'm the only one here right now, but sure. Hit me with your best shot.

Komiko: You had a chance to read the news story I linked to earlier, about Dr. Lan?

Torch: I did.

Komiko: She questioned HC's materials and practices, and she was diving back in for another lap. And then . . .

Komiko: Her whole lab was lost to a fire . . . along with all the samples and files. And a week later she sticks herself in the neck with a chemical cocktail.

Komiko: For anybody else, I'd say these were extreme measures for a cover-up. But I'm starting to suspect that, for Harrison, it's just another boring day at the office.

Torch: Take a step back, K. Fires happen. I'd guess they're even more likely to happen in buildings full of chemical samples.

Torch: The preliminary report from the fire investigator doesn't rule one way or another on arson.

Komiko: You have to imagine Harrison's people would know how to stage an accident.

Torch: But that's CONJECTURE, not evidence. It's not the smoking gun we need.

Komiko: I believe the fire was an accident about as much as I believe that Lan took her own life.

Torch: And if we could convict on your beliefs alone, half the world would be in handcuffs.

Lian gave a short, harsh laugh at this. "Gallows humor," they called it. Harrison held open the noose; first Jiao and then Lan had stepped into it. And try as they might, 06/04 couldn't saw through the rope.

12:11 AM HKT — *Crowbar has logged on*

Crowbar: Hi peeps, give me 1 sec 2 get caught up

Komiko: Switching subjects, then. There must be records SOMEWHERE that link Jiao to HC.

Komiko: We show that a worker died while in his employment, Harrison will have to face up to it.

Torch: Believe me, I'm doing all I can to find those records.

Crowbar: We do still have the 1st postmortem, the 1 that says she didnt drown

Komiko: Right. Put that together with her employment files, the timeline will be hard for the police to ignore.

Torch: The HC firewall is a lot tougher nut to crack than I anticipated.

Crowbar: U R the best hacker Ive ever known, T. I know U can break it

Torch: Vote of confidence duly noted.

12:13 AM HKT — *Blossom has logged on*

Komiko: Torch, if you really don't think you can hack them, maybe it's time we started thinking in more physical terms.

Torch: Meaning?

Komiko: One of us has to get inside the corporate office and find the file.

Torch: Way too dangerous.

Crowbar: Yeah K, if U really think hes responsible 4 those deaths, U cant think thats a good idea

Lian sighed, interlaced her fingers, and flexed them until her knuckles cracked. She had known that her suggestion would meet some resistance from the group, but she wasn't about to be steamrolled.

Komiko: Maybe those two dead bodies SHOULD scare me off. But instead, they're my reason to keep fighting.

Komiko: The authorities are seeded against us. The computer system is fending us off. All of Harrison's dice are loaded, and he has no reason to think he'll ever lose.

She thought of her father, cowering in Harrison's presence, and bit into her bottom lip in fury.

Komiko: Yes, what I'm proposing is dangerous. It's corporate theft, nothing less. And if you guys tell me you're out, I can respect that.

Komiko: But I'm in. All the way to the end. If I have to do this alone, I will. But I'd sure like to have you guys backing me up.

Blossom: Youre talking about meeting up in person?

Torch: That's pretty much the opposite of "anonymity." Which, as you might recall, is where we find strength.

Komiko: We've stayed anonymous this whole time, Torch—but now that things are getting serious, I'm worried we're not strong enough.

Nobody typed anything for almost a full minute.

Crowbar: Hell with it, Im in

Torch: This is very much against my better judgment.

Blossom: . . .

Blossom: I cant do it. Sorry, everyone, but Ive only been with 06/04 for a week. Its too early to ask me to blow my cover.

12:21 AM HKT — *Blossom has logged off*

Crowbar: OK dont sweat it, a triangle is the most stable structure anyway :)

Torch: NOTHING about this plan feels stable.

Komiko: Maybe not. But it's happening.

As she'd predicted, Lian got almost no sleep during the night. She found herself building up plans for infiltrating the Harrison offices, testing them for weak spots, and chastising herself when she found one. She fretted over her decision and had to reassure herself over and over that it was the only choice. She even wondered, briefly and frivolously, what she might wear to the first face-to-face-to-face meeting of 06/04.

In the morning, she rode the Twist N' Go to school, aware that her bleary eyes weren't the best choice for navigating the busy Central streets. More than once, at her periphery, she felt sure that someone was following her. She took a handful of one-way streets, off her usual route, to try to isolate the tail. When she dared turn her head enough to look, she saw nobody. Still, she couldn't shake the sensation.

And, weirdly, she couldn't help but think that it might be Matt.

There was no way to confirm it once she got to school because he didn't show up for the economics quiz. Lian sat at her desk, staring numbly at the paper. Even in her sleep-deprived state, she knew these answers easily; she was finished before even half of the allotted time had elapsed. But she read the questions again and again until the words became meaningless, simply because she didn't want to glance up and see the icy look in Mingmei's eyes.

When the bell chimed, she gathered up her bag, dropped the quiz on Mr. Chu's desk, and escaped into the hallway.

But she hadn't gone more than a couple of steps before Mingmei's voice struck her from behind like a dagger between the shoulder blades.

"He didn't show up because of you, you know."

Lian stopped in her tracks but did not turn around. "That can't be true."

"Come on, Lian. At least have the guts to call me a liar to my face."

This was the last thing she needed. So much was on her plate for the day, and a fight with her best friend would ruin the taste of everything else.

"I'm not calling you a liar," she said as she slowly turned to look at Mingmei. "I promise. I just mean, I can't believe that what I think of him has any bearing at all on what he does."

"Yeah," Mingmei said, biting off her words. "I wouldn't have thought so, either. Looks like we were both wrong."

"So," Lian said, trying for a smile, "that's one thing we can still do together. Be wrong."

"I think the era of us doing things together might be coming to a close. I prefer not to spend my evenings blotting my skirts in a failed attempt to get out the grease stains after popcorn's been dumped all over my date."

"I'm sorry," Lian said meekly. "I'll buy you another skirt."

"You're purposely missing my point, Lian." Mingmei's hands were on her hips, her voice frosty, her glare harsh. Lian hated this. Her stomach felt sour, and her head felt much as it had outside of the theater.

"Mingmei—" Lian broke off at the sound of a commotion at the far end of the hall. She wasn't certain what she had been planning to say in her own defense, and whatever it was fell right out of her head when she saw who was coming into the school.

The police.

All of the conversations in the hallway around Lian lapsed into silence, too. Was this who she'd seen following her? Were the police here to haul her in for what she'd done—or what she was planning to do?

Her feet rooted to the tiles, she watched as half a dozen uniformed officers strode up the hall toward her, their rapid footsteps the only noise in the eerily quiet space. Just when she was sure they were going to grab her, force her to the ground with a knee at her neck, tie off her wrists with riot cuffs . . . they brushed past without sparing a glance.

Down the corridor they continued and to the door of the computer lab. A barked command cleared out the students who were sitting in the room, and then the police entered. Another officer was coming down the hall, bringing up the rear with a wheeled shipping container. The students silently moved toward the banks of lockers, clearing a path for him.

Lian felt a sudden jolt when she recognized the newcomer as the baby-faced junior officer to whom she'd returned the blanket, back at the beach. Was it just coincidence that he was here now? Or had he been keeping tabs on her ever since she'd found Jiao's body? Lian was no longer sleepy but no less ill at ease. Her head swam with questions, but the police, in their wordless efficiency, offered no answers.

The young officer parked the storage bin outside the computer lab, and the six men inside the room began loading the computers, part and parcel, on board. The bell chimed for the next class, but nobody who could see what the cops were doing moved a muscle.

Lian was trying to reason with the voice in her head, the voice that was yelling the game was up—a mistake had been made. No mistakes could have been made, she told herself over and over again. Yes, she'd used the school computers to do plenty of research for 06/04 and had e-mailed herself several links that she'd explored in full on her laptop at home—but she'd been careful never to log into the chat rooms from school. Even with a nominally untraceable route through multiple proxy servers, it had seemed like a risk too far.

But, had even these protective measures been too little? Had the anonymizer failed somehow? A determined tracer—someone who had reason to suspect her—could have put two and two together. All it would have taken was a cross-referencing of her sign-in times at the school's computer lab with the times of "subversive" searches. As careful as she'd been, all Lian could think of now were the possible cracks in her armor and how they might have been pried open.

One thing was certain: Harrison was onto her. Maybe he didn't have enough evidence to have the cops haul her in quite yet. But this raid was a very public demonstration that he had her in his crosshairs, and that the authorities were at his beck and call to crack down hard.

06/04 was running out of time. Rand Harrison was laying down his final tiles. This was the endgame.

The break-in at Harrison Corp's offices would have to happen tonight.

TWENTY-THREE

It was like a blind date.

She'd known Torch and Crowbar for months, of course. She had followed their causes from the mainland even before she'd joined 06/04, and had come to think of them not just as fellow crusaders, but as friends of a sort. A friend with some control issues, and another with some apostrophe issues . . . but friends nonetheless.

But this was the first time they would ever meet in the flesh, and Lian found herself picking outfit after outfit from her wardrobe, discarding each of them after only a second's glance. She wanted to make a good impression. She wanted to impress. Should she pick something upscale, something that might create a mature look, at the risk of betraying her moneyed lifestyle? Or should she dress down and risk being dismissed as a juvenile teenager?

At last, she settled on a smart, dark gray suit over a silken cream blouse. With her hair pulled back and a brushing of dusky eye shadow, she could pass for a young professional, a serious-minded twenty-something who wouldn't disappoint her compatriots.

Lian picked a pair of sensible black flats from her large collection of shoes. After a moment's consideration, she also grabbed an extra pair of dark sneakers and some ankle socks and stuffed them into a messenger bag. If this break-in required speed and agility, all it would take was for her to switch shoes and ditch the suit jacket, and she'd be in good shape to outrun a pursuer or scale a fence.

They had finalized the arrangements only a couple of hours ago. Zan—whose poor, dead sister was the impetus behind all of this—would join them on the mission. Torch had gotten very edgy at the notion, but Lian had insisted; Zan was desperate to have a hand in bringing down the man responsible for Jiao's death. He had asked his factory coworkers to tell the floor boss that he was staying back at the Mansions, coughing up blood. In reality, he'd made his way across the harbor to Sun Yat Sen Memorial Park and was waiting, pacing nervously, when Lian arrived at half past nine to pick him up.

"Okay," he said, straddling the seat behind her on the scooter. "Are you ready for this?"

"More ready than I've been for anything in my life," she said, and then sighed. "Which is my fancy, face-saving way of saying that I have no idea."

"It's all come down to this, Lian. Tonight is where it all pays off. I know I've said it before, but, whatever happens, thank you."

Lian gave his leg a pat. "It's what we want, too. You brought the newspaper?" The members of 06/04 had agreed to have a rolled-up copy of the day's *Standard* in their left hands, as a way to identify one another without drawing undue attention.

"Got it," Zan confirmed, lightly swatting her arm with the paper.

It was all she could do to maintain a safe and inconspicuous speed as she drove them to the meeting spot—a little plaza nestled just north of where Queen's Road and Wellington crossed. There, only a couple of blocks from Harrison Corp's Central offices, they sat on a bench and failed utterly at trying not to fidget. They were an odder pairing than she'd have liked—she in her sharp tailored suit, he in his cheap gray T-shirt and black jeans—and she scanned the few passersby carefully, praying they weren't doing the same to her.

"Him, maybe?" Zan whispered, nodding toward a frowning middle-aged man in a suit who was walking purposefully around the perimeter. He was all business, except for a ponytail that stopped halfway down his back.

"He does look the part," she said. "But no newspaper."

After another minute or so, Zan tapped her and pointed out an obese, bespectacled young man on a waddling course that would take him near their bench. He did indeed have something rolled up in his left hand.

Lian felt her pulse quicken, and she sat up straight and gripped her own copy of the *Standard* tightly. The man's walking pace was agonizingly slow. Was this Torch, at long last? The master hacker, the naysayer, the firebrand?

"Nope, nope," Lian said, turning away quickly and blushing as she caught a glimpse not of newspaper, but a lewd comic book cover. "That's *hentai*. That's not our guy."

"That's *nobody's* guy," Zan said with a laugh.

"Excuse me," said a soft voice from behind them. Lian and Zan both turned at once, and the first thing either saw was a mass of dreadlocks in fierce, bright Gothic Lolita blue. Under these, like the delicate stem supporting some exotic azure flower, was a waif-like white girl of around twenty, in a black Joy Division shirt, a jagged skirt, and boots laced almost to her knees. She wore a spiked bracelet not unlike the one under Lian's bed, and her belt buckle was a wicked-looking brushed chrome crow with a small red jewel for its eye.

Lian knew, without knowing how she knew, that this was Crowbar. "I'm Komiko," she said, standing up and extending her right hand in greeting. "It's . . . it's really a pleasure to meet you."

"Crowbar," the girl said. She shook her hand, and the two of them spontaneously broke into big smiles. Lian's mind was scrambling to retrofit this new face to all of the many misspelled conversations and medical minutiae that she'd read after Crowbar's user name for so long. With her pale skin, slight build, and bubblegum-pink lips, this girl was far from the bruiser she'd imagined after Crowbar's takedown of ten heavily armed Junk Bay extortionists last winter.

"This is weird," the white girl said. "I mean, is it just me, or is this a little weird?"

"It's not just you," Lian said, laughing. "You haven't lived anywhere but inside my computer for so long. This is like meeting Super Mario in line at the market."

"Ha! I'd have accepted Lara Croft, too."

Zan stood up as well, and Lian introduced him.

"I'm so sorry about your sister," Crowbar said. "We're going to make sure Harrison pays."

"Thank you," Zan said. He shook her hand and then glanced away. Lian tried not to notice that he was wiping away a tear from his eye with his *Standard*.

"I, uh," she began. "I feel a little strange using code names out here in the real world. Is it okay if I tell you my actual name? You don't have to reciprocate."

Crowbar looked relieved. "Oh, thank God," she said. "I wanted to say the same thing, but I wasn't sure it was the right thing to do. I'm Eva."

"Lian."

"That's pretty. Does it mean anything?"

"By itself, it means 'lotus flower,'" Lian told her. "Which is a little less embarrassing than my full name, which translates to something like 'pious and incorruptible.'"

"We're a good pair, then," Eva said with a smile. "I'm named after the first woman corrupted in the Garden of Eden, so maybe we'll balance one another out."

Zan took a casual stroll around the plaza, keeping an eye out for the newspaper that would identify Torch, as the girls fell to chatting about Eva's year as a humanitarian aid worker in South Africa. Listening to the accounts of Eva's journeys in a nation struggling to be stronger than the legacy of apartheid and the scourge of HIV, Lian made a silent, personal vow: after she had dealt with Harrison, she would do more to help make a difference to people. University could wait.

Eva was in the middle of telling about her summer at a Siyathemba school when Lian stopped her. Out of the corner of her eye, she saw a figure in the shadows. Just like this morning, she couldn't help the feeling she'd been followed.

And just like this morning, she knew it was Matt Harrison.

"What the *hell*," she hissed through gritted teeth as Matt stepped out from behind a tree across the plaza and lowered the hood on his sweatshirt.

"What is it?" Eva asked her. "What's wrong?"

"We have to go," Lian said, taking Eva's hand and pulling her up from the bench. "We've been compromised."

"Oh, no," Eva said, her dark-rimmed eyes going wide. "Harrison's people?"

"Sort of," said Lian, quickening her pace. "Come on!"

The girls ran from their rendezvous spot, Lian leading the way, wishing she'd gone ahead and put on the sneakers. She didn't know where Zan had gotten to, but she hoped he'd spotted the commotion and was on his way to help.

Behind them, she heard Matt's footfalls on the bricks. "Lian!" he called after her. "Wait! Stop, dammit!"

Stopping was the last thing on Lian's mind. She pulled up short, nearly crashing into a decorative planter at the curb, and put up her arm to keep Eva from darting into the traffic on Wing Lok Street. Breathless, Lian pointed to their destination. They only had to make it across the two lanes, leap the railing at the opposite curb, and dash for the Sheung

Wan subway station, where they'd have a better chance at losing Matt.

But the cars weren't exactly cooperating. Lian took Eva's wrist and ran several yards down the sidewalk, away from the subway but toward a bus that was braking at Des Voeux Road. With one lane of traffic blocked, the girls sprinted between honking sedans and reckless taxis, leaping for the sidewalk.

Over the car horns and the pneumatic hiss of the bus, she couldn't hear Matt anymore. But he had to be back there—and he had probably brought Harrison's security with him. There wasn't a moment to slow down.

The girls ran headlong back up the sidewalk, Eva's dreadlocks bouncing, Lian's messenger bag slapping angrily against her hip. At last they reached the corner at Rumsey Street, where Lian turned to take them into the subway and instead smacked right into Matt's chest.

Eva skidded into her, and the two girls stumbled back, toppling onto the sidewalk. Matt stood over them, his gaze intense, and began to unzip his sweatshirt as he reached inside.

"No," Lian stammered. Her breath wouldn't come. "Matt, please, wh-whatever you're thinking of doing . . ."

He drew his hand out slowly, gripping something tightly, and extended it toward her face.

It was the Tuesday *Standard*.

"Komiko? Crowbar?" he said, dropping the paper and offering his hands to help them both up. "Nice to meet you. I'm Torch."

TWENTY-FOUR

"No," Lian said. "No way!" She batted away Matt's hand and got to her feet on her own.

"It's true," he said as he helped steady Eva. "I know how crazy this must seem . . ."

"You have *no idea* how crazy it seems," Lian cut him off. "Girls don't like to be followed, you freak! You were stalking me in the plaza just now, and I swear you were tailing me on my way to school this morning! What is the *matter* with you?"

"I had to be sure, Lian," he said, picking his *Standard* up from the sidewalk and tucking it back inside his sweatshirt. "I suspected it after the big dinner, but I had to be certain that you were who I thought you were. Komiko."

That word from his mouth was the most disconcerting thing Lian had ever heard. How could this slacker American boy, with his easygoing smile and surf shop mentality, be the infamous Torch, uptight hacker supreme and tireless crusader for justice?

"Wait," Eva said, her big dark eyes moving between the two of them. "Do you guys know each other?"

"We go to the same school," Matt told her. "We've run in some of the same circles, this last week or so. But from the look on her face, I'm pretty sure Lian had no idea that one of those circles was 06/04."

Before Lian could reply, Zan vaulted over the sidewalk railing and landed next to her. "Hey," he said, out of breath and pointing at Matt. "What the hell is he doing here?"

"Good evening, Zan," Matt said, calm and casual. "I'm here to help avenge your sister."

Zan shook his head like he hadn't quite heard what Matt had said. "Hold on," he said, propping himself against the metal rail. "You're the other guy? You're part of the little group, too?"

"I am."

Eva chewed nervously at the end of one of her blue forelocks. "So . . . you know him, too, Torch?"

"Matt," Lian said angrily. "His real name is Matt. I'll let him tell you his last name."

"Okay, all right, take it easy," Matt said. "We're all on the same side, here."

"Are we?" Lian spat back. "How are we supposed to trust you?"

"How was I supposed to trust you?" he countered. "Your dad is a Hong Kong trade envoy, after all."

"Oh, that's rich," Lian said with a short, mean laugh. "Considering that your father is the man we're taking down tonight."

Eva choked on her hair. "*What?*"

"Rand Harrison is not my father," Matt said in measured tones.

"What are you talking about?" Lian said. "Of course he is!"

"He's my stepdad," Matt said. "I had no choice in the matter. My real name is Cooper."

Lian stared hard at him. Was he lying? Even now?

"And from the moment he whisked my mom off her feet," Matt continued, "I've suspected that he was dirty."

It didn't make sense. Ever since she'd met Matt he seemed like a carbon copy of his dad . . . or stepdad, if his latest revelation was to be believed. Arrogant, brash, a foreigner with no feel or respect for different cultures.

"Why did you let me believe he was your real father then?" Lian asked.

Matt shrugged sheepishly. "It's all about the persona he wants to project in Hong Kong. Family man, trustworthy. But mainly because I didn't want to blow my cover. I've been watching him longer than any of you. Who do you think was feeding information to Mynah Bird?"

"And look how that worked out," Lian said.

"Mynah got sloppy," Matt retorted. "His arrest had nothing to do with me, or with his looking into Harrison Corp. All the same, it scared me off. I sat on my hands for months. But when we started connecting the dots to the dead girl on the beach, I knew I couldn't stay idle any longer. It was time to bring Rand Harrison down, once and for all." He looked straight at Lian and flashed his perfect smile. "Whatever you think of me, at least we still agree on that, right?"

Zan stepped between the two of them. "It's hard to believe you'd use teeth that nice to bite the hand that feeds you, Harrison."

"Maybe I'm overstating the obvious, Zan," Matt said, "but you really don't know a damn thing about me."

"Okay, enough!"

Lian and the boys all stopped to look at Eva. There was a resolve in her eyes and an edge to her voice. Under all that blue hair, there was probably less than a hundred pounds of flesh, but there was no doubt in Lian's mind that—at that moment—Eva could have taken them all on and won hands down. This was the determined trouper who had toppled the Junk Bay gangsters, and who seemed like she was not in the mood for infighting just now.

"I don't care what his real name is," Eva said. "I don't care about his story. He's Torch, and we know Torch. We trust him. As far as I'm concerned, 'Matt Harrison' or 'Matt Cooper' don't even exist."

Matt smiled at her. "Thanks, Crowbar. I think that's a very sensible way of looking at it." He ran a hand through his hair and frowned. "But, the problem is, Matt Harrison does exist. And the people in his stepfather's offices have a pretty good idea of what he looks like."

"Meaning what?" Lian prodded.

"Meaning, I can't go with you guys," Matt said. "I'd be a liability."

"Oh, right," Lian said. "So we go charging into the belly of the beast, while your hands stay clean?"

"My hands are dirtier than anyone's," Matt said. "I'm all over the office security footage for today. But you can thank me for that later."

"And why would we do that, exactly?" Lian asked.

"Because," Matt said, "the building security codes are updated at 4 A.M. every morning. It's a random alphanumeric string, generated on a stand-alone terminal. If it doesn't have a net connection, I can't hack it."

"So you had to retrieve it in person," Eva concluded. "And it had to be today."

Matt nodded, checking his watch. "Exactly. And it's only good for another five hours and forty minutes."

"Then we've got to go now," Eva said. "We've got to see this through."

"I hate everything about this," Lian said. "Some secret code that only Matt could get us, and that keeps him from coming with us on the raid? It just reeks of a trap."

"I'd go with you if I could, Lian," Matt said, looking genuinely hurt by her words. "I'd do the whole thing by myself, if that was an option. But I can't. So I've done everything I can to get you in and out without getting caught. Without getting hurt."

There was real concern in his eyes. Lian tried to ignore it. "How can we trust you?"

Matt spread his hands. "If I'd wanted to sell you out, I could have done so before now, couldn't I?"

"I hate to say it," Zan spoke up after a moment. "But I think he's right. You guys have been planning this, working toward tonight, getting everything in place. It doesn't make sense to back out at the last minute."

"Listen," Matt pleaded with her. "We all know that my stepdad has got cops in his pocket. And after what happened at the school today, it's a good bet that they're onto me already. Onto us."

Eva frowned. "What happened at your school today?"

Suddenly, it clicked for Lian: "The police raided the computer lab. Confiscated everything. I was sure they'd been cross-referencing my log-ins with my searches, putting together the puzzle from the tiny pieces I couldn't help leaving behind." She rounded on Matt. "But it was you they were after, wasn't it? You left them a big fat puzzle piece."

He blushed, unable to meet her gaze for a moment. "I logged on to 06/04, yeah," he admitted. "A couple of times. And mostly it was to throw you off, if you were starting to suspect anything. I figured that a few posts during class hours would scotch any notions that I was a fellow high school student."

Lian smirked. "Well, that's equal parts clever and idiotic."

"Yeah," Matt said. "That pretty much sums me up."

"Okay," Eva said. "We've got security codes that are set to expire, and corrupt police are going to kick down Torch's door any moment now . . . so we've got no choice. Either we do this right now, or else we call those cops and tell them where they can pick us up. Me, personally, I'm voting against jail time."

Jail time will be the least of it, Lian thought. Still, out loud she said, "I'm in. Eva and I can handle the break-in. It might go better with just two of us, anyway. Matt, you and Zan head back to the plaza."

She shrugged out of her suit jacket and began to tug her sneakers on. "I've got the blueprints loaded on my phone. You guys keep watch, and if we're not out in one hour . . ."

"I'll come in after you," Zan offered with a brave smile.

"Okay," Lian said, handing him her messenger bag with the jacket and dress flats stuffed inside. "Matt, let me give you my number."

"No need," Matt said. "I swiped it off Mingmei's phone a week ago."

"Good. The one-time invasion of privacy is helpful," Lian said, forcing a smile to offset any hostile tone that might creep into her voice. "If the cops show up, you text me 911 so we'll have a chance to make a run for it."

"No problem," he said, handing her the slip of paper with the day's security code on it.

Lian read the code twice, committed it to memory, and passed it back to him. "Thank you. And hey, Matt?"

"Yeah?"

"Do me a favor? Smile for me?"

He gave her a confused look for a second, then shrugged and complied.

"Good. Now, if this turns out to be a setup. . . . I swear I will personally smash every one of those perfect teeth out of your skull."

She didn't even turn around to watch his smile fade.

TWENTY-FIVE

"That was pretty badass, back there," Eva said as they moved through the shadows of the underground parking garage. "If we do get popped tonight, at least you bowed out with some famous last words."

"I'm just hoping I didn't use up all my bravado making Matt wet himself," Lian replied. "I could use a little bit for what we're about to do."

"Relax," Eva said. "We're just two hip young girls, out on the town, who happen across a big shiny skyscraper, and then happen to punch in the right door code on our first guess, and then happen to stumble across evidence in a ninth-floor records room that will happen to bring a global corporation to its knees. It could happen to anyone . . . right?"

Lian smiled. "Not exactly what I'd call an airtight alibi."

At a run, the two of them crossed a dimly lit expanse of white concrete and painted yellow parking stripes. Lian stopped with her back against one side of the support pillar closest to the building's rear doors; Eva drew up next to her. They peered in opposite directions around the post, holding their breaths, scanning for movement and finding none. The lot was nearly deserted in the 10 P.M. hour. If luck was on their side, they could make it in and out and not encounter a single soul.

Lian reached around the corner of the pillar, grabbed Eva's hand, and squeezed. "Here we go," she said, as Eva squeezed back.

They dashed to the rightmost of the four glass entry doors. Lian stopped when she reached the keyed security pad. If she entered the code, she would leave fingerprints. She cursed herself for the oversight, until she saw Eva reaching into her pocket and pulling out woolen gloves the same shade of blue as her hair. As Lian whispered the code, Eva keyed it in.

The door slid open with a whisper.

No alarms sounded, no guards pounced from the darkness. As the girls stepped inside, the door slid purposefully back into place and anchored itself.

Lian finally let herself exhale. So far, so good.

She pointed down the hallway to their left. All clear. The blueprints showed a service lift back here, as well as two banks of elevators in the heart of the building, but they'd agreed that these were likely to be fitted with cameras. The better bet was the emergency stairs at the end of the hall.

Thankfully, the lights weren't on motion sensors. Matt had reassured them, but Lian was braced to discover his mistakes—or *lies*—with every step she took. Eva gingerly pressed the bar to open the stairwell door, making only the tiniest of metallic clicks. She opened it just wide enough for the two of them to slip through, before gently letting it click back into place.

A single yellow bulb lit each floor's number. Lian tugged the sleeve of her blouse down over her left hand so her bare skin wouldn't touch the rail, and they made their way quickly and quietly up eight flights.

"Jiǔ," Lian said, a little out of breath, when they reached the painted symbol.

Eva nodded. "Nine."

"Yeah. But everything in Chinese means ten different things. It's a lucky number because it sounds like the word for 'everlasting.' And it's all bound up in dragon symbolism. It wouldn't surprise me at all to learn that Harrison's people did their homework and chose the ninth floor on purpose, as some kind of talisman."

"Where would big business be without ridiculous old-world superstitions?" Eva said with a smirk. "Now, knock on wood, we're about to find something that'll keep this dragon from being everlasting."

"Fingers crossed," Lian said, smiling.

"You brought your lucky rabbit's foot, right?"

"I never commit corporate crimes without it."

Eva turned the handle, and they stepped onto the patterned gray carpet of the ninth floor. Lian hoped that they had got all their nervous laughter out in the stairwell. Now was the time for seriousness and silence.

At the far end of the hall, a swaybacked cleaning lady slowly moved her vacuum back and forth in the dull glow of the maintenance lights. She didn't hear the stair door open and close, and in a few moments she had rounded the corner without noticing the intruders.

Lian brought up the blueprints on her phone and confirmed their destination. Harrison's corner office took up nearly a quarter of the finance department that lined almost the entire east face of the building. If any hard evidence of Jiao's brief employment with Harrison Corp was to be found, it would be there.

The girls moved quickly and stealthily along the corridors. Their eyes quickly adjusted to the gloom, and they peeked around each corner before turning, keeping a lookout for lingering workers or lights coming from under office doors. The sound of the vacuum cleaner faded until it disappeared.

The glass-walled finance department was dark, as still as a tomb and twice as foreboding. Taking a steadying breath, Lian entered the door code with her middle knuckle—8, 9, Q, 5—and stood frozen in the world's longest half second before the door unlocked.

Eva immediately crossed the room toward the tiny white glow that hovered over a desk. "How nice," she whispered. "Somebody left out the welcome mat."

One of the accounts officers—his nameplate read CHEN MENGYAO—had neglected to shut his computer down before leaving for the day. Eva nudged the mouse, and with a crackle of static, the monitor came to life. Lian allowed herself a smile: this saved them valuable time waiting for the system to boot up or trying to hack a personal password.

Lian suspected that Mengyao's next performance review would be harsh.

If he got to have one.

The corner office—Harrison's seat of power—was an impressive thing to behold, with a clear view straight to the ferry piers in the harbor. Lian peered through the glass into the office, careful not to touch it or leave any prints. Inside, she could see that the walls were lined with smartly framed photographs of Harrison with other men in suits, shaking hands or raising a glass in a toast. Occasionally, a well-dressed woman would decorate the scene. Lian didn't know who most of them were, but she recognized the TVB actress from the denim ad campaign, as well as at least one former American president.

The massive, dark wood desk was Spartan in its decoration: just a new-model Macintosh, a silver inkpot with a molded quill pen, and a two-foot-tall bronze statue of a baseball player—a Colorado Rockies batter, she guessed—preparing to swing for the fences. No photo of the family whose image was supposedly so important to the corporation.

Lian wondered what Matt thought about that.

The door to this inner office had both a keypad— presumably programmed with the same sequence as the other doors, although Matt had neglected to specify—and a traditional deadbolt. There would be no way in, other than to break the glass. This was the very definition of an emergency, Lian thought. A plan of last resort.

She turned away from Harrison's office and began reading the drawer labels on the banks of horizontal filing cabinets that bordered two walls of the department. There were four additional islands of these massive drawers in the middle of the room, not to mention at least two standing files visible in each walled office and two below-desk rolling cabinets in each cubicle. It was an ocean of paperwork, and Lian was without a compass.

The flashlight app on her phone illuminated label after label: quarterly stock reports; filings with the Securities Regulatory Commission and the United States SEC; operational logistics studies; bills of lading; shipping and receiving contracts. Lian opened some of these drawers and inspected files at random. Whether there was anything incriminating to be found among them, she'd never know; they all appeared legitimate enough, at first blush. Certainly, though, none of them had anything to do with Jiao.

Lian let a drawer click back into place, and was just about to hook her sleeve-covered fingers under the latch of the next one, when Eva waved her over with a loud whisper of "Got something!"

In seconds, Lian was peering over her shoulder at the widescreen monitor. Eva had wormed her way into the server and sniffed out the payroll database. "Ta da," she said humbly. "The Crowbar strikes again."

Lian's heart leapt. This was it: the name of every employee who had ever worked for Harrison since the transfer of operations to Hong Kong. They'd found the mother lode.

Even in gloves, Eva's fingers were fast and confident as they flew across the keyboard. "Now we just type in the name 'Jiao,' hit Find, and . . ."

No Results Matched Your Criteria

Search Again? Y/N

"Impossible," Lian said, crestfallen.

"Maybe they delete the dead employees?" Eva ventured as she backed out to the main screen.

Lian scanned the names. "No . . . here's one. Yè Tingfeng in manufacturing. Listed as deceased a couple of days ago." A sudden chill ran through her; hadn't Zan's friend with all the kidney stones been named Tingfeng?

Eva leaned forward on the desk, cracking her knuckles. "No need for despondence. I can trick any database into telling me what I want to hear."

Eva set up a laddered search, filtering out males, eliminating anyone over the age of twenty years old, defining a window for the start date of the employment. One by one, these qualifiers narrowed down the list to just eleven names. Eva clicked on the name at the top to open the employee file.

A photograph of a dull-faced teenage girl stared back at them. Her employment info ran down along one side. This was a seamstress at the complex. Too young for that kind of work, paid next to nothing, probably in desperate need of being rescued.

But she wasn't the girl Lian had found floating in the water.

Eva continued down the list, opening the files, frowning, and moving on. Lian felt worse with each passing moment.

And then, three files from the end—lucky number nine—she saw a familiar face.

"That's her!" she said, louder than she'd intended. "That's Jiao!"

"Not according to this," Eva said, squinting at the dossier. "Says her name is Kong Nüying, from Lau Fau Shan in the New Territories."

"That's . . . weird," Lian allowed. "But it's definitely the girl from the beach. In fact, that's the same exact photo that Zan has in his wallet. He showed me, the day we met."

"Fair enough," Eva said. "Let's get this on a memory stick and get out of here."

Lian pulled her rabbit's foot out of her pocket, twisted it at its center to extend the USB connector, and handed it to Eva.

"You actually had a rabbit's foot," Eva said, sounding as impressed as she was amused. She took it from Lian, and plugged it into the computer. Then dragged the girl's record to it.

Lian stretched her sleeves over each palm and leaned back on an adjacent desk, still trying to reconcile the disconnect between what the computer said and what she knew (or thought she knew).

"Huh," Eva said, scratching her head. "This file's not with the main database doc. It's in a subfolder."

"Really?" Lian said, standing back up to look at the screen again. Eva had brought up the file's properties, and they both looked at the word in all caps at the end of the metadata, after the final slash.

DELETED

Lian felt the chill pass through her again. Eva ejected the rabbit's foot, logged out of the database, and then disconnected from the server, putting Chen Mengyao's desktop back just the way she'd found it. She started to get up from his chair, then got a sudden, wicked grin on her face.

From the top of his Start menu, she pulled up the calculator. It appeared in the lower right corner of the screen. Her gloved finger tapped out four digits and a decimal on the keyboard, and Lian instantly realized what she was doing. As calling cards went, it was subtle but satisfying. When Mengyao got to work the next morning, he might wonder for the briefest of moments what he'd been doing on his computer that had added up to '0.604.'

Eva pocketed the memory stick, and the girls quietly let themselves out of the finance department and back into the hallway. They heard the sound of the vacuum, blocking the way they'd originally come and flattened themselves against a wall.

Lian brought up the blueprints on her phone. The only other path from here took them deeper into the building; they'd need to cross it to the southwest corner to access the other stairwell. It was a lot of ground to cover, but they couldn't just stand there waiting for the custodian to spot them. Lian drew their route on her phone. Eva watched and nodded, and the two of them took off down the corridor.

Everything was going perfectly, until they rounded the corner to the main elevator banks just in time for the doors of the nearest one to open with a cheerful ping.

Lian gasped as she was struck by an almost physical blast of déjà vu. In an instant, her mouth went dry and her palms broke into a cold sweat as she flashed back to the Fàn Xī foyer.

Dressed in a suit, the potbellied man stepped off the elevator and directly into their path.

Only this time, instead of Harrison's overcoat, he'd brought half a dozen armed security guards.

TWENTY-SIX

"Hey!" the fat man shouted, starting toward them with surprising speed.

Eva grabbed Lian's wrist and ran back the way they'd come. The vacuuming janitor was now the least of their worries.

"Matt sold us out after all," Lian growled. "That lousy, treacherous—"

"Not important!" Eva said. "Just run!"

Behind them, they heard the fat man directing the guards. "Split up! Cover both stairwells, and the service elevator! You stay here in case they're stupid enough to double back. And radio down to have them suspend the door code!"

"Oh, God," Eva said. "What are we gonna do?"

"We're going to be faster than radio waves," Lian said, diving for the keypad at the nearest door and punching in the code, still using her middle knuckle. The door opened and the girls bustled inside, pushing it closed behind them.

It settled back into its frame just as the pad outside buzzed and its display began glowing red.

She moved to the closest freestanding desk and started trying to shove it toward the door. Eva joined her, and soon they managed to get their makeshift barricade in place.

"Okay, okay," Lian said, fighting panic. "There has to be a way out." She wasn't sure she believed it, but saying out loud seemed to make it sound more plausible. She flicked through the blueprints until she found the office they were in.

Eva looked over her shoulder. "It's a dead end," she said.

"The air ducts," Lian said, pointing to the cooling system on the drawing. "We should be small enough to fit inside them."

"And then what?" Eva asked desperately, grabbing the phone. "We'd have to crawl more than halfway around the building before we could drop into a hallway by the stairs. It would take us hours! Even if they don't hear us clanking around over their heads, they'll have the whole place on lockdown well before we can get out."

"It might be the only plan we have," Lian said, taking her phone back from Eva. There was no "911" text from Matt. Of course there wasn't. Why would he have warned them about a trap he'd orchestrated himself?

She paced the office, teeth gritted, adrenaline the only thing keeping her headache at bay. The whole world was crashing down, and she was powerless to stop it. With an angry, growled sigh, she beat her fist on the glass of the window, nine floors above the darkened streets of the

Central District. Some equally dark part of her hoped that the glass would shatter and offer her some sort of escape—however permanent—from this nightmare situation.

That's when she saw it.

To either side of her, on the other side of the glass, thick cables ran vertically up to a roof rig. And right below her, just ten feet down, was a window washer's suspended scaffold, paused at the end of the workday on the eighth story.

"Eva!" she hissed. "We have a way out!"

Eva ran toward her, but drew up short a few steps shy of the glass. "Are you kidding me?"

"There's a window washer's gantry, one floor down. Look, this big pane opens."

"Forget it, Lian. This is not a Jackie Chan movie."

"It will be fine," Lian said, muscling open the latch. "We just have to—"

The end of her sentence was stolen from her mouth by the whipping wind that buffeted the building.

Eva's black-rimmed eyes were wide with fear, and she shook her head emphatically, every dreadlock like a shocking blue exclamation point. Lian took one tentative step over the sill, and then held out her hand, beckoning Eva to come with her.

"I can't!" Eva shouted. "I can't do it!"

"You can do anything!" Lian encouraged her. "You're the girl who cleaned up Junk Bay!"

"Junk Bay is at sea level! I'm afraid of heights!"

"You should be more scared of a Chinese prison," Lian said.

There was a loud clang from over by the office door. Eva turned to look over her shoulder. Lian looked past her and saw the propped-up desk shudder, as someone on the outside tried to get to the inside.

"They're here," Eva exclaimed, her eyes welling. "They're coming in. You have to go!"

"Not without you!"

The desk jumped again.

Eva stepped as close as she dared to the open window, and reached for Lian's outstretched hand. But rather than grabbing it, she dropped the USB rabbit's foot into Lian's palm.

"I can't go with you," Eva said tearfully. "But you can still get this to the authorities."

The desk toppled, followed by the sound of shattering glass.

"If we're both caught, it's all been for nothing," Eva said, pressing Lian's fingers around the furry memory stick. "So *go!*"

Lian saw the potbellied man charge into the office. Eva screamed. Lian gripped the rabbit's foot tightly, swung her other leg over the sill, and then let herself drop onto the platform below. She landed on her feet, but felt the window washer's scaffold judder. She spilled onto her side, snatching out her free hand to clutch at an edge. For one terrifying moment, the building and sky seemed to slide over her like a waterfall, but then she hauled herself into the right position.

She propped herself up on one elbow as she caught her breath, and willed her heartbeat to slow down. Then she grabbed for the control box. The "down" arrow was big and yellow. When she pressed it and the platform actually started to descend the face of the building, Lian thought she might cry with relief.

Overhead, the potbellied man's furious face appeared as he leaned out the window to see where she'd gone. He bellowed something into his cell phone, but Lian couldn't make out a word. She lay on the mesh floor of the scaffold, breathing hard, watching as the sidewalk seemed to swell and rise to meet her.

Her exhilaration was shredded by the guilt she felt at leaving Eva behind. They'd gotten the file they'd been after . . . but at what price?

She was two stories high when a security guard shouted up from below her. She peered through the mesh, saw the handgun aimed for the scaffold, and was instantly on her feet. She backpedaled up to the railing farthest from the guard, nearly tripping over a metal bucket of soapy water that sloshed onto her sneakers.

Without thinking, she grabbed the bucket by its edges and dumped its contents over the side, directly onto the guard. He sputtered for a moment, turning away and wiping his face. Lian leapt over the rail, covering the last few feet before the platform reached the ground. When the guard had got his bearings back, she swung the metal bucket with both hands, striking him on the head and sending him to the pavement.

For an insane second, Lian thought of picking up the gun he had dropped. But instead, she kicked it away from his unconscious form as hard as she could, and then took off at a run, rabbit's foot still clenched in her hand, her shoes leaving wet prints on the sidewalk behind her.

When she reached the plaza for the rendezvous, Matt was sitting on a bench next to her messenger bag, flipping through his *Standard*.

"Lian!" he said, looking up. "Wait, where's Crowbar?"

"Where's Zan?" she countered, trying not to look like she didn't trust him. She didn't want him to know—yet— that she had figured out his treachery.

"I don't know," Matt said. "He went to get a milkshake, like, twenty minutes ago. He hasn't come back yet."

"Do you have any idea how made-up that sounds?"

Lian felt her lips curl. "It's what he told me!" Matt protested.

"Liar!" she said, shoving him hard in the chest. Matt stumbled back, taken off guard. "You handed him over to your dad's goons the second Eva and I were out of sight, didn't you? Right before you sent them in after us."

Matt's eyes narrowed. "What are you talking about?"

"You sprung your trap, and Eva got caught in it! And I damn near had to chew my own foot off to escape!" She still had the rabbit's foot clenched tight in her hand. She felt a thrill of victory—if Matt hadn't planned for her to get back out of the building, then he certainly hadn't accounted for the notion that she might have gotten what she'd gone in for. It was followed by a shudder of dread when she pondered what he would do if he did become aware of it. What lengths he might go to in order to take it from her?

"Lian, you have to believe me," he said. "I didn't turn Zan in, and I didn't send anybody after you. I didn't sell you out."

"Then how did the potbellied man know right where to find us?" she demanded.

"The potbellied . . . wait, Mr. Yeung is in there? He has Crowbar? Oh, no."

"Eva!" Lian screamed. "Her name is Eva! That's a real person you just handed over, not some name on a message board."

"No," he said, arms held up in a gesture that was half placating, half surrender. Distant police sirens were growing louder. Flashing lights flickered, reflected in the glass and chrome of the buildings around the plaza. "I swear, this had nothing to do with me."

But Lian was done talking and done listening. She sprinted for her parked scooter, fired up the engine, and sped away, her eyes burning.

TWENTY-SEVEN

I know you're mad at me. But I hope we've been friends long enough that I can ask you for one small favor.

Lian hit Send on the text. It was after midnight, and she was hiding in the bushes, hunched over the glow of her phone. The knees of her pants were stained with grass; her blouse was soaked in sweat and torn at the shoulder where she'd nicked it on a branch. Her whole life depended on the next words that showed up on her phone screen. The seconds became a minute, and geared up to do so again.

One, and only one.

She heaved a sigh of relief and quickly texted back.

Okay: Open your front door, right now.

There was no reply on the phone. But moments later, the door opened, and Mingmei stood in a salmon pink silk nightgown, backlit by the lamp in her living room.

"Okay, I did it," she said to the night. "Can I close it now?"

"All right, two favors," Lian said, standing up from her crouch and pocketing her phone. "Please, Mingmei. Please let me in."

Whether it was because of the desperation in her voice or the twigs in her hair, Mingmei fell uncharacteristically silent and waved her into the house.

"What the hell, Lian?" she asked, once the door was closed. "Are you hurt?"

"I'm sorry, I'm so sorry," Lian said in a rush. "I didn't know where else to go. Things are falling apart, and I didn't think they'd come looking for me here."

"Back up a second. Who's 'they,' and why are 'they' looking for you?" Mingmei was clearly trying to piece things together in her head. "Wait, does this have something to do with the cops at the school this morning?"

"It does, yes. In a manner of speaking. Mingmei, could I use your computer?"

"So they can march in here and throw my laptop in their evidence wagon, too?" Mingmei looked skeptical. "Come on, Lian, what's going on?"

Lian heard the panic in her own voice. "Mingmei, if I get through tonight, I promise I'll explain everything. But right now, there's no time. I just . . . I need you to trust me."

For a long moment, silence settled over the room. Lian thought she might collapse on the spot.

"Whatever else happens between us," Mingmei said at last, opening her arms, "I will always, always trust you, Lian."

"Don't hug me, I'm gross."

"I trust that you are," Mingmei said, and embraced her anyway. "Now come on, my laptop's in the kitchen."

12:38 AM HKT — *Komiko has logged on*

"Who's Komiko?"

"It's me. I promise, I'll tell you all about it later."

12:39 AM HKT — *Blossom has logged on*

> **Blossom:** Got your ping, K. Im surprised youre here. Did the raid not happen?

"Who's Blossom?"

"I don't know."

"What raid?"

"Mingmei, later, I promise!"

> **Komiko:** It happened, but it went south fast.

> **Blossom:** Where are the others?

> **Komiko:** I doubt you'll see Torch on here again. He double-crossed us, and we walked right into it.

"Who's Torch?"

"You don't want to know."

> **Komiko:** Torch got the security codes but didn't go with us into the building. Crowbar and I got in just fine and even made it to the HC finance offices, but our luck didn't hold.

"Who's Crowbar?"

Lian didn't even bother answering.

> **Komiko:** We found the file on the dead girl . . . but her name's not Jiao, and she's not from Yah Tian. Still, we downloaded the document onto a memory stick.

Komiko: We thought we were home free, but the fat man showed up, the one who was at the beach and later the Family Hand.

Komiko: He nabbed Crowbar. I made it out and got to the rendezvous, but Torch was the only one there. He'd turned Zan over to the cops and then sicced them on us.

"Wait," Mingmei said. "I actually know who Zan is. The cops have him? What did he do?"

"Nothing," Lian said. *He trusted me,* she thought to herself. That's what he did. But it didn't seem like the most sensible thing to tell Mingmei at the moment.

Blossom: Wow! Thats insane. Where are you right now?

Komiko: Somewhere safe, that's all that matters.

Blossom: And you have the memory stick with you?

Komiko: Yes. I've got to get this file to the authorities. I don't know who's clean, but I'll make copies and send them out anonymously until somebody steps up to help.

Komiko: I just pray I can draw them out before anything bad happens to Crowbar.

She let her head drop, seeing those last images of Eva pressing the rabbit's foot into her hand, the eyeliner running down her cheeks, the terror on her face.

"Could I have a glass of water?" she asked Mingmei meekly.

"Of course," Mingmei said. "My house is your house."

Lian got a glass from the cabinet and filled it with cold, filtered water from the fridge door. It chilled her parched throat like a snowstorm blowing into a desert. She closed her eyes and thought that she had never tasted anything so pure in her life.

"Hey," Mingmei said, nodding toward the laptop. "I can't keep track of all the players without a scorecard, but I think you want to see this."

The chill that flooded Lian's body when she looked at the screen had nothing to do with the water.

12:50 AM HKT — *Crowbar has logged on*

> **Crowbar:** You will want to pay very close attention now.

Lian blanched. Seeing Crowbar's name, followed by "You" and "to" instead of U and 2, was absolutely horrifying.

> **Crowbar:** We know you have data that doesn't belong to you on a memory stick.

> **Crowbar:** You will hand this memory stick over to us, or Eva and Zan will die tonight.

Mingmei took a step back. "This . . . this isn't some weird online role playing game, is it? Are they serious about killing people?"

> **Crowbar:** You will not copy the data. Any copies you have already made, you will destroy.

> **Crowbar:** If you choose to disobey, there will be consequences.

12:52 AM HKT — *Crowbar has uploaded four JPGs*

Lian gasped. On the laptop screen were photographs. Her family's apartment building. The door number of their home. Her father's office in the city. Qiao's dorm at the University of Neuchâtel.

"Lian?" Mingmei said, her voice a little shaky.

Crowbar: You will call the following number within the next five minutes and arrange to deliver the memory stick. Alone.

A phone number popped up on the screen.

12:53 AM HKT — *Crowbar has logged off*

Komiko: . . .

Komiko: That was him. It had to be.

Blossom: Who? The fat man?

Komiko: Mr. Yeung is his name. Torch sounded scared of what Yeung could do.

Blossom: With good reason, it seems.

Blossom: Are you going to take the memory stick to him?

Lian pondered the question for a moment, until an antsy Mingmei prompted her to reply.

Komiko: I don't see any other choice. We have every reason to think Crowbar and Zan are in real danger. Protecting the brand is apparently worth killing for.

Komiko: I couldn't live with myself if their blood were on my hands.

Blossom: Or if they washed up on Big Wave beach.

"Wait a second," Mingmei said. "The girl from the beach? She's wrapped up in this, too?"

"It's a really, really long story."

Komiko: I'm going to call Yeung and make the trade. You said you didn't want to be outed, and I respect that.

Komiko: But if I, or Crowbar, don't get out of this . . . you're the only hope we have. You're the 06/04 insurance policy now.

Komiko: So promise me you'll find out everything you can about the girl. Her file says she was named Kong Nüying, from Lau Fau Shan. See this thing through to the end.

Blossom: Count on it.

Komiko: And if Torch logs on here again . . . don't trust a word he says.

Blossom: I absolutely wont.

12:56 AM HKT — *Komiko has logged off*

Lian dialed the number; the voice that answered was the same one that had directed the guards earlier. Yeung.

"There is a disused school building, the Golden Hill Academy, off Tai Po Road, north of the city," he said, with no pleasantries. "Do you know it?"

"I can find it," Lian answered, bringing up a browser window on Mingmei's laptop and searching for the school.

"Come alone, and bring the memory stick. Alert no one, especially not the police."

Sure, Lian thought. On the slim chance that I find one who isn't in Harrison's pocket already.

"If anyone but you arrives . . . or if you try anything stupid once you get here . . . I will be certain you're looking into your friends' eyes as I pull the trigger."

"I'll do what you want. There's no reason to hurt them," Lian said, trying to keep her voice calm.

"Oh, I'm not sure about that. Your boyfriend Zan is practically begging for it."

There was a rustling sound, and then Lian heard Zan's voice, fast and panicky.

"Lian," he said. "Oh, man, I'm so sorry. I messed things up so bad. I should have stayed with Matt. I just wanted a milkshake, and then these guys grabbed me, oh, man. I'm so, so sorry."

"Don't worry," she said, as much to him as to herself. "Everything's going to be okay. You don't have to apologize."

"Just . . . please . . . get here fast. These guys aren't screwing around, they've got this power drill, and I don't know what they're planning with it, but I—"

The rustling again, and Mr. Yeung's voice returned.

"Yes," he said evenly. "Get here fast. Because who knows what we're planning?"

There was a high-pitched whirring sound in the background. Something like the noise of a power drill.

And then the line went dead.

TWENTY-EIGHT

"I can't believe you're not letting me go with you."

Lian fastened the straps on her panda-painted helmet and then shook her head. "He said I had to come alone. If they see another headlight on the road with me, Eva and Zan could be dead before we ever got there."

Mingmei looked more worried than Lian had ever seen her. "You're going to the middle of nowhere, in the middle of the night, absolutely alone, and the only thing you know for sure is that the guy you're dealing with has a gun and a drill. How are you not totally freaking out right now?"

Lian considered the question. "I don't know." She could have added, that she'd pushed well through the part where she was feeling anything at all, other than wanting this to be finished. What little sentiment she had in reserve, she'd poured into a hastily written but sincere document on Mingmei's computer. She'd made Mingmei leave the room while she wrote it, and then had saved it with the password "littlepanda" to lock it away, unless and until it was needed.

"Tell my parents," Lian said, "that the key is their pet name for me. All one word."

"I won't need to tell them about it at all," Mingmei said. "Because you're going to be fine, and you're going to save your friends, and everything's going to turn out okay. Right?"

Lian looked at the ground and said nothing.

"Dammit, Lian," Mingmei said, throwing her arms around Lian with such force that the girls and the scooter nearly toppled over. "You tell me I'm right!"

"You're always right," Lian said, hugging her best friend. "You told me so yourself."

She fired up the Twist N' Go and patted her pocket, making sure for the hundredth time that the rabbit's foot was still there.

"When you're done," Mingmei said over the purring motor, "I don't care what time it is, you text me. Or call. No, just come back by here. I just want to see you on the other side of this."

Lian nodded.

"And if I don't hear from you by sunrise," Mingmei said, "I'll come looking for you. I'll get Matt, and we'll find you, no matter what."

Lian swallowed. "Don't bring Matt. Don't tell him anything at all."

"What? Why not?"

"You can't trust him, Mingmei. He's not who he seems to be."

Mingmei looked a little stunned, but she didn't argue. She just watched silently as Lian motored out of the driveway and disappeared into the Hong Kong night.

Central was still bustling at two in the morning, the sidewalks packed with late-night drinkers and the streets filled with taxis, produce trucks, cyclists, and pedestrians crossing as they pleased. Lian discarded every traffic regulation she knew and just concentrated on moving forward: weaving between cars, taking corners without pause, even heading against traffic for a block on a one-way street after a bus had blocked her road.

She chose the Western Harbor Crossing so she could skirt the western edge of the city, up the Kowloon Highway and through the port at Lai Chi Kok. The map had suggested that it would take her half an hour to reach her destination, but Lian was shaving seconds off anywhere she could. She leaned into the curves of Ching Cheung Road and barely slowed for the hairpin turn onto Tai Po.

Under any other circumstances, this might have been a pleasant night drive among tree-dotted hills, the wind in her face crisp but not cold, the leaves still green and vibrant in the last few weeks before they began to turn red and brown and gold. Lian had never been out this way before, and she very nearly missed the turnoff onto Caldecott.

The buildings here seemed new enough, and nice enough. Past an apartment block, there was even a construction site, with two cranes resting for the night outside a boxy, skeletal frame. She hadn't seen another vehicle for a while, though, and there were only a couple of lights on in the apartment. After the throngs in Central and the glow from Kowloon, this felt like a strangely sparse and unpopulated corner of the world.

Her final turn was onto an unlit and poorly paved road. Here, she eased off on the throttle to navigate the gaping potholes. The weather-beaten sign for the Golden Hills Academy had already broken free from one of its posts and was making a solid attempt at abandoning the other. The school building lay at the end of the road like a toppled gray tombstone.

Outside of the glow of her headlight and the purr of the motor, there was nothing but darkness and silence. A scream would go unheard; a plea for help would go unanswered. If Yeung planned to do away with her and her friends, he'd chosen the perfect setting.

Still, Lian thought as she killed the motor and removed her helmet. There's still Blossom. If all else fails, there's still one seed of 06/04 left, and from that seed a forest could grow in time.

Blossom had been cautious all along, staying in the shadows, finding strength in anonymity. Lian let herself wonder, just for a moment, whether things would have gone differently if she and the others had kept to that credo. If they'd never met in person, would she be here now, climbing the front steps into a pitch-black abandoned school?

It didn't matter. Because they'd met, she now knew Matt was a traitor. That 06/04 had been rotten at its core. Better to root him out than to continue living the lie.

"Hello?" she called into the blackness as the door shut behind her. There was no response. She took a couple of cautious, groping steps forward but heard nothing more than the crunch of her own sneakers on a debris-strewn concrete floor.

She was just reaching for her phone to illuminate her path, when suddenly she heard a sinister metallic click, and a blinding light shone directly into her eyes. She slammed them shut and shielded her face with her hand, but not before she caught a glimpse of a gun barrel held up next to the light. However she blinked, the afterimage danced before her, a blood-red cylinder seared onto her retinas.

"Whatever you were reaching for," Mr. Yeung's voice said, "take your hand away."

"My phone," Lian told him, continuing to blink as she adjusted to the flashlight in the dark. "Just my phone."

"There is no one you need to call. Everyone left in your world is in this room already."

His voice was a cold, bloodless thing that slithered out of him like a reptile. Lian felt the hairs on the back of her neck stand up. Perhaps she should have been terrified, but that emotion, too, had been used up completely over the course of the night.

"Now," Yeung said. "Slowly take out the memory stick and place it on the ground at your feet."

"First show me Eva and Zan," Lian demanded. She couldn't help the little waver in her voice. "I need to know they're all right before I give you anything."

Without a word, Yeung swung his flashlight so the beam fell on Eva, seated at a school desk in the corner of the room and bound to its chair with plastic riot cuffs. Her mouth had been stuffed with a wad of cloth, and duct tape had been wound around her head to gag her. Eva's black-rimmed eyes were wide and panicked, and she was struggling, clearly trying to say something that Lian couldn't begin to make out.

"The memory stick," Yeung repeated. "Now."

"What about Zan?" Lian asked. "I want to see him, too."

Yeung strode purposefully over the corner and held his handgun to Eva's knee, just above her boot. "You are finished making demands of me. Give me the memory stick, immediately, or know that you're about to cause this young lady a great deal of pain."

Eva wriggled and shook her head. Lian tried not to think about what a gun that size might do at point-blank range. When the light swung back to her, she held up one hand in a gesture of surrender, and moved the other one very slowly to her pocket.

"A rabbit's foot?" Yeung said, like a machine trying to approximate amusement.

Lian twisted it to expose the USB connector and then bent down to set the stick on the ground.

Before she'd stood all the way back up, two men had appeared from the shadows behind her, grabbing her and pinning her arms behind her back. She shouted and kicked at them, but they took no notice. The men smelled like aftershave and gasoline, their muscular arms covered by track jackets emblazoned with that hateful H logo.

They dragged her across the room and forced her into an empty desk near Eva. Lian felt the plastic cuffs dig into her wrists and then into her ankles. She thrashed in the small chair but to no avail; one of the men pushed the desk hard into the wall, and Lian grimaced at the impact. She was face to face now with the captive Eva, but still couldn't understand what she was trying to say.

"Let us go," Lian said, wrenching her neck to look at Yeung. "I did everything you asked. I came alone. I brought the only copy of the data. So set us free."

The overhead fluorescent lights switched on suddenly, and the inky blackness before them coalesced into the smiling form of Rand Harrison.

"Lian, Lian, Lian," he chided. "My associate already told you, you're done making demands. And here I thought you were such an intelligent girl. I'm disappointed that we have to repeat ourselves."

"I don't give a damn what you think about my intelligence," Lian spat back. "I was smart enough to beat you."

"Beat me?" he said with a laugh. "One of us has the dead girl's file, the multibillion-dollar corporation, and the wherewithal to keep the former from causing even a moment's concern to the latter. And the other of us?" He put one expensive loafer up on her desk and leaned down to meet her blazing eyes with his black ones. "The other of us has nothing. No data, no escape, no hope. No reason to go on living at all. So how, exactly, do you imagine that you've beaten me?"

Lian set her jaw defiantly. "It doesn't matter if I don't walk out of here tonight. I'm part of something bigger than myself, and our whole focus right now is taking you down, Harrison. You and your backstabbing son." She inclined her head toward Eva. "When we don't report back, another activist named Blossom will pick up where we left off. And Blossom is cautious, completely anonymous. You won't have any idea who they are, or how to stop them. But I promise, they will destroy you."

Eva squirmed and made a noise that Lian took as agreement.

"You know," Harrison said, taking his foot off her desk and walking a few paces away. "I take back my doubts. You're a very intelligent girl, after all. Because that, I must say, is a marvelously apt description of your friend Blossom."

"Please," a familiar voice said from behind Lian. "That name sounds so ridiculous out here in the real world."

Footsteps drew closer to her, and then a smooth hand in an expensive suit fell on her shoulder. The cufflink was polished silver, an embossed oval surrounding the stylized H. Lian couldn't turn enough to see the speaker's face, but she didn't have to.

"I've told you," he said. "Just call me Zan."

TWENTY-NINE

"No," Lian said as the realization washed over her. "No, this can't be right."

Zan stepped up next to her desk and crouched down to look at her. He was wearing an impeccable black suit with thin silver pinstripes, over a rich blue dress shirt. His hair was perfectly styled, and he was clean shaven. His aftershave was the same one the muscled goons were wearing. It made her gag.

"I think this is what they call irony," he said with a smile. "You swallowed everything I told you, and trusted every word Blossom typed . . . and yet when you find out we're the same person, you *just can't believe it.*"

Lian felt sick to her stomach. Her head swam. Her wrists ached.

"Hey, thanks for getting here so quickly," Zan said. "Did you like the thing about the power drill? I just threw that in for flavor, but it sure got you to come running. Good old Komiko, always ahead of the timetable."

Eva's mouth was still stuffed with cloth, but Lian was pretty sure she was calling Zan a number of nasty names.

"I'd say I was sorry that I had to lie to you, Lian," he said, stroking her cheek with his fingers. "But that would just be another lie in itself."

She jerked her head away from his hand. "Eva was trying to warn me."

"You bet she was," Zan said, standing. "But she didn't do a very good job, did she? She really needs to work on her communication skills." He grabbed a handful of Eva's dreadlocks and yanked her head up. "Learn how to type, you dumb bitch!"

"Stop it!" Lian shouted. "Don't touch her!"

"Stand up and say that again," Zan sneered.

Lian struggled in her seat, to no avail.

"Speaking of communication," Zan said, "I should probably apologize for swiping your phone while we were on the run that first night." He removed her old smartphone from his pocket, and she watched as he popped it out of its decorated rubber case. "I know it must have been a pain, having to re-upload all those apps and contacts. I wish I could do something to make up for your trouble."

He threw the phone to the floor as hard as he could, where the glass cracked and one side popped open. "There," he said mockingly. "Does that help?"

"Wait," Lian said, shaking her head and trying to piece the deception together. "This doesn't make sense. Blossom's been active for months. We vetted the alias thoroughly before we extended the invitation into 06/04."

"Oh, my God!" Zan exclaimed, throwing up his hands. "Do you really imagine you're the only people in the world who know how to use a computer? Do you seriously think we couldn't plant those stories, falsify the timeline, and create some sort of wide-eyed crusader out of zeroes and ones?" He smiled wickedly. "We even left you a little clue, if you'd looked for it. The first day of Blossom's supposed history? The first time that character surfaced? It was backdated to the same day, the same minute and second, that your arrogant friend 'Mynah Bird' posted his first screed against Harrison Corp."

It was such a weird little detail, such a bizarre digital signature . . . but as she thought about it, she realized he was right.

"The thing of it is," Harrison said, "I don't like being looked into. My secrets are my own. The backroom deals, the greased palms, the little favors that are done off the books . . . those are what business is built on, sweetheart. They're what keep the machine running smoothly. Everything else is just for show."

"And, hell, even the illegal stuff is more fun if you add a little theatricality," Zan said, making a wide, sweeping gesture as if the schoolroom were a stage on which some pageant was nearing its end.

"At first, I couldn't work out where 06/04 was getting its information on me," Harrison said. "So Zan started researching and reporting back. It's almost embarrassing how trusting you people were of the fox in your henhouse. You tout your anonymity as your greatest strength, but there's something to be said for knowing who's on the other side of the curtain before you start shouting your secrets. And once I understood how the online activist community worked, I ceased viewing it as a threat and started thinking of it as a tool. One that was exceedingly simple to use."

"What do you mean?" Lian said, frowning.

"The Drax Plastics takedown? The one that secured Blossom's place in the group?" Zan said. "I asked around for a little info and got handed more than I could read in ten lifetimes. You show up on the Internet with a cute nickname and an axe to grind, and every wannabe crusader for the common man will fall all over themselves trying to cozy up to you."

"And if Drax just happened to be making plans to expand into Harrison Corps' markets—plans that, sadly, had to be scuttled when the company went under and its assets were sold for pennies on the dollar—well, what a nice little bonus for me," said Harrison with a smug laugh. "Why pay for a piece of candy when you can have the whole candy shop at the same price?"

"Once I'd ingratiated myself to you guys through the Drax thing, it was just a matter of steering the conversation back to Harrison and figuring out how the information flowed," Zan said. "And now that we've closed that loop, we can get back to business as usual."

"So how do you close that loop?" Lian said. "You kill us?"

"How do you think this ends?" Zan said with a shrug. "Oh, and what's worse," he continued, "is that you won't even get to die a martyr because nobody's left to carry on in your wake. Your 'insurance policy' is null and void." He shot his cuff to check an expensive-looking silver watch. "3:18 A.M., Hong Kong time . . . Blossom has logged off."

"Wait," Lian said again. "Your sister . . . ?"

Zan threw his head back and laughed harshly. "You *cannot* be this naïve! No, Lian, I'm an only child."

"Then the dead girl . . ."

"Was nobody. Some small-town girl who won't be missed, a blank book of a person that I filled with my stories," Zan said. "She was as much flotsam in life as she was in death. The most useful thing she ever did for anyone was to turn up on that beach and get the do-gooders sniffing around Harrison Corp again."

"She was *somebody*," Lian said defiantly. "Her name was Kong Nüying. She came from Lau Fau Shan. She was a human being, you monster."

"She was *bait*," Zan snapped at her. "Unintended, yes, but you bit nonetheless." He came over to her again, one hand on either side of the desk, looking right into her eyes with something like glee. "The fact that you were on that beach, Lian—that Komiko herself was first on the scene— that was a gift from the gods. A one-in-a-million stroke of luck. That made things personal. You weren't going to stop until you got to the bottom of it."

"And now you've gotten to the bottom of it," Harrison interrupted. "And you're going to stop."

"But . . . why have Zan working us, online and in real life," Lian asked him, "when you already had Matt as Torch, telling you every move we made?"

"I *said*, you're going to *stop*," Harrison growled. He turned on his heel. "The press conference is in five and a half hours, Yeung. Take care of this in your usual manner, and you'll still get five hours' sleep."

Yeung nodded to Harrison, then motioned to his goons in the track jackets. They disappeared into an adjoining room and quickly reemerged, each carrying two gas cans. Yeung moved to one side as the men began to douse the walls and floor with gasoline. Zan stood next to him, arms crossed, enjoying the scene. Harrison exited through the front doors and into the night without looking back.

Lian shot a wide-eyed look at Eva. She'd never seen someone looking so afraid.

The goons emptied their cans and tossed them aside, then made for the door as well.

"Ladies," Zan said. "I'm so glad we could have this official send-off party for 06/04. But it's getting awfully late, so I think I'd better be on my way."

Yeung had taken a Zippo lighter out of his pocket and snapped open its cover. With the barest hint of a smile, he flicked the thumbwheel.

Nothing happened.

He cursed, shook the lighter, and tried it again, but it didn't even spark.

Zan sighed and rolled his eyes melodramatically as he reached into his suit jacket. "What would you people do without me around, Yeung?" he said, handing the fat man a matchbook. With a droll wave, Zan opened the door, and then switched off the overhead lights. The room plunged back into a darkness broken only by the rectangle of the open doorway framing the traitor.

Yeung tore a single match from the book, closed the cover, and struck it. It flared up and danced, excited to be set loose on this stage, the final act before the curtain dropped.

Leaning between the two girls, Yeung tucked the matchbook into the pocket of Lian's pants, like some paltry exchange for the rabbit's foot she'd had there. He straightened up, looking first at Eva and then at Lian, his face unreadable.

"It's nothing personal," he said, his placid features flickering in the tiny light. "Just good business."

Then he walked to the door that Zan was holding, tossed the match over his shoulder into the room, and was gone.

THIRTY

In an instant the pitch black of the schoolroom gave way to violent orange. Flames raced over the concrete floor, curdling the bits of trash into ash-gray husks, and chased up the walls to devour arithmetic charts and inspirational posters. Lian watched as a photo of four multiethnic hands gripping one another by the wrists split up its middle and fluttered from its thumbtacks. TEAMWORK, the caption read.

The goons had left the small area around the desks free of accelerant—the better to prolong their captives' suffering, Lian thought—but the heat was upon them, and the smoke was everywhere. She and Eva strained at their plastic cuffs, rocking the desks in their panic. Lian's vision doubled and trebled as she blinked away sweat and stinging tears. The smoke and the stink of the gasoline filled her nose and mouth, tore at her lungs, left her coughing and sputtering.

Eva screwed up her eyes, and her pale face went bright red. She was only breathing through her nose, Lian realized;

she must be coughing up soot, too, with nowhere for it to go.

The flames touched the acoustic tile of the ceiling and began to crisp the squares and warp their plastic frames. Lian throttled back and forth, making the desk move in little hops, but she couldn't get enough distance from the wall to do any good.

One last, hard kick, and a sharp pain shot up her leg. She looked down, confused, to see that the sole of her sneaker had become lodged in the mortared space between bricks. The pressure she was putting on her foot just by sitting was excruciating. Not thinking, just acting, she hurled every ounce of her weight away from the wall.

The desk moved, but the shoe stayed.

It was enough. She bruised her knee as she wrenched her leg up rapidly toward the underside of the desk. The loop of plastic around her ankle caught for a moment on her sock, and then her left foot was bare and unbound.

If she hadn't been crying from the smoke, she might have wept for joy. Her other foot was bound tight, and her hands were pinned behind the chair. But with her free foot, she could drag herself in a tight arc until her desk was behind Eva's, their backs to one another.

The flames were growing curious about this mystery play in the corner of the room, coming closer to investigate. Lian swore under her breath and paid for the sin with a wracking cough. She pushed herself backward, and her fingers found the riot cuffs at Eva's wrists.

If I can't save myself, Lian thought, maybe I can save my friend.

She blindly felt around the cuffs, trying to understand how to release them without being able to see them. Without being able to see much of anything, really; the smoke was getting thicker, and it seemed to pry into her through every pore. She couldn't find her breath. Her fingers fumbled. Fire kissed her bare toes.

Bizarrely, the room felt as if it tilted for a second, all of the flame bowing briefly toward the door. A shape appeared at the edge of Lian's vision, darker than the dark gray, more insistent than the blaze. Above the roar and crackle, she heard the horrible, high-pitched whine of a power drill.

Yeung, she thought. Come to finish us off. Just good business.

And then, glistening even through the plumes of smoke, she saw a white smile.

"Don't move," Matt shouted. "This is delicate work."

He forced the drill bit into the plastic that bound her ankle to the leg of the desk, and her whole body thrummed with the vibrations. But in fifteen seconds he was through it. He grabbed the chair and swung it out so he could free her hands as well.

She leapt from her seat the second she was able. Matt began working on Eva's cuffs, and Lian dashed around him to check on her. The girl's eyes were bloodshot slivers ringed in sticky black. Her head lolled on her neck. She seemed to be on the verge of passing out.

"Eva, I'm so sorry," Lian said, her hands on Eva's shoulders. "This is going to hurt like hell, but it'll wake you up."

With both her hands, Lian grabbed the loose edge of the duct tape wound around Eva's mouth and pulled as hard as she could. The tape gave way with a sick, sticky sound, and stole two small blue dreadlocks from the back of Eva's head before it let go. The skin around her mouth was a deep red rectangle of burst blood vessels. Her eyes were wide open now, and as soon as Lian pulled the wad of cloth from her mouth, Eva unleashed a stream of expletives that caused even Matt to pause in his work for a moment.

"You were right," Eva rasped. "That did hurt like hell."

Matt severed her last ankle bond, dropping the drill and helping her to her feet. Lian got on Eva's other side to prop her. As quickly as they could, the threesome made for the door, staying close to the one brick wall that the fire had not yet consumed. Burning ceiling tiles and wisps of pink insulation rained down on them. Matt gave the girls a sudden shove and took the brunt of a falling wall clock on his back.

Their last few steps to the door were unavoidably blocked by flames. Without a word, Matt swept Eva up in a fireman's carry, wrapped his free arm around Lian's waist, and charged for freedom like a man with nothing left to lose.

He didn't stop running until he reached the top of the steps outside, where he first deposited Lian and then knelt so she could help with Eva again. They supported one another down the stairs and ten yards or so onto the unkempt grass, turning only when the school building seemed to moan at their absence and then collapse in on itself, support beams at last giving way to the inferno.

Lian's eyes were on the burning building even as her feet continued to move away from it, so she nearly tripped on a large, dark lump in the grass. With a gasp, she realized that it was the prone form of Mr. Yeung. The tall grass around his head was deeply stained by the blood seeping out of a large gash in the side of his head.

"So," Matt said between lungfuls of clean night air, "now do you guys trust me?"

Eva smiled, sat on the ground, and fell into a coughing jag. Lian looked up at Matt, her eyes softening. "So you never were a mole," she said. It wasn't a question; she had no doubt of the answer now.

"As much as my stepdad hated Torch, he had no idea it was me until tonight. Zan went for a 'milkshake' and told him everything."

"What you did in there," Lian said breathlessly. "Coming to rescue us. That . . . that was really—"

Her sentence ended in a shriek as she felt meaty fingers close around her bare ankle.

"You aren't . . . rescued yet," Yeung said groggily.

Lian kicked at him until she was free. He was no longer moving quickly, but with his head wound she was amazed he was moving at all. His hands went to his pocket.

"Which were you looking for, Yeung?" Matt asked, holding up the memory stick in his left hand. "This?" From his right sweatshirt pocket, he then pulled out Yeung's handgun. "Or this?"

"Pretty boy," Yeung said, spitting blood. "You wouldn't dare use it."

Matt fired a shot that split the grass three inches from Yeung's face.

"Lucky shot," Matt said, in a tone that told Lian luck had nothing to do with it. "Must be the rabbit's foot."

He put the memory stick back into his pocket, then handed the gun to Lian, who accepted it gingerly. "Oh, I also nicked your car keys when I was rooting around in your pockets, Yeung," he said, jingling the keys on their ring. "So I guess we'll be on our way."

Lian stared at the gun in her hand, then looked at Matt questioningly.

"Just stay here and cover him while I get his car. I'll pull up so we can load Eva in."

Lian nodded, and Matt took off at a run toward Yeung's black Mercedes, parked at the head of the drive.

"Lian," Eva whispered.

When she turned, Lian saw it: the glint of metal that leapt from Yeung's ankle holster to his hand. He had gotten to his feet somehow, grinning the first grin Lian had ever seen on him, his teeth stained with his own blood. He looked directly into her eyes and swung his arm back to throw the knife.

She put a bullet through the center of his chest.

The grin faltered. The hand trembled, and the blade fell silently onto the grass. Lian dropped the gun, feeling a sudden swim of nausea. Yeung staggered backward, clutching at his heart, mouth moving but making no sound. He collapsed onto his back at the foot of the school stairs, and a flaming corner slid off the roof to bury him.

Lian was still staring at the gun on the ground, when Matt pulled up behind her.

"I . . . I killed him."

"See, that's why you're such an effective activist," Matt said through the rolled-down window.

"He had a knife," she muttered.

Matt climbed out of the car, picked up the gun and flung it into the heart of the fire, then held the car's passenger door for her as she climbed in. He ran back to get Eva from the lawn, lifted her as if she were weightless, and eased her into the backseat of the Mercedes. Then he jogged over to retrieve something from behind a stump.

Lian felt numb. She'd just shot a man. In the chest.

Matt handed something to her before climbing back behind the wheel. It was her messenger bag.

"That was good thinking," he said with a smile as she opened it. "Knowing that Eva might want to cover up with a suit coat, and you might need a replacement pair of shoes."

"Yeah," Lian said, turning around in her seat to lay the jacket over Eva. "Everything went exactly the way I planned it."

She removed her right sneaker and sock, slipped her feet into the black flats, and then lay back in the leather seat and closed her eyes.

"Hey," Matt said as he pulled away from the ruined schoolhouse. "Buckle up, Lian. You don't want anything bad to happen to you tonight."

Lian fastened her seatbelt, marveling at how steady her hands were. As they turned back onto the main road, a cell phone in the car's center console lit up and gave the double chirp that indicated a new text message. Lian picked up the phone; the caller was identified only as RH.

Is it done?

She showed it to Matt, who nodded. She tapped out a reply and sent it.

Of course.

"But it's not, quite," Matt said. "So what's our next step?"

"We have the information," Lian said. "Now we just have to get it to the people who can do something with it."

"Don't worry," came Eva's tired voice from the backseat. She tapped her belt buckle with a fingernail. "A little bird told me that everything's going to work out fine."

THIRTY-ONE

Lian had stayed at the Mandarin Oriental hotel only one night in her life, two years ago when her father had been wooed for his current job on the island. She had never experienced such luxury before or since. Winding herself up with sweet delights from the Cake Shop and then calming back down under the Vichy showers in the spa, she had spent nineteen enchanted hours through the looking glass in this five-star wonderland.

Now she stood at one side of the lobby, with Matt and Eva at her side. Harrison was prepping at the front, accompanied by an eight-man security detail, serious guys in serious suits, little curls of translucent wire leading from their ears into their shirt collars. Lian's father and his bosses were there as well, talking amongst themselves. The higher-ups looked self-congratulatory, but Hung Zhi-Kai seemed empty; to Lian's eyes he appeared exhausted and disheartened, a shadow of the father she loved.

"I think Taylor almost told me about you," whispered Lian, "on Harrison's yacht. He said you wore hand-me-downs. I didn't get it."

Matt blushed, and for once he didn't look comfortable in his own skin. "My folks made ends meet, or at least got within shouting distance. But the, uh, when my dad got sick . . . that's where all the money went. I'd pick up little odd jobs around the neighborhood, mowing lawns or washing cars for a couple of bucks. When Rand met my mom she was waitressing on the graveyard shift. It seemed unreal; he plucked us from small-town Colorado and suddenly we're living in his huge house…"

Rand Harrison cleared his throat, calling the press conference to order. Lian glared at him across the vast room through sunglasses that hid her face but did nothing to dim her hatred.

A sea of journalists representing new media and old had gathered to report on the occasion. These same writers, or ones very like them, had covered Harrison before; in her research, Lian had read enough press on the man and his company to know that he'd feed them sound bites expertly chosen to reflect precisely the image he wanted for his company. Any hard questions would be subtly but artfully evaded; any softballs would be seized upon to the room's amusement. And every one of these reporters would file almost the exact same story: the story that Harrison's publicity people had written for them even before he'd opened his mouth.

That's how things had gone up until today, at any rate.

"Good morning," Harrison said to the crowd. "Zǎo shàng hǎo. I'm so pleased that you could join me here today. I think, when all is said and done this morning, you'll feel that you've witnessed something . . . just a little bit extraordinary."

The convivial tone and warm smile did nothing to betray the fact that, six hours earlier, the man behind the podium had casually ordered the death of two teenage girls.

"We stand today," he continued, "at the precipice of a bold and exciting new era of Chinese–American business cooperation. I had to sign an awful lot of dotted lines to get us to this point, too." Harrison held up his hand, cramped into an exaggerated claw. "Does anybody know if there's a good acupuncturist anywhere in town?"

This drew laughs from the press. Harrison shook the stiffness out of his hand and ran it through his hair, smiling. "But if writing my name a couple hundred times is the worst thing I have to do to usher in a period of unprecedented prosperity for Harrison Corp, well then, I guess it'll all have been worthwhile. Now, I'd like to spend a few minutes talking about exactly—"

There was a tiny squeal of feedback, and then Rand Harrison interrupted himself.

"Beat me?" his voice asked through the sound system. "One of us has the dead girl's file, the multibillion-dollar corporation, and the wherewithal to keep the former from causing even a moment's concern to the latter."

Harrison gripped both sides of his podium, his eyes suddenly wide and furious. He was saying something, but Lian couldn't hear it. Nobody could; the microphones had cut out completely. The lobby echoed with the sound of a voice from just a few hours before, sinister and taunting.

"And the other of us? The other of us has nothing. No data, no escape, no hope. No reason to go on living at all. So how, exactly, do you imagine that you've beaten me?"

"*This is how*, you smug son of a bitch," Lian said under her breath.

"You know," Eva said, stepping up behind her and handing her grapefruit juice in a champagne glass. "This is a really nice way to spend a morning."

"I couldn't agree more," Lian said as they clinked their glasses together. Eva's eyes were still a little pink, as was the square around her lips, but she smiled nonetheless. She was wearing a black overcoat and had her dreadlocks tucked up underneath a dark gray snood. At her waist, the eye of the chrome crow glittered.

Hours earlier, from the backseat of Yeung's Mercedes, Eva had detached the belt buckle and explained that it hid a digital recorder. She never left home without it, and when she suspected that a situation might become noteworthy, she pressed the bird's eye and started taping. Last night the crow had been served quite a meal.

Matt had nearly lost control of the car when Eva had told them about the recording. Lian had plugged the device's cord into her phone, and the three of them had taken a lazy drive through Kowloon at four in the morning as they listened to Harrison and Zan gloat over their dirty doings.

There had been no sleep for them after that. At an all-night coffeehouse back on the island, Eva had downloaded an audio editing app to Lian's phone and had set about isolating Rand Harrison's greatest hits. Matt had hacked the hotel's server to discover the make and model of the soundboard they'd be making available for the press conference. Lian texted Mingmei and reassured her that everything was fine, that the mystery letter to her parents could be deleted unread, and that Mingmei might wish to feign illness so she could stay home and watch the local news.

"The thing of it is," Harrison's oily voice said from the speakers, "I don't like being looked into. My secrets are my own. The backroom deals, the greased palms, the little favors that are done off the books . . . those are what business is built on, sweetheart. They're what keep the machine running smoothly. Everything else is just for show."

The reporters were already buzzing, but Lian watched her father's face darkening in his chair.

"I said, stop the damned recording!" Harrison bellowed from behind the podium, loud enough for the room to hear even without the microphones' amplification. His security guards were all jabbering into their earpieces, but none of them seemed able to do anything to silence the speakers.

"And if Drax just happened to be making plans to expand into Harrison Corps' markets—plans that, sadly, had to be scuttled when the company went under and its assets were sold for pennies on the dollar—well, what a nice little bonus for me." Harrison laughed on the recording. Lian thought he might never laugh again in real life. "Why pay for a piece of candy when you can have the whole candy shop at the same price?"

"That's a man who's had too much candy," Matt said as he joined the girls. "It was bound to catch up to him."

"He certainly looks sick to his stomach," Lian agreed.

"Oh, just wait," Matt said. "It's about to get better."

The playback ended. Harrison just stood before the crowd of reporters, his brow glinting with sweat, his eyes bulging fiercely, his face as red as that of a New Year's dragon.

A pretty young Web journalist near the front of the throng held up a manila envelope, addressed to her in Lian's measured script.

"On the assumption that we've entered the question-and-answer phase of the conference, Mr. Harrison," the woman said, "I'd like to ask about your thoughts on this. It's a very interesting package that was waiting for me this morning. Files from a number of sources linking your corporation to police and governmental corruption. Chemical poisoning and cover-ups. The recent death of Dr. Lan Ming. Arson at her building, as well as at a disused schoolhouse south of Kam Shan Park." She paused for breath.

"And the formerly unidentified girl found ten days ago at Big Wave Bay Beach, here shown to be one Kong Nüying . . . dead under mysterious circumstances while under your employ. Any comment on these connections, Mr. Harrison?"

"None whatsoever," Harrison sputtered. "This press conference is over. Good day to you all."

The security men swarmed around him, as much to prop him up as to protect him. They began to duck and weave, pole handlers dancing their dragon through the swarming crowd.

Lian took off her sunglasses and stood blocking the path of the processional. To either side of her, Eva removed the snood, and Matt simply smiled.

Harrison skidded to a stop as his eyes met Lian's, then took in the other two. "That's . . . not possible," he said.

"This is the question-and-answer session," Eva said. "The lady asked you a question. It's time you started offering up some answers."

"I . . . have . . . *nothing* to say!" he said, apoplectic. "And especially not to you!"

"Well," said Lian's father, tapping Harrison on the shoulder. "Maybe you'll have something to say to the police." The life had returned to his face; the fire was back in his eyes. "You may grind me under your heel all you wish, Harrison. But don't take me for a fool."

"Hung—" Harrison began.

Two police hands clamped down on Harrison's arms; two more snapped the metal cuffs onto his wrists. The security detail supporting him was turned away, and in their absence, Harrison collapsed, his legs giving out beneath him.

Lian thought back to the beach, to the day that had set her hand to Harrison's downfall. And as he was dragged limply from his own festivities, the poetry of a phrase returned to her, and she heard herself say it aloud to her two new friends as they smiled in agreement:

"The dragon's back is broken."

Sunday

THIRTY-TWO

Komiko: So this is it, then?

Torch: It's going to be strange, isn't it?

Crowbar: 4 sure, but were doing it 4 all the right reasons

Komiko: Right. I know that. As much as we've talked it over, I feel like we were all in agreement from the beginning.

Komiko: It's time to log off the message board for good.

Torch: Knowing that we did more in the last two weeks than most groups like ours dream of doing in a lifetime.

Crowbar: & knowing well meet again face 2 face soon

Crowbar: U guys R probably already sick of meeting face 2 face at school every day, huh? :)

Lian laughed at this.

Komiko: You'd be surprised. For some reason it doesn't bother me like it used to.

Torch: And all I had to do was carry you from a burning building.

Komiko: A girl's got to have her standards.

Crowbar: Theres still plenty of threads 2 follow from this harrison mess

Crowbar: Im putting out new feelers every day, but Zan still hasnt popped his head back up

Komiko: If that's even his real name. Big "if."

Torch: My stepdad is still in custody, but he's lawyered up and not saying a single word to the police other than to request better coffee.

Torch: The good news is, today the last of his shareholders backed out of the new deal.

Torch: The company's value is basically nil, and that's BEFORE the criminal investigation has even begun.

Crowbar: U were right, that IS good news

Torch: And on a personal note, I'm looking into having my last name legally changed back to my birth father's. I've been a Harrison a lot longer than I cared to be.

Torch: The change has been kind of a hassle to do, though. You ladies might not believe this, but Hong Kong bureaucracy can be somewhat difficult to work with!

Crowbar: Say it aint so!

Lian loved knowing who was on the other side of those code names now, imagining the smiles on Matt's and Eva's faces as they typed their little jokes and repartee. 06/04 had claimed strength in anonymity, but she felt that all of them were stronger for having revealed their true selves.

Komiko: Maybe the best news in all of this is that Kong Nuying's parents finally have an answer for what happened to their daughter.

Komiko: That in and of itself is some closure. The answers that will be pried out of Harrison eventually can only help ease their pain.

Her bedroom door suddenly opened a crack. Lian quickly switched to the Desktop view.

"Oh, sorry," said her mother, closing the door again. She gave a sharp rap on the other side. "It's your mother," she added unnecessarily through the door. "May I come in?"

"Just a second, Mama," Lian called.

Komiko: Guys, I need to go now. I'll be back online in time for the big shutdown this afternoon. 4:06 p.m. See you then.

11:47 AM HKT — *Komiko has logged off*

She closed the laptop and ran to answer her door. Her mother was there, waiting patiently but with a concerned look on her face.

"Could I have a word with you, Lian?"

"Of course," Lian said, holding open the door. She had been dreading this conversation for days. She'd left Wednesday's press conference too wired to sleep, and had spent the afternoon switching channels on the television and updating the news Web sites, looking for any morsel of information. After dinner she'd crashed hard and was surprised to wake near noon the next day, her mother having already called the school to say that Lian was ill and might not return until after the weekend.

To her surprise, it had been left to her father alone to nudge her for the truth about her involvement with Harrison. Her mother instead had worn a continuously worried expression, but had shown her concern through frequent spontaneous hugs and just as frequent offers of food. Her father had done his best to remain stoic, but he'd wanted to know how it was she came to be at the press conference, and what exactly her links were with the recording that sealed Harrison's fate. She had pleaded ignorance, no connection outside of an economics class with the man's son, and her father had accepted the explanation—just. As he too hugged her tight, he'd said in her ear, "You're not telling me everything, little panda, I know that. However, I am going to trust you."

But her mother's curiosity had obviously reached its limits.

"Lian," she said haltingly, "our maid found something in your laundry that needs an explanation immediately."

Lian cocked her head. This certainly wasn't how she'd expected the conversation to go.

"Tell me the truth, please," her mother said. "Have you started smoking?"

Lian broke into a smile. "What?"

Her mother held up a matchbook, its cover open and a single match torn out. Lian recognized it after a second of confusion: Yeung had slipped it into her pocket as a farewell gift. Just good business. She started laughing and tried to stifle it, her hands over her mouth.

"This isn't funny, Lian!" her mother said sharply. "I asked you a question. I need an answer."

Lian took a deep breath and forced herself to put on a straight face. She reached for the smallest and most believable fib she could find.

"Those are from Mingmei's house, Mama. She asked me to light a scented candle, last time we were studying. I must have just hung onto them by mistake."

The relief that washed over her mother's features was beautiful. "Oh, thank goodness," she said. "For a moment . . . it seems silly now, but for just a moment I thought you might have done something you shouldn't have."

"No," Lian said, throwing her arms around her mother. "I would never, ever do that. I'm still your good girl."

"Still my little panda," her mother agreed, hugging her back and kissing her on the forehead.

She closed the door behind her, and Lian lay back on the bed. It was such a little wisp of a lie, comforting to hear yet completely insubstantial.

But it was what her mother had wanted to hear. Scented candles were at the lower end—while still making an appearance—on a list of risks that Lian might take. Cigarettes were, she supposed, the upper limit of what her mother could imagine in this case.

So it wouldn't have done any good to bring up the activist group that had staged the midnight office break-in that had led to her escape from a ninth-story window. Or to mention the hostage situation that had turned into a blazing inferno and ended with a well-placed bullet.

Scented candles were just fine.

Lian was about to open her laptop back up when her eyes fell on the matchbook, still open and resting on her comforter. Its cover was emblazed with words she knew all too well.

THE FAMILY HAND CAFÉ. The simple characters for *mahjong*. The dirty little dive where she'd first followed Harrison and Yeung.

Except that these matches had come from Zan. At some point, he'd been there, too.

Which meant that, at some point, he might go back. Especially if he had nowhere else to run.

Lian pocketed the matchbook and went to put on a jacket. She would text Matt and Eva on the way there. Before she left her room, she practiced the café's code on her wall: three fast knocks, a pause, then two more.

Just a tiny courtesy before she kicked down their door.